Panic in Pee

CW01432232

The Peesdown Series, Volume 2

Carole Williams

Published by Carole Williams, 2021.

PANIC IN PEESDOWN

First edition. February 8, 2021.

Copyright © 2021 Carole Williams.

ISBN: 978-1393540700

Written by Carole Williams.

This book is dedictated to my mother who died in
December 2019.

This is the first book I have written that she hasn't
read and I have really missed the support and input
she gave me with all of my previous books. She was
definitely my biggest fan.
Just hope you have a kindle up in heaven, Mum.
God bless. Xx

PANIC IN PEESDOWN

TABLE OF CONTENTS.

PANIC IN PEESDOWN

PROLOGUE

JANUARY

Bob Watkins pulled on his jogging top and trousers, did up his trainers and left his rented terrace house on Unwin Street to the north of Peesdown. It was just getting light but was bitterly cold and he blew on his hands to keep them warm as he ran down the High Street, across Miller Lane, skilfully missing the icy bits of pavement, and into Peesdown Park. He kept to the grass as he was less likely to slip and headed down to the lake. It took around fifteen minutes to jog all the way round. He usually did five laps every morning and then headed home to shower, have breakfast and go to bed, having been at work all night.

He looked around with interest as he sped along. There were the usual early morning dog walkers, a couple of cyclists and three joggers, one male and two females. He recognised them all and nodded as they passed, no-one keen to stop and chat in the cold.

He reached the point where that woman had been found, raped and strangled a few months ago ... Tanya something. The bloke who did it had never been caught and people, especially women, were very scared, not only in Peesdown but all the other parks in Leeds too ... Roundhay, Meanwood, Golden Acre. Occasionally he jogged in one of them instead of Peesdown, fancying a change of scene but it was rare to see a woman alone since the murder. Most females now walked or ran in pairs or groups and kept a keen eye out to see who was around and even though the parks tended to be quieter in the winter, this year they had been almost abandoned during the week although busier with families at the weekends. Even so, everyone was on alert and little went unnoticed.

1

He wondered why the man had killed the woman. It was too extreme. He could understand the rape, the thrill of it, the power, the urgent need to dominate but to actually kill someone afterwards? That was too much. He could never go that far ... or could he? He could cheerfully have killed that stupid bitch he went out with last year who had declared her undying love, then stolen all his savings from under his mattress. Nearly £5,000 he had amassed. It had been his dream to travel the world so he had saved hard and had been intending to chuck in his job next year and go, starting off in America and Canada. He had spent hours planning his route and researching all the countries he wanted to visit; India, Thailand, China, Australia, New Zealand. He had intended working his way around and his savings would have given him a good cushion but that bitch had cleared him out and buggered off. He had tried to track her down but she had disappeared off the face of the earth. Rumour had it that she had hidden herself away in London but as that was like looking for a needle in a haystack and he didn't want to waste any more money searching for her, he gave up. However, if he ever saw her again, he would dearly like to place his hands around her neck and squeeze tight. Bitch!!

He supposed he could have just gone ahead with his plans anyway but she had taken every penny he possessed and he didn't want to depart on his big adventure with absolutely nothing to fall back on so he had started saving again but now his job was in jeopardy. The firm he worked for was folding and he would be out of a job next month with little in the way of redundancy money. He had a couple of interviews lined up but as there were so many looking for work at this particular time, he didn't hold out much hope.

Yes, he could kill that cow for what she had done to him, messing up his life. It wouldn't have even mattered about losing his job as he could have just gone now if he still had his savings. Blast women. He despised them all, starting with his useless prostitute of a mother and his needy, whiny, pathetic older sister who became a junkie and was found dead in her bed after an overdose. Bugger them all but especially that bitch who had cleaned him out.

He had gone a bit wild after her departure, convinced every woman was out to get what they could. She had utterly destroyed the little trust he had ever had in her gender. Women who went out with him were now treated with disdain and he used them for his own gratification, abusing them with rough sex when he took them home, threatening he would return and kill them if they ever breathed a word of it. He had convinced himself it wasn't actually rape, that they had wanted it as they had willingly gone out with him but in the back of his mind he knew it was wrong, especially when they cried "no!" and made it very plain it was what they meant.

He grimaced and concentrated on completing his final circuit of the lake and was just about to leave the park when he noticed a lone female jogger, running with little effort, almost gliding on the path. She wasn't even breathing heavily. Fascinated, he watched her coming towards him. She was utterly beautiful; her slim, long-legged body encased in dark pink lycra, her long dark hair pulled back into a ponytail and her face, oval, with high cheekbones, big eyes and a pert nose.

He stood aside to let her pass. She didn't even glance at him or say thank you. Snooty cow. He had never seen her before and wondered if he would again. It certainly looked as if she could do with a bit of rough sex to sort her out. He chortled and went on his way. He was tired and relaxed now and wanted his bed.

CHAPTER 1

JANUARY

William Pemworthy leaned over the railings of the cruise ship and looked down at the sea. It was calm, like a millpond ... virtually turquoise with the odd ripple of white. The sky was a perfect azure blue. It was all picturesque but, even with the sea breezes, it was hot ... too hot for him. He rubbed his handkerchief across his brow and pulled his white canvas hat further down over his sunglasses. He wanted to return to the cool of his cabin, to collapse on the bed under the air conditioning but if he did, he would miss seeing Tilly Pargeter when she came out of the dance class she was presently enjoying.

Line dancing. He pursed his lips and turned up his nose. Daft buggers. Shouting and hollering and waving their ridiculous hats around when they jumped up and down. Tilly had asked him to go with her but he had declined. There was no way he was going to be seen making a fool of himself.

He looked at his watch. The class would be finished soon and then they would all flood out, laughing and joking about how much fun they had had. Tilly would be hyped up too. She always was when she had been line dancing. She gradually calmed down though when they went to the Juniper bar for a drink afterwards. She would chatter on excitedly for a little while, and then listen to him, looking at him with adoring eyes, hanging on to every word that came out of his mouth.

He loved it. Her adoration. He wasn't used to it. It was a novelty for him. No woman had ever looked at him the way she did but it wasn't right. Something was missing and he knew what it was. She wasn't Miranda ... and she never could be. For a start, she looked nothing like her. Tilly was red-haired. It was frizzy and coarse. Her skin was covered in freckles ... her face, her neck, her arms ... even her legs. She was overweight too and was always

4

complaining about how much she was putting on since the cruise had begun but it didn't stop her ramming down as much as she could at every meal and the snacks between were large and frequent. He knew that because for the last two weeks they had spent most days together.

Just the sort of woman he had been looking for, on her own, lonely and looking for romance, he had targeted Tilly on first clapping eyes on her, sitting alone in the Juniper bar sipping slowly from a straw in her ghastly sickly lime-coloured cocktail. He had watched her for a while to see if anyone was going to join her but after half an hour and she had spoken to no-one, he decided to try his luck.

"Hi," he said, smiling down at her as he stood beside her and gestured to the barman that he would like to be served. "Interesting looking drink you have there."

She had smiled shyly. "It's a witches' brew."

"Glass of lemonade please … with ice and a slice of lemon," he said to the small, rotund, swarthy skinned barman. "Would you like another … witches' brew?" he asked the woman.

"That's very kind. Thank you … I shouldn't have too many though. They make me terribly squiffy."

She was right. Having downed two more during the evening, it wasn't long before she was slurring her words. They had left the stools at the bar and sat on the comfy seating overlooking the sea. It was getting late and they virtually had the place to themselves as most passengers had either gone to bed or were engaged in dancing the night away under the stars two decks above.

Their conversation had been mainly about Tilly. William had no desire to tell anyone much about himself and any questions she did have, he managed to field fairly well back to her. He did tell her two things though. He told her he lived in Peesdown. He told her there was a beautiful park. He didn't tell her about Miranda.

****

"God, I'm fed up with this cold," moaned Miranda, blowing her nose loudly, disturbing Nellie, her chocolate Labrador and Charlie, her black and tan mongrel, who had been fast asleep on their red velvet sofas. They both opened their eyes and looked at her reproachfully. They were tired after a day running around the parks in Leeds with their groups of friends and needed their rest. How dare she disturb them?

"Never mind," Anna replied. "It will soon be spring. Then we'll all feel a lot better."

"Oh, Lord, Anna. It's only the end of January ... we have February and March to get through yet. More snow, sleet, gales and rain ... and as much as it makes my life a lot easier not having many people about when I'm walking groups of dogs in miserable weather, since poor Tanya Philips was attacked and murdered, I can't say I like walking in Peesdown Park much now. I was always careful before then but now I'm becoming paranoid, imagining murderers behind every tree, jumping at every movement, watching the dogs anxiously when their heads go up in the woods ... and if they bark ... well, my heart leaps into my mouth ... and I have the protection of six dogs! Most people only have one or two and everyone I bump into, who still have the nerve to go to the park, are just the same. Everyone's scared and no-one wants to walk alone ... or venture into the woods ... they're staying out in the open."

Anna sighed. "I know. I have so many customers in the shop commenting on it and saying they're driving over to Roundhay or Temple Newsam instead and even then, they're taking precautions and walking with others ... why don't you walk with Belinda or one of the other girls you have working for you? Then you'll have twelve dogs for protection as well as each other."

"We can't unfortunately. Professional dog walkers aren't allowed to walk together as it's too intimidating for others ...

which is understandable. It's difficult enough for some people to encounter six dogs, let alone twelve. No. We have to walk on our own but none of us are going to enjoy it very much until this damned madman is caught. Has your Sergeant Wilkinson any more news on that front?"

Anna smiled and blushed. "He's not *my* Sergeant Wilkinson."

"Oh, come on, Anna darling. I've seen how you look at each other ... and he's nice. I've known him for years and he's one of the good guys ... and not just because he's a policeman. He really is and I think you would make a lovely couple," Miranda teased. "Perhaps when Jeremy can get up from London next ... he won't have time this weekend with the party ... we can all go out for a meal together ... that would be nice, wouldn't it?"

She looked longingly and proudly at the photo of Jeremy in his army uniform on the sideboard. God, he was gorgeous. Every time she looked at him, either in real life or in a picture, she couldn't believe he wanted to go out with her ... and how hard she had fallen for him. She couldn't wait to see him this coming weekend. It was his birthday and his sister, Daphne, was throwing a party for him at her house in Headingley to which so many of his local friends and colleagues from his London barracks would be attending. It would be wonderful to be with him again but she was a trifle nervous, and that was putting it mildly, about meeting all those people who had known him far longer than she.

"Um, well," Anna blustered, wishing her cheeks would return to their normal colour, "anyhow, I'm not sure ... we'll have to see ... and no, in answer to your first question. No progress has been made on the murder investigation for weeks apparently. No new leads, no new forensic evidence ... but Andy assures me they're still working on it."

"Which means there's every chance they're never going to get this guy. Blimey. I'm beginning to wish I'd never decided to become a professional dog walker and have to risk life and limb every day. People have no idea that we do you know. They think we have a lovely life, swanning around the park in beautiful weather with perfectly behaved dogs and visiting cats to cuddle and pet them. They have no idea how dodgy it can be, what with weirdos in the parks and then having to enter people's homes when they're away to feed the cats, never knowing if someone has broken in or maybe still be there. It's not all it's cracked up to be, believe me ... let alone the fact that it's damned hard physical work."

Anna grinned. "But you love it and you know perfectly well you wouldn't want to do anything else."

Miranda smiled back. "No. You're right. I wouldn't but sometimes I wish I was rich and could go off for weeks at this time of the year ... on a cruise maybe ... like William. I expect he's having a lovely time. I hope he comes home well again. He certainly looked very peaky when I popped round to see if he was okay before he went."

"He must be pretty wealthy," Anna remarked, slipping on her shoes. It was time for her to go home, having popped in after closing up Pampered Pets for the day to drop off the food for Charlie and Nellie which Miranda had ordered. They had spent the last hour chatting over two cups of tea and Miranda had offered her something to eat but Anna had a stew in her slow cooker at home and was looking forward to eating it.

"I should think so, with that huge old house of his in Miller Lane. The one next door is up for sale. Did you know?"

"Oh, is it? I should love one of those lovely old Victorian houses but it just wouldn't be practical ... oh, by the way ... I've an appointment with an estate agent tomorrow evening. He's coming to take details and photographs of the house ... I've finally decided I'm going to put it on the market and move into the flat above the shop."

"Good," sniffed Miranda before blowing her nose again. "You need to get yourself more settled. The shop is doing really well now word is getting around but you've been looking really tired lately and driving backwards and forwards every day in heavy traffic isn't exactly a stress-free occupation. Life will be so much easier once you are above the shop .... and get yourself a furry companion to keep you company," she finished with a grin.

Anna laughed. "You won't be happy until you see me with a dog, will you?"

"No. You said yourself you always wanted one. It's just a matter of time."

Miranda walked with Anna to the door while the dogs raised their heads and wagged their tails but were too comfortable to move.

"Bye dogs, bye Miranda. Get an early night. You look done in."

"I will … and you do the same."

****

"Bastards!! Bloody bastards," yelled Sonia, throwing the phone down on the kitchen table where it nearly missed landing in a bowl of mushroom soup.

Josh, who was loading the dishwasher following their evening meal, jumped, as did the cats and dogs who had all settled down for the evening on the sofas and in their baskets.

"Who?" Josh asked, having a pretty shrewd idea of what his mother was going to say. It had to be something to do with some poor abandoned or neglected animal from the venom in her voice.

"Someone's tied up two old dogs to a gate down a lane somewhere near Walton, you know that lovely village near Wetherby. Luckily, the farmer who owns the land just drove down there and found them, otherwise they would have been there all night. Poor little buggers. It's bloody freezing. They probably wouldn't have survived until the morning by the sound of it. He says they are terribly underweight and terrified. Anyway, he's bringing them here … in about half an hour."

"Right," Josh said, putting on his coat. "I'll go and get the isolation room sorted for them and prepare some food."

Sonia nodded. "And I'll ring Jemma. I hate to drag a vet out at night but the dogs need to be checked to make sure there's nothing else wrong with them apart from starvation and cold. Jesus. I wish I could get my hands on the bastards who did this."

"You and me, Mum. You and me," Josh muttered, heading out of the kitchen door to stride over to the isolation room next to the dog kennels.

Jemma was happy to oblige. She was tired and had a date with her boyfriend later but she was as passionate about dumped and neglected animals as Sonia and always put their needs first.

"I'll be over in about an hour," she told Sonia. "I just have two more patients to see at the surgery and then I'll be on my way."

Josh returned to the kitchen, having turned on the heating in the isolation unit, made up two comfy dog beds with thick, woollen blankets and defrosted some rice and chicken which they always kept in the freezer for dogs who had poorly tummies and needed to be on a light diet.

"I think the farmer is here with the dogs," he said to Sonia. "I can see car lights coming up the lane. I'll go down and open the gate for him."

Sonia put on her coat and stood at the kitchen door, all the family cats and dogs now awake and raising their heads to see what was going on at this time in the evening.

All the outside lights were on and Sonia could see the van was dark blue as it pulled up beside her. A man with a beard and thick, curly hair got out and grimaced at her.

"John Marchant," he said, nodding his head in greeting. "And you must be Sonia. I've heard a lot of good things about what you do here at Happylands and it's good of you to take these two as you're probably full to bursting after Christmas with so many dogs being dumped. I could have taken them home but my old dogs would have given them what for and I think the poor little devils have had enough to contend with."

"It's no problem, John. We were up to capacity yesterday but today we managed to re-home four dogs so we have availability and we're all geared up for them. What breed are they? You never said on the phone."

"Bit of a mix-up really … might have a bit of Lab in them but see what you think."

He opened the side of the van slowly so as not to frighten the dogs more than they already were. They sat, a pathetic, heartbreaking sight, shivering at the back, their eyes wide with fear and misery.

"I gave them a couple of blankets and had the heating turned on full blast all the way here but I don't think it's done much good. I've no idea how long they've been tied to that gate. I haven't been up there for a couple of days and it was only by chance I did this evening."

He tried to coax the dogs out of the van but they refused to budge. Reluctant to pull them out, he turned to Sonia. "Any ideas?"

Josh had joined them and Sonia turned to him. "Josh, could you please get some of the chicken from the isolation unit. We'll have to tempt them out."

She talked to the dogs softly while waiting for him to return while John stood and watched her. One of the dogs began to respond to the sound of her voice and crept a little closer while the other remained where it was.

Keeping her tone gentle, Sonia looked up at John. "I think you're probably right. A bit of Lab and a bit of something else but not quite sure whether it's Border Collie."

The first dog responded to the smell of chicken Josh handed Sonia and after the first furtive nibble, gulped down a few handfuls, gradually growing closer and closer to the woman with the kindly voice and delicious food.

11

The other dog began to creep closer too and buoyed by the fact that her companion was growing in confidence, warily took a piece of chicken Sonia placed on the floor of the van.

"What sex are they?" asked Sonia. "Did you notice?"

"The first is a male and the timid one is a female," said John softly.

Gradually and slowly both dogs ceased shaking as Sonia kept up a soft dialogue, telling them how lovely they were and how they were going to be all right now.

It took nearly half an hour before they trusted her enough to allow her to clip on long leads to their collars and encourage them to leave the warmth and safety of the van. Josh and Sonia walked them slowly into the kennels, followed by a curious John who even though he had been well aware of the presence of Happylands, had never set foot in the place before. He was also intrigued with Sonia; her plain-speaking but inherent kindness.

When the dogs were settled into nice comfy beds, with a little more food in bowls beside them, Sonia looked up and smiled at him.

"Do come into the house for coffee, John. I think you've earned it."

"Well, I didn't do much apart from bringing the poor little devils to you. It's you who will have all the hard work ... building them up and finding them new homes."

"I know ... but at least they're safe now and no-one, over my dead body, will ever abuse them or their trust again."

John followed Josh and Sonia into the house and while drinking coffee and enjoying an enormous slice of chocolate cake, surrounded by several rescued dogs and cats Sonia told him she couldn't part with, decided he liked her more and more by the second. He made a mental note to pay Happylands a few more visits. After all, he had the excuse that he wanted to see how the two dogs were faring ... and looking at the place, there might well be a few jobs he could help with in his spare time. Yes, this wouldn't be his last visit to Happylands.

****

Tilly was feeling exhilarated. Line dancing always made her feel like that. She had never done it before ... until this cruise ... but it was an activity she had always fancied having a go at and was pleased she had signed up for the classes. With a bit of luck, the exertion would help her lose a bit of weight ... or at least work off some of the calories she was consuming. It was proving impossible to resist all the fabulous food which was set out in such a dazzling spectacle every day. Her taste buds were constantly being teased and Tilly had no will-power. None at all.

Anyhow, she wasn't going to worry about that as her new friend, William, didn't seem at all bothered by how tubby she was. Her new friend. Her new lover, hopefully. She had come on this cruise, a desperately lonely woman. She had never married, never had children and her parents had died in the last year, one after the other, her mother with breast cancer and her father from a broken heart as they had been inseparable. It had left her devastated. Apart from her job as a librarian, she had never felt the need to have much contact with others and had very little social life. Her parents had been her world. She had lived at home with them, never wanting to leave the cosy bubble they had made for the three of them. Why would she have wanted to live in a flat by herself or with people she didn't know when she could have the closeness of a fabulous family life? She had barely socialised, preferring the company of her family and the books she devoured from the library but once her beloved parents had died, she had to think about what she was going to do with the rest of her life. Her colleagues had persuaded her to get away and enjoy herself on a cruise, meet new people, have some fun. So, she had gone mad and booked a long trip around the Caribbean, courtesy of the generous life insurance policy and ample savings her parents had bequeathed her.

She had embarked nervously and for the first twenty-four hours began to think she had made a big mistake. The hordes of jolly people, loving couples and happy families, had made her feel even lonelier and more depressed but on the second evening she met William and had been bowled over by his kindness, his interest in her and his olde-worlde charm. He had made the past few weeks more than bearable. He had shown her there was life after death and she could be happy again ... if he was in her life. She knew she was falling in love with him ... had fallen in love with him ... and prayed he was feeling the same about her. She began to dream about a white organza wedding dress, a bouquet of lilies and pink roses ... and best of all, the honeymoon ... maybe another cruise ....

CHAPTER 2

EARLY MARCH

William was on his way home to Peesdown … and couldn't wait to get there. He had been away for the whole winter and was fed up with heat, ships and never being able to get completely away from the human populace. Now it was the beginning of March he wanted to be in England for the spring. He craved peace. He craved his lovely old Victorian home. He wanted to walk in Peesdown Park. He wanted, more than anything, to see Miranda.

His taxi pulled up outside his house at 2.00 a.m. so no-one witnessed his homecoming, which was just as well as he wasn't in disguise, although he now had the perfect excuse if someone did see him without it. He did a grin. He had been hatching a plot while away and couldn't wait to put it into action.

He paid the driver, who turned the taxi around quickly and sped back towards the High Street, desperate to get back to Leeds railway station to pick up another passenger. William stood outside his gates with his suitcases on the ground beside him and with the aid of the illuminated street lights, studied the road he lived on; Miller Lane, with the church at the far end, the Vicarage, the pub, the park gates. He noticed with interest a 'for sale' sign in the garden of the house next door. He had never had anything to do with the elderly couple who lived there as they were frequently away and if he had bumped into them, they only nodded and made no attempt to be friendly. That had suited him admirably. He certainly didn't want neighbours who bothered him repeatedly. He hoped the next lot would be the same. He didn't want to have to move. He liked his house and it was so perfect … being right next to Peesdown Park. He breathed in the cool night air and could feel himself relaxing. It was a welcome relief after months of stifling heat, even when cooled down by sea breezes. God, it was good to be back.

With a smile on his face, he opened the new solid oak gates which he had ordered to be erected during his absence. They were perfect as no-one would be able to see up to the house at all now the wrought iron ones had gone but he would have to affix some good strong bolts on the inside as soon as possible to stop unwanted visitors intruding on his privacy. He walked up the drive, the security lights bathing him in a warm glow as he approached the house. He turned the key in the lock of the original Victorian wooden door and stepped into the hall. All was as it should be. Nothing out of place, nothing disturbed. He knew from experience that when the police searched a house, they weren't exactly fastidious about how they left a place when they departed so he was satisfied no-one had been inside during his absence and, therefore, he couldn't have been linked to that woman who had been raped and so tragically killed in the park before he left home in December.

He dumped his suitcases in the hall and grinned as he entered the kitchen and made a pot of tea, although he would have to drink it black as he hadn't any milk. He looked at the clock on the wall. It was only a few hours until morning and he could go for a walk in the park and see her … Miranda. They would have a lot of catching up to do. He had a lot to tell her about his cruise … where he had been and what he had done … although there was something in particular he could never tell her. That was his secret and his alone … and he had another trophy to add to his collection. In the morning he would have to retrieve his special box from where he had hidden it in the garage before he went away and enjoy an hour or two reminiscing on all his special activities. He chortled. 'Special'. He had never thought of it like that before.

****

"Will you stop kicking me, Charlie," groaned Miranda as she turned over in bed and pushed his legs away from hers. She never

16

allowed the dogs on her bed normally but cheeky Charlie had decided during the night that she wouldn't mind for once. She had been vaguely aware he had joined her but had been too sleepy to resist. It was a surprise Nellie hadn't decided to join the party too but she could be heard snoring heavily downstairs in the lounge.

Miranda turned on the light and looked at the clock on her bedside cabinet. It was nearly 5.00 a.m. .and she had to get up soon so there was no point in trying to get back to sleep. She had to feed the dogs and let them out in the garden before heading off to feed four lots of cats before the traffic built up. If she could make a start while the roads were reasonably quiet, she could get it all done in about an hour and a half and then be free to crack on with all the dog walking and all the paperwork she had to do that day. Her business was expanding fast now and she was finding it difficult to keep up with the massive amount of office work and was thinking about hiring someone to help her on that front. She had considered turning the spare bedroom into an office but it was too much effort to move everything and she simply didn't have the time but she ought to as it made downstairs look so damned untidy. An office upstairs and someone to deal with all the different forms, letters and wages would be a real bonus. She hated being bogged down with it all. She wanted to be out and about with the animals. After all, that was why she had started the business in the first place.

Charlie thumped his tail on the bedding, always eager to get up and have breakfast.

"You're a very greedy young man," Miranda remarked, throwing her arms around his solid black and tan frame and kissing his nose. She had loved all her dogs but somehow this one was just a little more special. He was desperate to be a good boy and always wanted to be as close to her as he possibly could, probably because he had such a bad start with some unkind person and now appreciated his good fortune. Darling Nellie, on the other hand, was a different kettle of fish. A confident Labrador, oblivious as to whether she was naughty or not and only behaved when it suited her. Naughty Nellie!

Miranda kissed Charlie on the head and headed for the bathroom to get ready for the day, throwing a desperate look at the photograph of Jeremy beside her bed. She thought, for the hundredth time, how it should be put away, thrown away even. She had picked it up several times to do just that but something always stopped her.

It had been taken on Boxing Day when they had taken the dogs up to Ilkley Moor and walked, hand in hand, for miles. The Army had generously granted him a few days leave over Christmas and although he stayed with his sister, Daphne, and her family, a good proportion of his time in Leeds was spent with Miranda. They had been so happy, getting to know each other, she actually dared to look forward to a future together but then he had been given the news he was going to be posted to Germany for an indefinite period. It had been a dreadful blow. His posting in London had been bad enough but at least he could get back to Leeds fairly easily and frequently but once he was in Germany, they wouldn't see much of each other at all. Miranda had been devastated and dreaded the day he would go and was desperately unhappy when he informed her that it would be at the very beginning of February, just a couple of days following his birthday.

Daphne decided his birthday party would double up as a leaving party, to which Miranda, as his girlfriend, was naturally invited. She would have much preferred to cook a delicious meal for him at her home, just the two of them and the dogs, and then curl up in bed together but it wasn't to be. Daphne had put in a lot of work organising the bash and there was nothing for it but to get through it as best she could.

She had been nervous, dreadfully nervous, at meeting Jeremy's old friends and some of his colleagues who were also on leave before their posting to Germany with him.

The evening was a miserable, heart-wrenching blur now and she could feel the tears welling up in her eyes as they did every time she thought of what had occurred.

She had managed to hold her own quite nicely to begin with. With Jeremy constantly by her side, she had been introduced to everyone and they had all been nice and included her in all their conversations. The only person she hadn't been keen on was a tall, willowy, blonde-headed woman who was introduced to her by Jeremy as Captain Karen Watkins. Miranda felt instantly at a disadvantage as Karen towered above her, the same height as Jeremy, her hair flowing beautifully over her shoulders and ample bust. She was dressed in a green velvet sequined dress and looked stunning. Miranda had held her hands instantly over her stomach to hide any kind of bulge, wishing she was inches taller and had stuck to her New Year's resolution of losing some weight.

"How nice to meet you," Karen had purred. "Jeremy has told us so much about you."

Miranda had been mortified to feel her cheeks turning pink, which would make her blusher look ridiculous. She had already wondered if she had applied too much. Excusing herself, she disappeared upstairs to the bedroom Daphne had set aside as a powder room for the female guests.

Her fears were realised. Her cheeks, thanks to Karen's remark and the two glasses of champagne she had consumed since arriving at the party, were ablaze beneath the blusher, making her look as if she were having an extremely hot flush. She took one of the tissues from the pretty pink box Daphne had left out on the dressing table and scrubbed at her face but it only made matters worse. She was just contemplating washing it all off in the bathroom when the bedroom door opened and the elegant, beautifully formed Karen Watkins entered with a smile which Miranda could only describe as somewhat triumphal.

"Oh, dear. Are you having a problem with your make-up, Miranda? I'm lucky, alcohol never seems to affect me in that way."

She sashayed across the room and sat on the bed near to Miranda and crossed her long, slim legs.

"You know," she said quietly with just a hint of venom, "you're wasting your time. Jeremy won't stay with you. He's been seeing me on and off for a long time now and in that time, he's played the field ... and so have I, come to that, but he and I have an understanding ... and once he's sewn all the wild oats he needs to, it's me he's going to end up with ... marry and have a family with ... and you will be just another notch on his bedpost. So, if I were you, I wouldn't stick around too long to be humiliated ... it really wouldn't do your self-confidence much good now, would it?"

Miranda had stood like a statue, unable to move, unable to believe what she was hearing. Her heart had been thumping wildly, she had felt nauseous and wanted to run to the bathroom and throw up but she wouldn't give the woman the satisfaction of seeing that. So, she hadn't said a word and concentrated hard on her breathing.

With yet another triumphal smile, Karen stood up and left the room, tossing her long tresses over her shoulder as she closed the door behind her.

Miranda had sunk onto the king-sized bed draped in thick gold brocade and tried not to dissolve into tears and ruin what was left of her make-up. All she had wanted to do was disappear, to get home, to get back to Charlie and Nellie who loved her unconditionally and would never let her down. All the old feelings of rejection the Beastly Bastard had left her with returned with full force. Her marriage had never been a particularly good one, fraught with money problems due to Barry's need to spend every penny both of them made as fast as possible and then rack up thousands of pounds of debt, but his final betrayal with her best friend, Charlotte, had been the most humiliating and traumatic end to their relationship. It had taken a long time to recover and push all those feelings away and regain her self-confidence and self-esteem and stupidly she had placed her trust in another man and found herself back in the same position ... well not quite. Although mortified, thanks to Karen flaming Watkins, she had been spared any further heartbreak and she should probably thank the woman for preventing the relationship from continuing. Better she should find out now what Jeremy was really like than further down the line.

She could have kicked herself. She hadn't wanted to get involved with another man, had always said she wouldn't but when she had set eyes on Jeremy that day outside his father's shop which she and Anna had turned up to view a few months ago, she had been utterly smitten. How stupid she had been. Stupid, stupid, stupid. She had known deep down she would never be good enough for him. They were worlds apart. It was ridiculous and she had to extricate herself from her predicament as fast as possible.

She hadn't felt able to face him again that evening. Taking her coat off the hanger from the rack of guests' coats in the bedroom, she had hurried downstairs and praying she wouldn't bump into anyone, crossed the spacious hall and slipped out of the front door.

She had arrived at Daphne's in a taxi, not wanting to drive because she would be drinking. It was a long walk home and the silly high heel shoes she was wearing would cripple her. She walked around the corner, out of sight of the house and called a taxi on her mobile. She had cried while waiting for it to arrive, uncaring if her make-up was utterly ruined. The taxi driver wouldn't care and neither would Charlie and Nellie, who would be the only other eyes set on her that night.

She sent Jeremy a text. "I'm sorry, I had to leave. Terrible headache. Enjoy your party, good luck in Germany and please don't contact me again."

He didn't reply. More than likely his phone wasn't switched on but even if it had been, he probably didn't hear the ping of the text arriving due to the high volume of the music. Still, he wouldn't care too much about her departing. He would have

Karen to keep him happy … and they would be off to Germany in the morning and that would be that. She would never see him again. It was over.

She arrived home in the taxi half an hour later, still with no answer from Jeremy. She collapsed onto the floor with Charlie and Nellie, who realising she was distressed, tried their best to comfort her by licking her and cuddling as close as they could. She had wrapped her arms around them and wept, resolving that she would never, never fall in love with a man again. It just wasn't worth it. Her entire focus in the future would be her business and her dogs.

CHAPTER 3

MARCH

The phone was ringing as Anna opened up the shop and stepped inside. She dropped her handbag on the counter and answered the phone.

"Pampered Pets," she said cheerily. The name rolled off her tongue now she had become used to it and as the shop was doing so well, she was immensely proud of it too.

"Mrs Stapleton?"

"Yes."

"Hello, good morning. It's Rendell's, the estate agents. We have a couple interested in your property and were wondering if you would be available to show them around this evening ... around 7 pm?"

"Oh, brilliant. Yes, that's perfect," Anna smiled. "What are their names?"

"A Mr & Mrs Merridew ... they're cash buyers so if they like your residence, you could be moving fairly quickly."

"Right," Anna said as her tummy lurched. This really could be it. The house had been on the market since early February and two other couples had viewed it but failed to put in an offer but perhaps this time she would be lucky. "Gosh. That's good. Thank you ... I'll look forward to seeing them."

She put the phone down and perched on the seat beside the till and stared into space. She wanted to sell the house, of course she did but now someone might actually be wanting to buy it, it felt strange. She and Gerald had bought it when they had married and never wanted to move as they loved it so much ... and now she was doing just that. She felt like a traitor ... guilty ... as if she was turning her back on their old life ... but that was just silly. She was moving on ... doing the sensible thing, moving into the flat above the shop to save time and money and make life a lot easier.

After all, what did she want with a three bedroomed house and large garden now? The flat here was perfectly adequate for her needs and there was the gorgeous garden outside which she was looking forward to caring for now the winter was over.

She stood up and went through to the back, through the pretty garden room and into the kitchen and made herself a cup of coffee. She had an hour before the shop was due to open and Emily, her new member of staff was due to arrive for her first day. It would be marvellous to have real help at last and enjoy a proper lunch hour. Since opening the shop a few months ago, she had struggled more or less on her own, working all day, keeping a sandwich and a flask of coffee beneath the counter and darting to the loo for a few minutes while she locked the shop door and put a 'back in a few minutes' sign on it. She could have shut the shop at lunchtime but that would have been silly as that was often the busiest time when people were shopping in their breaks. She had taken on a couple of people but neither had suited. One had lasted a month, another about seven weeks but they had been young and became bored easily of the chitchat, mainly about customers' pets. She had learned her lesson since then. Emily was in her forties. She hadn't worked for years, having stayed at home to bring up her three children but they had now fled the nest and she wanted something to occupy her.

"My George, he's a fireman," Emily had said proudly at her interview, "he's quite happy for me to have a little job and I've always loved animals ... we have our little Sammy, our Chihuahua, and adore him ... in fact, I think we might have seen you in Peesdown Park when we were walking him ... you were with Miranda from Four Paws ... we like her very much. She looked after Sammy for us when we had to go to a funeral in Scotland last year ... it was George's cousin ... died of a stroke ... poor man. My George was really upset."

It was difficult to get a word in with Emily. She certainly liked to talk but she was nice, kind and friendly and Anna was more than willing to give her a chance and was looking forward to her arriving today. It would be possible to pop into the park for a walk with Miranda too once Emily had been shown what was what. That would be a refreshing change.

Anna smiled. It was going to be an interesting day, having Emily join her, the Merridew's looking over the house this evening … and a walk with her best friend, who no doubt would talk about nothing but Jeremy. Miranda was still suffering badly from the trauma she had suffered at Jeremy's birthday party and it was hard to jolly her along as she was sunk in despair that she would never see him again and he would probably marry the beautiful, clever, posh Karen Watkins. Poor Miranda. Anna felt so sorry for her. She liked Jeremy enormously and was disappointed he hadn't been straight with her best friend that he had another woman in tow.

****

Freddie Fletcher was looking forward to today as his replacement as park keeper, Bob Watkins, was joining him on his rounds of Peesdown Park so he could be shown the ropes before Freddie hung up his uniform and took a much welcome retirement.

Beryl, Freddie's darling wife, with whom he could not live without, had finally persuaded him to hand in his notice two weeks ago. He had intended to stick it out until he retired but had never recovered from that awful day when he found that woman's body in the lake … Tanya Phillips. He simply couldn't forget it. Every time he closed his eyes, he could see her again … and it wasn't pretty. The poor, silly woman, must have had a terrible end. He hadn't known it at the time but the police had informed him afterwards, and it was soon common knowledge, that she had been raped before being strangled. Stupid, stupid woman. He could feel deep anger towards her at times, even while feeling deeply sorry for her. Why the hell did she have to be so crazy as to walk around the park at night? He had warned her that there was a rapist about who had never been caught and she had just shrugged it off, totally oblivious to her own safety and welfare … but she had paid the price … and so had he.

He had enjoyed his job for years but since that awful morning he hadn't. It had become a nightmare, wondering who could have done such a dastardly deed. He had always been observant, after all, you had to be, in charge of a place such as Peesdown Park with all the goings-on, especially in the summer with the younger generation and their antics but now he studied everyone more closely, engaging more than he normally would in conversation, trying to get an idea if they could be capable of such a terrible act.

It all played on his mind, day in and day out, night in and night out. Who was it? Was it a park regular? Was it someone he knew well? Had he missed something? He kept having nightmares if he did manage to get some sleep and frequently woke Beryl. She was looking more and more drawn and tired as time went on. It wasn't fair on her … and on him. They had talked it over a couple of weeks ago, both at the end of their tether with it all.

"I don't think you have any choice, Freddie," Beryl insisted. "You have to hand in your notice. It's going to make you ill, going to the park every day, walking around the lake, never being able to forget or put it to the back of your mind and then not sleeping properly. You … we … simply can't go on like this."

"I know you're right," he had agreed "but it's a while before I can claim my pension. We need the money, Beryl … I can't give it up … not yet."

"Nonsense. If we don't have a holiday this year … have one of those staycation thingies people are talking about … you know when you just remain at home but go out for days, we can save a lot of money … and we have those premium bonds Aunt Mary bought us for our silver wedding anniversary. They've only netted us twenty-five pounds so far. We could cash them in, which will help. Then there are our savings and my job … and then perhaps you could find something part-time … gardening maybe. We'd manage, Freddie."

He had felt a huge weight being lifted off his shoulders at her words. "Oh, Beryl. If you're really sure."

"Yes, I am," she had said determinedly. "I want my old Freddie back and once you're away from that park, you can start forgetting what happened … at least not forget exactly but put it to the back of your mind and find something else to think about. We could start planning a holiday for when you do get your pension … somewhere we've never been … we could splash out and go abroad … see some of the sights we've always wanted to before we're too old to enjoy it … so … hand in your notice today. Promise me, Freddie, you will."

He had. He rang Reginald Barrington Senior from Barrington and Barrington, the solicitor who looked after the affairs of the Pee family who owned Peesdown Park, and informed him of his decision. Mr Barrington had expressed his disappointment but was most understanding when Freddie explained how he felt after finding Tanya Philips and the effect it was having on him.

"I'll find a replacement for you as soon as I can," Mr Barrington had said. "I'll try and get someone to start as soon as possible so you can familiarise them with the park and your duties before your notice expires."

He had been true to his word. Young Watkins was commencing this morning which made Freddie look forward to going to work himself for a change. It would be good to have someone with him, someone to chat to and rely on if there was any need for backup … and the best bonus of all was that there weren't many days left before he could hand in his uniform and be free of Peesdown Park and all who entered it for good.

****

Robert Watkins, Bob as he liked to be called, was looking forward to his first day at work in the park. He hadn't been able to believe his luck when he saw the advert for a park keeper for Peesdown with a decent salary and the prospect of working only during the day and being in such a beautiful and clean environment. With his job as a security guard on the construction site coming to an abrupt end, he hadn't hesitated in applying for the park keeper's job and was chuffed to bits when he was told it was his.

He knew the park well and not just from using it for jogging every day. He had hung out there a lot with school friends, using his free bus pass to get there from the horrid little back-to-back in Harehills where he had lived with his mother and sister. It had been good to escape into the fresh air and get away for a few hours from the seedy life his mother lived, bringing man after man back to have noisy sex in her bedroom, right next to his and from where he could clearly hear every grunt and groan. God, it had been good when he had finally grown up and could leave and find a place of his own. He had shared a house with two other lads for a few years while he worked as a labourer on a building site but when he found the security job, which paid much better, he rented his little terrace in Peesdown, pleased to be living so near to the park where he could jog every day and use it as a garden when he wanted to just sit and watch the world go by in nice weather.

However, using the park for recreational purposes rather than working there was going to be a different kettle of fish and he was looking forward to it, getting to know everyone who used it regularly and making sure everyone behaved themselves. He certainly wasn't going to stand for any nonsense from anyone, that was for sure… and there was the added bonus of all the women to meet and ogle, especially in the summer when they appeared in their skimpy outfits, lazing around on the grass, or running around the lake and walking their dogs. He looked good in his dark blue uniform … smart and trustworthy … and women liked a man in uniform. Yes, he had high hopes for a few more interesting encounters before he swanned off on his travels next year.

****

William woke up, opened his eyes and had to think for a moment as to where he was. It seemed strange not to be in his cabin on the ship and feeling some kind of motion. Everything was still and calm and instead of seagulls, he could hear garden birds twittering and tweeting outside his window.

He looked at the picture of Miranda by his bed and smiled. He would see her today. He would walk with her, talk to her, smile at her. He could feel the butterflies in his tummy at the mere thought. He wondered what she had been up to in his absence. Probably expanded her business as she was very ambitious … and hardworking. He would give her that. It couldn't be easy taking six dogs at a time to the park and keeping control and at the same time making sure her employees were doing their jobs properly.

He thought about some of the other people he knew from the park. Freddie Fletcher, the park keeper. He had found the body of Tanya Phillips floating in the lake, which must have been a hell of a shock for the poor old boy. William felt quite sorry for him.

Then there was Anna from Pampered Pets. No doubt her shop was doing well as she was such a warm-hearted woman and easy to like. He would pop in later and say hello if she wasn't in the park today.

He also had something to tell them too … an exciting plan he had been working on all winter and today he was going to start putting it into action. 'Operation Miranda' he was going to call it.

He grinned, got out of bed and looked out of the window at the gate at the far end of the garden. Yes, it looked good. Nice and solid and provided total privacy with the high hedging all the way around. He would pay a visit to the ironmongers along the High Street and buy a couple of solid bolts and fix them later ... and he had to go to the post office and collect his mail ... and he needed to retrieve his trophy box and scrapbook from the garage ... after all, he had more things to add to the collection now ... and a photo ... of a very drunk Tilly Pargeter, just before she so tragically died.

He remembered that day clearly. Their ship had docked in St. Lucia early in the morning where it was going to remain until the following day. They had gone ashore and hired a speedboat to take them to an uninhabited island a couple of miles out to sea. He had found out about it from a tour guide on their ship who had visited on a previous cruise. Apparently, the beach was particularly beautiful but it was rare for anyone to visit as there was nothing but deep, dangerous forestation in the middle and it was impossible to arrive or leave unless by boat so there was every likelihood visitors wouldn't be disturbed for hours.

William had told Tilly about it, enthused about how lovely it would be to get right away from the world for a few hours, to be alone on their own private island to swim, have a picnic, relax and soak up the sun.

Tilly thought it was an excellent idea, seemingly bowled over by the thought that he wanted to be totally alone with her for a few hours. Her eyes had widened and her smile had been broad as she nodded her assent and talked of nothing else but how she was looking forward to it.

The tour guide booked the speedboat and arranged a luxury picnic hamper, which included a few shots of Tilly's favourite Witches' Brew and a couple of bottles of champagne. An hour after they docked in St. Lucia they were being whizzed across the water by a charming young Rastafarian and deposited on their own, private island, William pleased as punch that no-one else from the ship had considered the trip worthwhile and had remained in St. Lucia soaking up the sights.

Tilly had jumped out of the red and white speedboat, her face wreathed in delighted smiles as she waited for William to come ashore with the hamper. They waved goodbye to the young man who grinned in acknowledgement and swung his boat and dreadlocks as he sped off again, having said he would be back to collect them around 5.00 p.m. As it was only 10.00 a.m., they had many hours to fill.

William put down the hamper in a shaded spot beneath some trees, while Tilly paddled happily in the sea.

"I do wish I could swim," she said sorrowfully. "It looks so enticing. I should have had some lessons on the ship."

"I could teach you," he said, "We could start your lessons now and then continue when we get back on board."

He stared at her. He could feel the old itch. It had been bothering him for days ... just as she had ... and now he had her ... completely at his mercy ... with no-one around to come to her aid. It was a completely different scenario to what he normally did. Usually, he carried out his attacks at night and didn't hang about but today it was going to be different. It was the morning, in brilliant sunshine and he had hours in which to play with his victim. Stupid woman, trusting him ... just as they all did.

Suddenly she whipped off her top and skirt to reveal a green swimsuit beneath. "Come on then. No time like the present," she giggled.

He removed his outer clothing to reveal his black swimming trunks and noticed her gulp as she looked his body up and down. She wanted him ... and it was going to be easier than he thought. He might actually have sex with her normally, without force. It would be interesting to see if he could manage it properly for once before he finished her off ... because that was the real thrill. The ending of the life, hearing the last breath, the final closure of the eyes, the relaxation of the body. He felt the excitement in the pit of his stomach. He couldn't strangle her though. He couldn't leave any signs that he had murdered her. It had to look natural ... like an accident. He stared at the water and then at her as she grabbed his hand and led him towards the stunning blue sea and they entered it together.

31

CHAPTER 4

Miranda received a text from Anna to say she would be able to take an early lunch and have a walk with her this morning as the new assistant, Emily, seemed to be coping well in the shop and was more than happy to be left for an hour.

Miranda smiled. It would be good to have Anna's company on a walk again. In fact, the day was going to be an interesting one as once the walk was over she was interviewing potential dog sitters to board dogs in their homes while their owners were on holiday or unable to care for them for short periods, maybe if they were ill or on jury service. Recently a couple of people had rung her in a panic because they were being called to sit in court for a couple of weeks and had no idea what they were going to do with their dogs.

The boarding side of her business was certainly beginning to pick up now she had more time to concentrate on it. With three girls walking for her, she could leave most of the group walks to them, just doing her one walk in the morning as Nellie and Charlie still had to go out and it was important for them to be with their friends.

There were two couples to see this afternoon, one who lived near to Meanwood Park and the other in Shadwell, a pretty village on the outskirts of Leeds. They sounded as if they could be satisfactory candidates with suitable homes and gardens to look after dogs for a week or two and if they were, that would make six families she would have on her books. The other four were already full for this coming summer and as she was beginning to be flooded by requests from dog owners, she would need a good deal more to cater for the demand.

Anna was just emerging from Pampered Pets as Miranda drove along Peesdown High Street. She honked the horn and pulled up beside her friend.

"Hop in."

Anna did as instructed, glad she had quickly changed into old clothes as Nellie and Charlie, who were on the back seat, pushed their noses through the dog guard and tried hard to lick her, showering her with dog hairs as they trembled with pleasure at her appearance. She grinned as she tried to find room for her feet in the pile of dog leads, balls, various chewed toys, dog bowls, bottles of water, packets of poo bags and two blackened banana skins in the footwell.

"Sorry," grimaced Miranda. "I do tidy it up occasionally but it's rare anyone ever sits there."

Anna giggled. "I'm sure you have much better things to do than clean. This is so nice," she sighed, "being able to escape for an hour."

"So, Emily is doing ok," Miranda stated, driving up the road, across Miller Lane and through the park gates. She pulled up next to a Subaru and a smart Volvo estate which made hers look old and tatty. She grimaced, making a mental note to chuck it through the car wash before she turned up for the interviews this afternoon. If it was clean on the outside it wouldn't look quite so bad and thankfully no-one would have to look inside.

"Really well, so far," Anna smiled as she got out and watched Miranda open the car doors for the dogs to alight. Today, in addition to her own, Miranda had two black Labrador sisters, Heidi and Bonnie, a Springer Spaniel called Ellie and a black and tan Working Cocker Spaniel named Alfie, who looked angelic and loveable with his big, brown eyes, but could be very naughty indeed if he wasn't kept an eye on and didn't give a fig if he received any chastisement.

Miranda nodded at the cafe. "Oh look ... it must be opening up soon ... that will be nice. The lady who usually runs it is lovely and makes some super snacks."

For the first time since Anna had started using the park, the freshly painted cafe door was wide open and there were lights on. It must be nice inside, she surmised, with the windows overlooking the lake. She would have to take a look as soon as it was up and running as it was going to be competition for her little venture in the garden room.

The two women walked along the path towards the lake, the dogs gallivanting happily beside them. It was a lovely spring day. The sun was shining and for the first time for a good few months, it was possible to walk without wearing gloves and scarves.

"So, tell me about Emily," Miranda, slipping an arm through Anna's.

Anna laughed. "She doesn't stop talking ... it's really hard to get a word in edgeways ... but her heart's in the right place and she's so eager to learn and work hard. I did wonder about the wisdom of leaving her on her first day but she's done so well this morning and insisted she's happy to be on her own ... and she can always ring me if there's a problem. After all, I'm not exactly miles away."

Miranda smiled. "I'm so glad. Perhaps we'll get to see a bit more of each other now."

"I do hope so ... oh, and I've a couple coming to see the house this evening. With a bit of luck, this pair might put in an offer."

"Oh, Anna. I do hope so. It will make your life so much easier."

"I know. I've still got mixed feelings about selling up but I know it's the most sensible action to take."

"Goodness," Miranda said, staring along the lakeside path, unlooping herself from Anna to scoop up two loads of poo deposited by Nellie and Heidi. "I think that's William over there ... talking to Fart Features and someone who looks very much like he might be the new park keeper."

Anna followed her gaze. "Oh, yes. It is William. He's been away a long time. I do hope he feels better now. He should do after such a long cruise."

Their footsteps took them towards the three men who were deep in conversation, Miranda taking the precaution of putting

Nellie on the lead in case she decided to jump all over Fart Features.

"I can't say I have a lot of time for the old boy but I think I'll quite miss him," giggled Miranda. "All his scolding and threats. It just won't be the same in the park without him … do you think we should have some kind of leaving party for him … in the pub … you know, the Red Lion just outside the gates … I'm sure quite a few would come … even if only to make sure he never comes back," she laughed.

Anna stifled a giggle. "Miranda. Behave. The poor old boy isn't that bad really … and he's been dreadfully shaken up ever since that poor woman was attacked and murdered."

Out of the three men, William saw them first.

"Miranda!" he said, leaning on his stick, his face lighting up as his eyes settled on her.

Miranda smiled back warmly. "Hello, William. It's so nice to see you. Have you had a good holiday? You certainly look well. You're very tanned."

"Yes … yes, thank you. I had a lovely time and yes, I feel much better than I did." He didn't add that seeing her was the best lift he could have had. His heart flooded with love for her. He wanted to take her in his arms and kiss her … her eyes, her cheeks, her lips. God, he loved her so much. He had to have her … and soon … in his house, in his arms … in his bed. He felt giddy at the mere thought of it as he smiled at Anna and said hello.

"I'm glad we've bumped into you this morning, Miranda," stated Freddie firmly, glaring at Nellie who was whining to be let off the lead so she could jump into the lake and harass the ducks. As a precaution, Miranda also snapped Alfie's lead on quickly in case he decided to disgrace himself.

"Oh … and why's that," Miranda asked, catching the gaze of the man standing beside Freddie. She smiled but his face remained impassive. Her heart sank. She had hoped Fart Feature's replacement would be far more companionable than him but perhaps not.

"This is Bob Watkins, your new park keeper. He's spending a bit of time with me before I leave ... to get a feel of the place and meet people."

"How nice ... Bob ... I hope you'll enjoy your new job. You'll certainly be seeing a lot of me ... I'm here most days ... and this is Anna," Miranda waved a hand at her friend, "she runs the pet shop, Pampered Pets, just down the High Street. She's going to get a dog soon so you'll be seeing much more of her too."

Bob nodded in acknowledgement as he looked at Anna, who gave him a bright smile.

"Yes, well .... You'll have to make sure those dogs of yours behave themselves now," remarked Freddie. "Young Bob is going to be a right stickler for making sure everyone keeps their animals under proper control."

Miranda grinned. "Well, as you can see, Bob. Mine are ... oh, whoops," she muttered as Bob nodded his head in the direction of Bonnie who was doing a nice big poo on the grass a few yards away.

Miranda headed off quickly, whipping a poo bag out of her jacket pocket and hauling a disgruntled Nellie and Alfie with her. "Don't think I'm letting you two off the lead just yet," Miranda hissed. "You'll disgrace me badly if I do. You'll have to wait until we get to the woods."

"Well, Bob," said Freddie. "We better move along. There's a lot more I need to show you. Goodbye William. It's nice to see you again ... and looking so well. Anna," he added, doffing his cap at her.

The two men disappeared around a bend in the path.

"Whew!" gasped Miranda, re-joining Anna and William. "I'm not sure about this new chap. Did you see the way he glared at me just because I hadn't noticed the poo? I do hope he's not going to be more of a little Hitler than Fart Features."

William gave a wry smile. "I see you haven't changed, Miranda. The poor man's name is Freddie."

Miranda laughed. "Sorry. Can't help it ... will have to think of a name for our new park keeper now, won't I? Something with 'poo' in it, I think, by the look of him."

She brushed her hair away from her eyes as she spoke and William was startled by the look of misery in them, even as she laughed. Her usual sparkle wasn't there and there were tension lines around her mouth. It struck him that she was unhappy. Whatever had occurred in his absence? He couldn't ask now, in Anna's presence, but he'd try to get Miranda alone this week and find out. He couldn't bear the thought of her being upset about anything. He had to sort it for her if he could. Her happiness was paramount.

****

"You'll have to watch these professional dog walkers," Freddie remarked as he and Bob continued on their way around the lake and turned into the woods. Paths were running in all directions and Bob needed to know his way around and Freddie was determined to show him everything.

Even though the sun was shining, there had been a lot of rain in recent days and the ground was muddy and slippery but as both men wore heavy boots, they strode along confidently.

"There are more and more of them every week," continued Freddie. "I suppose they think it's easy money, taking six dogs for a walk, but most of them soon find out it's not as cushy as they first thought and disappear fairly quickly with their shiny new vans and their daft logos. Miranda, however, although a cheeky young madam, is a stickler for hard work and seems to be growing quite a big business. I believe she has three other dog walkers working for her now. I've met Belinda ... she seems quite a capable young woman and I've never had any bother with her ... or her dogs ...

and the other two women go to Roundhay or Temple Newsam so we don't see them here. Anyhow, don't take any nonsense from Miranda as she can certainly be a bit of a handful at times."

"Oh, don't worry, Freddie," Bob replied. "I've no intentions of doing so. Some of these so-called professional dog walkers are a menace ... I've encountered a few when running ... and been chased by their blasted dogs. It's not funny, believe me, having them snapping at your heels."

He vividly remembered an encounter with a nasty little Jack Russell which had sunk its teeth into his flesh at Golden Acre Park. He had given it a good kicking and sent it flying across the grass as its owner screamed profanities at him. He had jogged away, leaving her to scoop up her injured pooch and rush off in the direction of the car park, no doubt to take it to the vets. He had never seen her or her blasted dog again.

"No. I'm sure it's not," Freddie agreed, thinking it was bad enough running into them when just walking. "Now, this is the boundary wall ... on the other side is the golf course. It's rarely used and there's talk of closing it down and using the land to build houses but how true that is, I'm not sure. I don't frequent the place. Could never understand why anyone would want to spend hours trying to get a little ball into a hole a long way away ... but then I never can understand why people have an obsession with balls ... rugby, football, netball, hockey ... it's all beyond me."

Bob nodded in agreement. He had never been one for games either. Running and spending time at the gym yes but ball games and participation with others was a definite no. Bob liked his own company and his own pursuits. He had no wish to make friends.

The two men followed the boundary wall until it meandered back down to the lake via a woodland path and they could return to the car park and the cafe.

"Come and meet Trudy. She runs the cafe every year. You'll like her," Freddie said. "Although the poor woman has had a hell of a lot of problems, she remains remarkably cheerful. Her husband died a couple of years ago in a terrible accident at the factory where he worked. Fell into a vat of boiling oil. Ghastly death, poor man. She was left with two teenagers who then went off the rails, leading her, a grieving widow, a merry dance. Bunking off school, shoplifting, drugs. The boy, Carl, ended up in prison for burglary, trying to steal money for his drug habit and the girl, Rebecca, got herself pregnant and is now living in a council flat in a seedy part of Leeds with her child. Trudy offered to have Rebecca and the baby live with her but the stupid girl refused, preferring her independence. From what I gather from Beryl, my wife ... she's friends with Trudy ... Rebecca's now working as a prostitute, is also dependent on drugs and the child has been taken into care. Poor Trudy's battling to get custody of it, although if she does, I have no idea how she will manage to work. Blimey, people do have their problems."

A white transit van with 'Temptation Foods' written on the side in gold lettering was parked beside the open cafe door. The driver, whistling tunelessly, was busy unloading boxes, carrying them inside and dumping them on the counter behind which stood a tubby middle-aged lady filling a fridge with canned drinks. Her dark hair was pulled back into a bun on the top of her head and she wore a dark blue overall, which gave her a somewhat matronly appearance.

"Hello, Freddie," she smiled. "It's that time of year again ... but I must say I was sorry to hear you won't be here for much longer."

Freddie smiled back, pleased to see Trudy again, especially as she gave him freebies of coffee and a sandwich on his break every morning and tea and a bun in the afternoons.

"Yes," he replied. "Just a couple more weeks and then I shall be free of the place ... and this," he nodded at the man beside him, "is Bob Watkins, the new park keeper."

Trudy and Bob shook hands.

"Sit yourselves down and I'll make some coffee," Trudy instructed. "There aren't any snacks yet as we're not open officially until tomorrow."

The two men walked across the room to a table by the window overlooking the lake and the woods beyond and sat down.

Bob looked around with interest. It wasn't a big space, only ten tables with four chairs around each one, then the counter and the food preparation area behind but it was adequate for snacks and customers also had the benefit of the fabulous view over the park.

"I presume you and Trudy know there are plans afoot to increase the size of this place ... and do other things too," he remarked as he pulled out a chair and sat down. "The owners want to put in a big play area for the kids and run events here too ... Mr Barrington told me when I was interviewed."

"Oh?" Freddie looked surprised. "Goodness knows why. The place has been a little haven of peace and quiet for many years and the Pees live in Ireland and seem to have little interest in what goes on here."

"I heard they're having to tighten their belts," Trudy remarked as she approached the table with three cups of coffee on a tray. She placed it on the table and sat down beside Freddie.

"That's what Mr Barrington told me when I went to pick up the cafe keys and that I'm to expect surveyors and the like coming to assess the place and see what can be done to expand it. By all accounts the Pees have lost money on the stock market and have had to sell land in Ireland ... along with one of their homes in Switzerland ... and as Peesdown Park costs them so much, with only cafe takings in the summer as revenue, they need to start making it pay otherwise, I suppose, they will consider selling it too."

Freddie rubbed his chin. "Barrington didn't tell me about the financial situation when I popped into the office to hand in my written notice but thinking about it, the park must cost the Pees a pretty penny when they have a park keeper's wages to pay along with gardeners and then I suppose there is insurance and goodness knows what else, then keeping the cafe and toilets up to scratch and as you say, Trudy, the only revenue is from the cafe in the summer."

"That's right," she agreed. "I can understand why things are going to have to change, although I do hope we're not going to be swamped with people all the time as the main attraction is the solitude and there won't be much of that if there are hordes of screaming kids now we are going to open all year through ... and hold noisy events such as pop concerts, or the like," she shuddered.

Bob looked out of the window at the scene before him. The ducks and swans on the lake, along with the moorhens and coots ... a couple of elderly pensioners throwing bread to them, three women pushing toddlers in pushchairs, four female dog walkers chatting while their pooches busied themselves in the bushes. It all looked serene and charming with the trees and bushes springing into life and the hum of a grasscutter in the distance. However, this was late morning at the end of March and children were at school but Easter was nearly upon them and things could be very different then. Not that he minded. He was looking forward to having more people to keep under control.

Freddie sipped his coffee. "I think I've just picked the perfect time to retire," he said with a smirk.

CHAPTER 5

William enjoyed his morning in the park. He had forgotten what a lovely place it could be, whether or not he had the bonus of seeing and talking to Miranda. He loved the sense of freedom from the bustling Peesdown suburb, the fresh air, the flora and fauna, especially as it was all coming to life now it was spring. Daffodils were out in abundance in the flower beds and the trees were greening up, some already out in their finery, others taking a little longer but it was all so uplifting and made his heart sing with joy … until he noticed how miserable Miranda was.

He had accompanied her and Anna around the lake. It would have been better without Anna but he couldn't take exception to her as she was so damned nice. He genuinely did like her and was keen to see what she had done to the shop in his absence.

"I'll pop in later," he said. "Meet your new assistant too."

Anna grinned as they strolled amiably along in the sunshine. "Just be prepared. You might find it a bit hard to get a word in edgeways. Emily tends to talk rather a lot."

"So, how was it? The cruise," asked Miranda curiously. William certainly looked fighting fit now with his tanned face and bright eyes and he seemed to be walking better too, his limp not quite so distinct as it had been before he went away. Warmer climes must have been beneficial for his leg.

"Very good. Very good indeed … but as nice as it was, it's even better to be back in Peesdown … although I shan't be on my own for much longer," he added, realising this was his moment to start putting his master plan, 'Operation Miranda' into action.

Both women looked at him curiously.

"My cousin, Stephen, is coming to stay with me," he said with bated breath. His idea had to work. He couldn't bear the thought of never having Miranda as his own. She had to fall in love with Stephen. She had to come and live with him. She had to. He didn't know what he would do if she didn't. "So, you might well see him in the park in the coming days. He doesn't like to walk with me though ... he finds my pace a bit slow ... so we shan't be together ... but you'll probably recognise him as we do have very similar features."

"Oh, that's a shame," Miranda remarked and then added hastily, "not that he's coming to stay with you but that he doesn't want to walk with you."

"Oh, I don't mind. Not at all. We both like our own space ... indoors and out."

"It's just as well you own such a lovely big house, William. I shouldn't imagine you will have much trouble keeping your distance from each other." Anna remarked.

William smiled. "Yes, it's rather large and I do rattle around a bit so it will be nice to have company for a while. I don't know how long he will stay ... Stephen. He owns a construction business in the west country and is thinking of expanding up here in the north. If he's successful, perhaps he might like to buy the house next door, which is up for sale. Anyway, I certainly hope whoever the next occupant is that they're nice and quiet. It's been so pleasant with the present elderly couple but the houses are perfect for a large family and I can't say I'm a great fan of children ... especially when they're noisy," he grimaced.

Miranda had a dreamy look on her face. "I'd love it ... it would be so handy for the park ... and I could board so many dogs ... give them lovely holidays with all that space in the house and garden ... but," she sighed. "Pigs might fly."

William glanced at her. Bless her. She was going to get her wish. She could come and live with him and have as many dogs as she wanted. He saw the future clearly. He would make her fall in love with Stephen, they would get married in St. Edmunds and they would live happily ever after in his house with numerous dogs and cats ... and maybe even children. He didn't want them but if she did, he would tolerate the little blighters if it made her happy. He could hardly contain his excitement. It was all bubbling up inside him and he couldn't wait to get home and start bringing Stephen to life.

They reached the car park fifteen minutes later, Miranda having put all six dogs on the lead, William pretending his leg was beginning to play up and Anna beginning to worry about having left Emily for so long.

"I'll be off then," William said, wincing convincingly as he put his left foot on the ground. "I think I've done enough for today. Bye, Miranda. See you tomorrow maybe." He turned to Anna. "I'll pop in later, Anna. I've a bit of shopping to do this afternoon when my leg has had a rest ... have to get one or two things in for Stephen as his taste in food is a little different to mine."

He turned and walked out of the gates, leaving Miranda to put the dogs into her Volvo and say goodbye to Anna.

"That's the first time I've enjoyed a walk for weeks," she sighed contentedly. "It's been so nice, you having time to walk with me. Even with the dogs, it's a lonely occupation and although walking is supposed to release happy endorphins, it seems to do the opposite for me when I'm on my own and depression seems to descend pretty rapidly just lately."

Anna hugged her friend, knowing how much she was still hurting from her broken relationship with Jeremy.

"Well, if Emily hasn't frightened all my customers away, I'll be able to join you more often. Good luck with the interviews this afternoon. I'll ring you later so you can tell me all about it and also let you know how I get on with the house viewing this evening."

"Oh, yes, do. I'm dying to know. Good luck to you too."

Anna walked off in the direction of the High Street and Pampered Pets while Miranda jumped into her Volvo and started the engine. At the same time, Freddie Fletcher and Bob Watkins emerged from the cafe. Freddie nodded at her. Bob stared in her direction and then turned away. For some reason, Miranda shivered. She didn't like him. She didn't like him at all.

****

William went home with mixed feelings. He had seen Miranda. He had talked to her. He had told the girls about Stephen ... introduced the man's coming presence with a simple explanation of why he and his 'cousin' would never be seen in the park together and it had been accepted. He couldn't wait for Stephen to make his first appearance!

He reached his house and shut the large oak gates behind him. He would nip into the hardware store along the High street this afternoon, buy the bolts and get them on before it grew dark and that would be one important job out of the way ... but for now he had to go and rummage through his wardrobe and find clothes no-one had seen him wearing but as he hadn't many, that was probably going to be an impossible task. It was more than likely a trip to Leeds was going to be necessary to buy a new set of clothes for his 'cousin'. Oh, heavens. He hated shopping. He groaned.

"Helloooo ... William," called a voice just as he was about to step indoors. He turned, annoyed that someone had opened the gate. The sooner the bolts were on the better.

"Hello, William. I was just next door, saying goodbye to Mr and Mrs Smithson before they move out and saw you arriving home. I must say, William, your gates are very smart," he added admiring the solid oak. "I do hope you've had a good time while you've been away."

William forced a smile at the Vicar. He didn't feel like being chatty now. He had things to do. "Yes, thank you," he said, trying not to grit his teeth with annoyance.

"Good," the Vicar smiled. "I'm so pleased. Now that you're back though, I was wondering if you could find time to give us a hand on Easter Monday. We missed you when you were away for the Christmas bazaar, which I must add was very well attended and we did very well. Anyhow, we've decided to have a little event in the park this time ... a few stalls and games and things ... in aid of the local hospice … it should be quite busy as if the weather is good, which so far the forecast is saying it will be, there might be a lot of people out and about so we want to take advantage and try to raise some money … and for everyone to have a good time of course."

William's heart sank. The last thing he wanted to do was help out at Easter. He wanted to concentrate on bringing Stephen to life but he had to keep in with the Vicar, after all the man would be marrying him and Miranda very soon.

"Right," he said, trying to sound eager. "What would you like me to do?"

"Man one of the stalls … the books perhaps, or the bric-a-brac. It would be terribly kind of you if you could spare a few hours."

"Yes. I'm sure I could. I'll come to church on Sunday and you can fill me in then, Vicar. I'm afraid I must go now … I have a rather urgent job I have to see to." *Such as fixing bolts on the bloody gates.*

"Oh, right. Yes, of course. Well, that's tremendously kind of you, William. I'll see you on Sunday then."

The two men smiled at each other and the Vicar walked smartly back down the path and shut the gates firmly behind him.

William entered the house, closed the door and sighed with relief as the silence settled around him.

****

Emily was bubbling with having been given such responsibility so early in her new job and had sold several bags of dried dog and cat food, a dog bed, a very expensive dog lead, cat litter and several toys and treats, leaving Anna with a sense of guilt.

"Gosh, Emily. I'm so sorry. It's not normally that busy on a Monday morning. You should have rung me and I would have come back."

47

"No, no, Anna. I managed perfectly and enjoyed chatting to everyone and pointing out things they might have forgotten ... like the toys and treats." Her eyes twinkled merrily. "I'm sure there are some animals in Peesdown who will be delighted with my suggestions."

Anna laughed. If Emily kept this up, she would certainly pay for herself very quickly.

Refreshed and relaxed from her walk, Anna sent Emily for her lunch and settled down on the chair at the counter to flip through the latest details from Sonia about the newest animals at Happylands who needed re-homing. Her attention was immediately drawn to two arrivals, whom, according to the details, had been found abandoned and tied up on a local farmer's land.

Anna looked at the pictures. Both dogs looked wary and frightened. Her heart went out to them. What had they been through? What ghastly person had left them, in the middle of winter, at night, to probably die of exposure and starvation if the farmer hadn't found them? How could people be so cruel? She felt an overwhelming urge to see them, to give them as much love as she could to make up for their awful experience but it was doubtful Sonia would consider her as a suitable new owner for two dogs, after all with her inexperience, one would be a challenge. She looked at the other dogs and cats on offer but her eyes kept darting back to the first two. They looked so adorable and it wasn't as if they were young puppies and would rip the place apart. They might be nice and calm, perhaps even trained. Then she thought about her situation ... selling the house and moving into the flat. It was hardly the right time to be taking on one dog, let alone two.

She sat and bit her lip, thinking hard, considering what life would be like with two dogs, living here, above the shop, in the flat. They would have to remain upstairs during opening hours. They weren't puppies so wouldn't chew or soil the place, at least she hoped not. She could walk them easily in the park before she started work, then at lunchtime and again after work and then there was the lovely garden they could enjoy during the light evenings. Her heart leapt with excitement. She desperately wanted a dog but could she cope with two? She would ask Sonia what she thought. If Sonia was one thing, it was forthright. A spade was a spade as far as she was concerned and if she didn't think Anna was suitable, she would certainly tell her so.

She took one last look at the picture of the dogs and with her heart melting, Anna picked up the phone and dialled Sonia's number.

****

"Happylands," said Josh, holding the phone between his head and shoulder and wiping his hands on a tea towel. He had been making a broccoli and tomato quiche for tea while his mother was outside talking to someone who wanted to rehome one of the dogs.

"Oh, hello, Anna. What can we do for you?" he asked brightly. He liked Anna. But then, who wouldn't? She was so nice and kind and a pleasure to be around.

"Hi, Josh. It's about two of the dogs you've recently rescued … the two the farmer found on his land. I was … I was wondering … have you re-homed them yet?

"No … they're still here. Mum's only just started advertising them as she wanted to make sure they were well over their shocking treatment before they were re-homed. Lovely dogs. Much happier now they're used to Mum and the kennel maids. They're wagging their tails most of the time, which is always a good sign."

"Oh, I'm so glad they're getting over their terrible experience. I bet your mother had a lot to say about that."

Josh laughed wryly. "You could say. You know her. She doesn't keep her feelings to herself."

"No," Anna agreed with a grin. "Well, I was wondering, if no-one else is interested in them ... of course, your mother might think

49

I'm not the right person for them, especially as I've never owned a dog before and I would quite understand if she turned me down ...."

"Anna ... I can't think of anyone mother would find more suitable ... and we'll all help you. You know that."

Anna smiled. "That's very kind. Thank you, Josh. Look, should I pop over this afternoon? I have an assistant in the shop, Emily. She's at lunch now but I could leave her for an hour, come and see the dogs and have a chat with your mother. If she doesn't think it's a good idea ... me having them ... can you ask her to ring me before I set off ... probably about 2.00 p.m.?"

"Of course ... but I'm sure she will be delighted ... oh, here she is now. You can ask her yourself."

Josh handed the phone to Sonia who looked at him with a querying expression. "Who is it?"

"Anna ... and she wants some dogs," he grinned.

"Dogs!"

"Yes, dogs," he laughed and turned back to his quiche, having handed her the telephone.

"Anna? What do you mean you want some dogs?"

Anna giggled. "Yes, Sonia. Josh is right. I'm interested in the two who were found tied to that farmer's gate. I know I'm probably being a bit ambitious, thinking of taking on two when I haven't even had the experience of one and if you think it's a stupid idea and I'm not the right owner for them, I quite understand ...."

"Stop right there, Anna. I think they would suit you admirably. They're gentle and kind and seem pretty clued up. Someone has taken the time to train them and they respond very well to all commands. They get along fine with the other dogs and have shown no signs of aggression ... and as for your inexperience, we can soon teach you everything you need to know. What about the shop though? I know how busy you are."

"Well, I've taken on an assistant who, even though today is her first, looks as if she is going to become a real asset so I shall have plenty of time to walk them ... although I will be living at the shop soon. Would that be a problem?"

"No, I shouldn't think so. You have that lovely garden and are so near to the park. When do you move?"

"Well, that's the thing. I'm not sure. I have someone viewing this evening. If they want the house, it will be weeks and then there's all the upheaval of packing and moving and if they don't want it and I have to wait even longer for a buyer .... oh, Sonia. I'm wasting your time ... I'm not really in a suitable position at this time. I should have waited ... it's just the picture of the dogs did something to me. It's their eyes. It sounds so stupid but I felt a real tug in my heart when I looked at them."

"Look, come over ... and we'll have a chat. You might change your mind when you see them in the flesh and if you don't, we'll work something out. I refuse to separate them and finding a new home for two is far more difficult than just one so there's no rush. They are perfectly ok here and can stay until you are settled and ready for them."

Anna grinned. "Right. I'll be there around 2.30 pm. Thank you so much, Sonia."

"No, as usual, thank you, my dear."

Anna put down the telephone with a smile on her face as Emily opened the shop door, swinging an enormous shopping bag. A little overweight, short and with mousy shoulder-length hair, a round face and gold glasses, she was certainly no stunner but her demeanour was cheerful, there was a ready smile on her face and she had a willingness to put herself out for others and make them happy. All in all, Emily was a really lovely person.

"Gosh, Anna. I didn't mean to buy so much but I just got taken away with it all ... working so near to other shops is a boon but I'm going to have to watch my spending. Perhaps I better not go out at lunchtime. Perhaps I better bring a book and stay here ... or perhaps I could do what you did this morning and go for a walk in the park ... it will be okay on a nice day of course but I don't think

I would like it on a wet one. I should have to bring some clothes to change into, just in case, as I wouldn't want to work in wet clothes all afternoon. Now, Anna. What would you like me to do for the next few hours ... did you say something about cleaning some of the shelves?"

Anna grinned and nodded. She would never have to try and find something to talk about when Emily was around.

CHAPTER 6

Anna turned off the Wetherby road in her little red Mini-Clubman, beetled down the track for Happylands and pulled up outside the lovely old farmhouse at exactly 2.30 p.m. Her mother had drummed into her that turning up late for an appointment was extremely rude so she had a thing about being everywhere on time, often turning up somewhere early but today she had judged it just right.

Munching a mince pie, Sonia emerged from the farmhouse with a smile of greeting on her face.

"Hello, Anna. Do come in and have a cup of tea and a mince pie or two. Josh has just made loads and they are utterly delicious. We don't just eat them at Christmas as they are so damned good … I think he puts plenty of brandy *and* rum in them, between you and me, although he won't admit to it. Anyhow, whatever he does, I can't get enough of them."

Anna laughed. "I'd love to but would you mind if we saw the dogs first? I'm dying to see them."

"Of course. I do hope you like them. We'll let them out into the field and you can see how you all feel about each other."

They walked round to the kennels and as they entered all the dogs instantly rose to their feet staring curiously at Anna, some barking excitedly. They all looked adoringly at Sonia.

"It's these two," she indicated with her finger, moving to the kennel at the far end.

Both dogs were on their feet and wagged their tails madly at Sonia but one backed away a little at the sight of Anna.

"That's Dolly … she's still a bit timid but no-where near as nervous as she was. The male is Rio. We've had to name them as John Marchant, the farmer who found them, had no idea who they belonged to so we didn't know what to call them. He's been really kind. He's been up a couple of times to see how they are and brought loads of old blankets he didn't need any longer. He's turned out to be such a kind man."

Anna gave Sonia a sidelong glance. "Do I detect a note of interest?"

Sonia smiled. "Well … I haven't much time for many men … most are a complete waste of time and I'm too set in my ways to want to disrupt my life for another one … but he's ok is John. He'll make a damned good friend … and I'm quite happy with that."

"So, this is Rio," Anna said, smiling at the black dog trying to lick her hand through the bars of the kennel. "You look like a lovely boy … and Dolly." she said, turning her attention to the black dog with a hint of white fur on her chest and both paws standing quietly behind him. "Hello, Dolly. Would you like to come and live with me?"

Dolly eyed Anna cautiously but didn't move.

"How old do you think they are?" Anna asked.

"Well, when John brought them in, we thought they were getting on a bit but I suspect it was the trauma of what they were going through and they were starving and freezing cold. We had Jemma, our vet, check them out and she thinks they are four or five. Anyway, since they've been here, they look somewhat younger and fitter with decent food and plenty of rest. They're good with the other dogs and obedient in the field. They can't get out so we can let them off the lead and since they became used to their new names, they respond very well to commands. They know how to sit and stay and are good at recall. That's what's so puzzling. Someone, somewhere, has spent time training them and obviously loved them at some point."

"How very sad," Anna murmured sorrowfully.

"I know. How they ended up makes my blood boil … as you know. Anyhow, let's get them out into the field. Dolly might feel a bit more confident with you out there."

Sonia slipped into the kennel and put leads on both dogs and brought them out, handing Rio to Anna. "You take him as he doesn't worry too much who handles him."

To the cacophony of barking from the other dogs, they walked outside and round to the field. Sonia opened the gate and shut it firmly behind them.

"You can release Rio now," she instructed, letting Dolly loose.

Both dogs shot off to sniff around the hedges bordering the field, Dolly suddenly perking up and her tail beginning to wag with excitement.

Anna gulped. They were a bit lively. Would she be able to cope? Was she trying to bite off more than she could chew?

Sonia looked at her. "Having second thoughts?"

"Um ... I know I've been out with Miranda ... but she makes it look so easy ... keeping control ... but I'm not sure where to start. Will they listen to me?"

"Of course. You just need a bit of training. It makes me laugh when people say they take their dogs to be trained. It's the owners who need the training. Once you know what to do, you'll be fine. I'll teach you and we can start now. It's really easy ... as long as you have some nice treats to begin with," she added, pulling out some doggie chocolates from the pocket of her jeans.

Anna laughed. "Bribery."

"Well, if it works, don't knock it ... and once you have their attention you don't have to give them a treat every time. They just need to learn to respond to you. So, take these, call the dogs, and when they come back to you, tell them to sit and give them a chocolate each. They will love you forever, believe me."

"Ok," Anna replied, taking the chocolates. She looked at the dogs, who were still busy sniffing in the hedges. "Rio ... Dolly ... come," she called.

Neither dog took any notice of her and she looked at Sonia in despair.

"Your tone is too soft. Lots of dogs don't take much notice of women as their voices aren't pitched right. Make it much firmer and lower ... like a man."

Anna tried and was surprised to see both dogs turn to look at her. "Come," she commanded firmly, opening her hand holding the treats.

They came, surprisingly with Dolly arriving first, desperate to eat the chocolates she had grown to love.

"Sit!" Anna said firmly.

They sat. She gave them a treat each and patted their heads. "Good dogs. Oh, good dogs. That was so good," she said with pleased surprise as they both took the chocolates gently with no attempt to snatch.

She laughed at Sonia. "Oh, my. They listened ... to me ... and did as they were told."

Sonia grinned. "Told you. You're lucky with these two as they already know what to do so it will be really easy for you. Let's go around the field a few times and you can do it again every so often, which will increase your confidence and help them get to know you."

Half an hour later Sonia looked at her watch. "We ought to put them back now as the kennel maids will be letting out the others for their turn before all the dogs have their tea. So, how do you feel about Rio and Dolly now?"

Anna grinned at the dogs who now rushed up to her, sat down at her feet and eagerly awaited their treats. They both looked happy and relaxed now they had enjoyed some fun and exercise and had a kind new friend.

"I think we'll do very nicely, don't you think so too, guys?"

Rio and Dolly wagged their tails enthusiastically, as if they knew what she was saying.

Sonia laughed. "I think that's your answer, Anna. I'm so pleased. Now, what do you want to do about taking them home?"

"Well, I've some people coming to see the house this evening so I might well be packing up fairly soon. It's a crazy time to take on two dogs. I'm going to be pretty busy over the next few weeks … and I don't want to confuse them, moving from my house to my flat."

"No. They've had enough upheaval," Sonia agreed. "They can stay here until you're sorted … you can visit as much as you can to establish a relationship with them and continue your training in the field. You can take them for walks along the lanes and across the fields around here … or Peesdown Park with Miranda."

They walked the dogs back to the kennels and Anna shook up their beds and straightened their blankets so they were nice and cosy, rewarded by Rio nuzzling her gratefully and Dolly wagging her tail enthusiastically, her nerves with Anna having been dispelled after a goodly supply of doggie chocolates.

"It's a bit early for their tea and it's best to feed them at the same time as the others anyway but here is something you can give them for now," Sonia said, taking a handful of marrowbone biscuits out of a box on a shelf above the kennel.

Anna handed out the biscuits, feeling quite emotional. Rio and Dolly looked so adorable and were begging for love and attention and she could give it to them … in abundance. She wanted to make up to them for all the horrid experiences they must have endured and had a real desire to make them happy and to feel secure.

"I wish I could take them now. I don't want to leave them," she said to Sonia, glancing at her watch with dismay. "Gosh. Is that the time? I must get back to the shop. Poor Emily. It's her first day and she's been left alone for quite a bit of it. I do feel rather guilty."

"I don't suppose you have time for tea and mince pies then."

"No. I better not but thank you anyway."

"Just bear with me for a couple of minutes. I can't bear the thought of you not trying Josh's goodies. I'll put some in a box for you and you can enjoy them with Emily when you get back to the shop."

Anna drove away from Happylands a few minutes later, a box of mince pies on the seat beside her and an urge to get Dolly and Rio home with her at the very earliest opportunity. She couldn't wait to tell Miranda about them later. She was going to have a hell of a shock!

****

William had met Emily. He had meandered along Peesdown High Street, bought the bolts he required for the gate from the ironmongers and then popped into Pampered Pets.

"Oh, hello," he said when seeing Emily behind the counter. "You must be Emily. Is Anna not about?"

"No. She's had to pop out ... gone to look at some dogs who need a home ... at Happylands ... I do hope she likes them ... it would be so nice for her ... to have some companions ... as she lives alone ... it's so sad ... her having lost her husband as she did ... and she's so young. I do hope she finds a nice man to keep her company in the not-too-distant future. There's nothing like being married. Me and my ... well, sorry. You don't need to know about my marriage," she giggled. "Now, what can I do for you ... is it a cat or a dog you have? We have just about everything you could wish for to keep them well and happy."

William gave a wry smile. "Neither. I know Anna from walking in the park ... I saw her at lunchtime and thought I would pop in and see what she's done with the place in my absence ... I've been away for a few months you see."

"Oh? That's nice."

"Yes, yes it was," he said, thinking that Tilly Pargeter wouldn't have agreed. Her body had been flown back to England from the cruise ship the day after they were picked up from the island and his acting skills had been superb as he pretended to be distraught because he had supposedly been asleep when she got into difficulties in the water and he had been unable to save her. The passengers, crew and the Captain, who had questioned him carefully, had been sympathetic and kind and showed no sign that they thought there was any foul play involved. He had watched the helicopter head off with her body and felt a sense of awe and triumph. He had been successful again. It made him feel all-powerful, as if nothing could stand in his way of achieving what he wanted ... Miranda!

The shop door suddenly opened and Anna breezed in with a big grin on her face. "Oh, Emily, I am so sorry. It all took much longer than I thought ... and on your first day too. I do hope you've managed to cope. Hello, William," turning her smile on him.

"Hello, Anna. I've just popped in as I said I would ... just to see what you've done. I must say, it looks really good now and well established. I remember you mentioning about using the garden room as a cafe. Have you done anything about that yet?"

"Yes ... well, a bit. Would you like a cuppa and I can tell you all about it? And guess what, Sonia has agreed to me having two dogs ... yes, two," she laughed as he raised an eyebrow and Emily's face broke out into a big grin. "She's done a bit of training with me and I feel sure I can cope with them now ... Rio and Dolly. Oh, I can't wait to get them home."

She looked at Emily. "Go through to the garden room and put your feet up for a while. You deserve it. If you put the kettle on, I'll make some tea when it boils and William and I will have ours here."

William settled on the stool Anna had placed near to the counter for any customers who needed to sit down.

"I've obtained the necessary permissions from the council so we can open up the garden room as soon as we like," Anna remarked. "However, I think it might have to wait as not only do I have this place to run but I'm selling my house ... and then there are the dogs to settle in... things are going to be a bit hectic in the next few weeks so opening up the cafe is the last thing on my agenda."

"Well, if you need any help with anything," William found himself saying. He had no idea why but he always felt he had to lend Anna a hand.

"You're so kind, William. I certainly know who to call if I need to."

William smiled. Anna obviously trusted him … and that was the way he liked it. The more of Miranda's 'people' he had on his side, the better!

CHAPTER 7

Miranda was only yards from her first appointment when her phone started ringing. She stopped the car in a gateway to an empty field and felt the now familiar sense of despair when she pulled her mobile out of her trouser pocket to see it was Jeremy ... again.

He had rung continuously since his arrival in Germany two months ago. He left messages and he sent texts, pleading with her to speak to him and tell him what was wrong and explain why she had walked out of his party. It was heart-breaking and exhausting. It would have been so easy to turn off her phone or change the number but it wasn't possible because of her business. She had to be available at all times in case her staff needed her, present clients wanted to get in contact or new ones wanted to book her services.

Why couldn't Jeremy leave her alone? She had been doing so well without a man in her life after recovering from the divorce from the Beastly Bastard. God, why had she been so stupid to let herself fall in love again? Because that was what she was, totally and utterly in love with Jeremy and not seeing him, not talking to him, knowing he was planning to shack up with bloody Karen and not her, was tearing her apart. The pain was far, far worse than it had been with the demise of her marriage. But she wasn't going to relent ... and become just his plaything. Anyway, she hated to admit it but that Karen woman was far more suitable for him with her model looks, her plummy voice ... and the shared army career. It was impossible to compete with that and she didn't want to. She hadn't the energy for it. It was better to get over him and move on, concentrate on her business and the dogs ... she had her family and she had her friends, Anna in particular. She didn't want a man in her life to make it more complicated. She didn't! She didn't!

She let the call go to voicemail, guessing it would be another impassioned plea for her to contact him. Why he was bothering, she had no idea. Surely the blasted Karen woman had her claws well and truly into him, after all, they were in Germany together, working together, living in barracks together.

The tears rolled silently down her cheeks as the deep longing to see him overwhelmed her. She so badly wanted to talk to him but knew it would be the wrong thing to do. It would only stir it all up again and she had to be strong. Get on with her life, get on with her business.

She dabbed at her watery eyes and blew her nose. She had to pull herself together, put on a sunny smile and go interview her prospective doggie holiday people. Four Paws was what was important now. She had to focus on that and try and ignore the gnawing pain from losing the one man she truly loved.

****

William was sitting on his sofa in his front drawing room with a notepad and paper trying to make up a background for Stephen, who was going to make his first appearance in the park very soon, hopefully this week or next. However, there was a lot to do to bring his 'cousin' to life and he had to get Stephen's biography exactly right and then there were his clothes and he would need a car.

The biography was essential. He had to know all about Stephen, who he was, where he had lived, his likes and dislikes, etc., etc., and he had to write it down and get it firmly into his head as he didn't want any stupid slip-ups when talking to people in the park.

It was Monday today. If he got cracking, he could have Stephen ready for public scrutiny in a week, which meant he could supposedly arrive in Peesdown over the weekend so, first things first, he had to decide exactly on what Stephen was going to look like.

He stood up and peered at himself in the massive gilt-edged mirror over the fireplace. When wearing his bald wig, glasses and moustache he looked around sixty years old. Without it, as he was now, he was 32 and a decent looking individual. He liked his light brown eyes, his lips were a bit thin but his nose was ok, not too big or oddly shaped and his ears weren't too large or stuck out. His skin wasn't bad either with all the fresh air and exercise he enjoyed and he was sporting a nice tan from the cruise.

The only thing he really disliked was his hair, which since having to cram it under his bald cap for hours, made it greasy and unkempt and he had to wash it more often than he would normally and he abhorred the colour, auburn, inherited from his mother's side of the family. He had been teased relentlessly at school, which had infuriated him, leading to the purchase of hair dye on more than one occasion, which had led to even more ridicule. Stephen, therefore, was going to have dark brown hair. Certainly not auburn!

He smiled into the mirror. He had spent a fortune at a top dentist in London when he received his inheritance following his parents' death, having his much-disliked teeth whitened, straightened and all the ugly amalgam fillings removed and replaced by gold ones. He grinned. His mouth was worth a small fortune.

So, that was it. He would present Stephen as himself, just with a different hair colour and as he turned backwards and forwards in front of the mirror, he decided that there was no reason at all why Miranda wouldn't fall in love with him.

He returned to the sofa and wrote 'hair dye' on a separate piece of paper to the biography and then began to think more about Stephen's lifestyle. His cousin would need trappings of wealth to be a good catch for Miranda and that meant owning a decent car. A BMW was always a good bet as most women would be impressed, especially if it was brand new and if a convertible, even better with the summer coming up.

He looked up the local BMW dealers online and ordered a brand new 8 series convertible in silver. The salesman was shocked that a customer didn't want to come in and see it first before spending the best part of £100,000 but as far as William was concerned such a classy brand-new car shouldn't have any issues or problems and Miranda would be thrilled when Stephen asked her out for a drive.

As the dealers weren't open on a Sunday, he arranged to pick it up on Saturday and drive home, pretending he was Stephen if anyone saw him. So, that settled exactly when Stephen was going to arrive.

Although he would have to find somewhere to put the car when Stephen supposedly returned to the west country, which he would have to do if he had a large business there. It was annoying that there was only one garage in the grounds, in which he kept the van. He thought about leaving the van on the gravel if he hid the BMW in the garage but that would appear strange if anyone was keeping tabs on him. No, he had to remove the BMW from the premises when Stephen was 'away' but it would be a bit dodgy leaving it in a street somewhere in case it was stolen or even recognised … after all, it was a pretty stunning car and would arouse a great deal of interest. The only thing he could think of was renting a garage somewhere, although buying one would be better. He didn't want a nosy landlord asking questions.

He wandered back to the kitchen, made a coffee and thought hard. Why buy a garage? Why not an actual house, somewhere remote. It might not be a bad idea to have a bolthole in case things went wrong at any time. He felt pretty secure in his disguise in Peesdown and fairly confident he wasn't a suspect for any of his crimes but one could never be 100% certain that the police wouldn't come calling. If they did and he had to go on the run, it could be dodgy trying to flee abroad, although he had two false passports which he had secured from a forger in the back streets of Milan while exploring Italy a couple of years ago. With false identities, he had been able to set up Swiss bank accounts so he could access money at any time if it became impossible to use his normal current account.

Yes, another house, somewhere quiet with no neighbours might not be a bad idea … and if the itch returned, it would be somewhere to take his victims … although if married to Miranda that part of his life would be over. He would never want another woman again if he had her.

He returned to the sitting room and woke his laptop from its slumber. Where should he start his search? He didn't want to drive miles if someone was chasing him so the nearer the better. He looked at an estate agent's website, searching for properties in quiet locations in the immediate vicinity. Most were unsuitable, far too close to neighbours but then he found one, a four bedroomed seventeenth-century house tucked down a lane off a B road leading to Appleton Roebuck, not far from York. He had driven out that way once, cruising the villages looking for whores and had been taken with how quiet it was but still very near to the A64 and the A1 where one could get up a decent speed and make a quick get-a-way. He rang the estate agents and made an appointment to view it the next day. The property had been on the market for a month with no interest so with a bit of luck he could put in an offer and have it accepted fairly quickly.

Satisfied he could do no more on that front for now, he turned back to finishing off Stephen's biography, turning to the question of his employment. He had already told Miranda and Anna that his cousin owned a construction business in the west country. He would have to be based somewhere though. He looked at the map. Bath. He had been there once. It was a beautiful city and an expensive location. He could describe it in fairly good detail if asked so Bath it was. Stephen would also employ an efficient manager so he could spend more time in Yorkshire checking out possible expansion opportunities.

Marital status. Obviously, Stephen had to be single. William pondered on former relationships. It would seem odd at the age of

32 if Stephen hadn't been entangled somehow ... although, thinking about it, *he* hadn't. Miranda was his first ... his very first love. However, that was pretty unusual so Stephen must have had some kind of girlfriend but not been married or that would raise the question of children and make his biography far more complicated with the possibility of slip-ups ... and he couldn't have a divorce. William always thought of divorce as sordid and someone who obtained one as being tainted, not fresh. No, Stephen wasn't going to be divorced ... but he could have been engaged and she jilted him ... running off with another man. There, that would bring up the sympathy vote. Brilliant. Now all he had to do was think of a name for this unkind woman ... something sexy as Stephen would originally have been attracted by that kind of woman but had been so hurt, he was now looking for someone more genuine, kinder, less likely to bugger off. He ticked off the names in his mind but kept coming back to Charlene. Yes, he could imagine her; tall, willowy, fabulous breasts, long blonde hair, heavy use of make-up. He grinned, thinking of her draped naked over the BMW. Yes, Charlene it was. That would do very nicely.

As William wrote it all down, Stephen became a real person. He had a sad past, he had a good business, he had a decent car and he had plenty of money ... everything a girl could wish for. All that needed to happen now was for Miranda to succumb to Stephen's charms. Yet again, he could feel the excitement rising in the pit of his stomach.

He returned to the job in hand. All he had to do now was figure out how he, as William, would depart the scene permanently once Miranda had fallen in love with Stephen. He would have to say he wanted to live abroad again and then Stephen could buy this house and live here with Miranda. That should make her very happy, after all, she had that very morning expressed a wish to live in the property next door. Well, she wouldn't have to. She could live here … with Stephen. Oh, God. It was all fitting together. It was perfect. Absolutely bloody perfect!!

CHAPTER 8

William felt exhausted when he opened and rubbed his eyes the next morning. He had sat up most of the night practising how he was going to appear as Stephen, frequently checking in the mirror to see if Miranda would recognise him ... if anyone would recognise him... without his bald wig, moustache and glasses ... and the walking stick of course. He would have to remember not to walk with a limp, which would be difficult as he had trained himself to do so and it was second nature now. However, in Stephen's clothes, which would include new shoes, he would feel different to how he normally did when in the park or out and about in Peesdown so that should keep his mind on what he was supposed to be doing.

He had breakfast in bed. He felt like treating himself so he trotted down to the kitchen, toasted a couple of thick slices of wholemeal bread loaded with seeds ... he loved the seeds ... and smothered them with butter and thick-cut marmalade. He made coffee in a soup mug as it was bigger than an ordinary mug and would last longer, added loads of sugar and then took it all back upstairs, threw open the curtains and tucked up in bed. Even though he was tired, he had still woken up reasonably early, probably because he had such a lot on his mind and was excited and apprehensive at the same time. Munching his toast, he stared out of the window. The weather didn't look too good. It was overcast and quite chilly which didn't make one want to rush to get outside ...but it might improve and he had loads of time. Miranda wouldn't be at the park until after 11.00 a.m., although he couldn't linger long there this morning. He had an appointment with the estate agent to see the property near to Appleton Roebuck at 1.00 p.m. and then he was going into Leeds to buy some clothes and toiletries for Stephen, including the hair dye.

He took the photo he had of Miranda from his bedside table, placed it on his lap and stared at it. As she had approached him one day in the park, concentrating on the dogs and calling them, he had hidden behind some trees and quickly snapped her just as she lifted her head. The picture was stunning. Her beautiful dark brown eyes, her pretty little nose, her luscious mouth, her gorgeous fair hair. God, he loved her so much. He couldn't wait to have her beside him, in this very bed, and be able to hold her, kiss her, love her ... and she would love him back and never want to leave his side. He was becoming all of a dither just thinking about it. He was sweating with desire, his heart was thumping and he could have fainted just imagining what they would do to each other; naked, panting, groaning, sighing, kissing, thrusting. Oh God, the thrusting. It would be sheer heaven.

He knew he would be able to do it with her. That he wouldn't have any problems. It would be so very different from all those other women ... and he could trust her never to say anything negative about his sexual prowess ... and she would never know about all those other embarrassing attempts. She would make him feel like a king ... he would finally be potent and powerful without having to resort to violence. He couldn't wait!

****

Anna was at the shop early, tremendously excited now she had a firm offer for the house. Mr and Mrs Merridew had decided not to go ahead but another couple had turned up promptly for their viewing, moved around the rooms, smiling and making positive comments and even though it was obvious they liked the property, she hadn't expected the estate agent to ring her half an hour after they departed to advise they were happy to pay the full asking price. They were also cash buyers and could move in as soon as all the paperwork was complete.

Tremendously excited, she had rung Miranda immediately, not only to tell her about the house but also the dogs, which had made Miranda laugh.

"Oh, my goodness, Anna. You don't do things by halves. Gosh. I'm staggered. Really pleased about the house and your move ... but the dogs! Blimey. I can't wait to see them."

"I shall value your opinion. I'm just hoping I haven't been a bit ambitious with two but Sonia seems to be happy and, oh Miranda, they are so lovely and so badly need a loving home and as soon as I'm settled properly at the shop, I can give it to them. I'm going to spoil them rotten. They will want for nothing and now I have Emily I can give them so much attention and have lots of lovely walks ... and it's amazing how they respond to me now Sonia has shown me what to do. I never thought I would be able to make two dogs do what I want them to so easily."

Miranda laughed. "Oh, Anna. I'm so pleased ... and you know I'll help in any way I can ... and if you get stuck and can't walk them, I can do it for you ... no charge of course as it's you," she insisted.

"That's so kind of you. Gosh, I'm so excited. I've wanted a dog for so long. Have you any time this week when you could come with me over to Happylands to see them?"

"I'll check my diary when I get home and see when I can squeeze you in."

"Lovely. How did you get on with the interviews you did today?"

"The first pair, the Hutton's, were useless and it was bloody obvious they were only in it for the money. They had only ever owned one dog and it appears that was put down because it turned nasty but after some questioning on my part, it seemed they never took the poor thing for a walk and as it was a Staffy cross it must have been demented with frustration, went for one of the kids when the stupid child disturbed it in its basket, so had to pay with its life. I'm glad Sonia wasn't with me. She would have made her feelings quite plain."

"Oh, dear," Anna had added, feeling desperately sorry for the poor dog. "How about the other couple?"

"Brilliant. Retired. Lots of experience. Both of them have had dogs all their lives, their most recent Labrador has just died ... cancer, poor thing and they have decided not to get another but still want doggie contact and thought boarding would be just right for them and I agree. They have a massive, secure garden, their grandkids are all grown up so no little ones to upset the applecart and they are keen walkers. I think I can keep them pretty busy."

"So, your day wasn't a complete write off then?"

"No ... but I did get another call from Jeremy," Miranda had added sorrowfully.

"What did he say this time?" Anna asked. She did wish Jeremy would leave her friend alone. It was odd that he kept trying to contact her when he had that other woman in tow.

"I don't know. I haven't listened to his message but I expect it's more of the same."

They had ended the call, promising to meet up in the park again today when Anna intended to try and cheer up her friend. She did ponder on whether or not to ring Jeremy herself and tell him to leave Miranda alone but she didn't think it was her place to interfere.

With mixed feelings of excitement and sadness with so much to think about; selling the house, living over the shop, the dogs, Miranda, she had hardly slept either and deciding there was no point in wasting time in bed she got up, had a shower and drove over to the shop before the morning rush got under way.

She wanted to get upstairs and measure up for curtains and think about where she was going to put some of her furniture. A lot would have to be disposed of as it wouldn't fit in the flat. She had walked around the house after speaking to Miranda last night and made a list of what she would keep, what would go to charity and what she could sell. Gosh, there was so much to do. Then there were the dogs. She had to make time for them. Thank God it looked as if Emily was going to be a blessing as she would have to be relied on a good deal in the coming weeks.

Having measured up for the curtains, deciding as it was spring, she would buy some light, pretty ones, she went down to the shop, placed the float in the till and went through to the kitchen and made a coffee. It was still half an hour before opening time and she liked this time of day when she could sit in the garden room and look out over the lawns and flowerbeds which were now looking spectacular with all the daffodils and crocuses. Jeremy's father had certainly been very busy when he lived here and made sure the garden was well stocked. It would certainly be interesting to see what else was going to pop up in the next few weeks.

Surprisingly, the doorbell rang and Anna looked at her watch. Perhaps it was Emily arriving earlier than expected. She went through to the shop and couldn't help smiling when she saw it was Sergeant Wilkinson, Andy, as he had told her to call him on one of his frequent visits.

"Hello," she said with a smile as she unlocked the door. "This is a nice surprise. I was just having a coffee before we opened. Would you like one?"

Andy smiled and took off his cap. "That would be very welcome indeed, Anna. I've been on duty all night and it's a bit nippy still but I don't want to keep you from anything if you're busy. I saw your car in the car park and thought I'd just say hello before I went home."

"Honestly, I was just daydreaming in the garden room. I've had an offer for my house and am moving in here in the next few weeks so have lots to organise and think about."

He followed her and sat down at the table where she had been sitting. He liked this room and the view of the garden. It was a very pleasant place to while away a few moments with a steaming cup of coffee and good company to boot.

"Here we are," Anna said, placing a pretty mug painted with red roses in front of him. "So, have you been on duty all night?"

"Yes. We're short-staffed at the moment and I've been out on patrol in Peesdown and circled the park a few times ... just in case."

"Um. No more news on finding out who the killer of poor Tanya is then?"

"No. It seems not but the case is still open of course ... not many people are working on it now but it won't be closed completely ... but it's still a mystery. No real concrete evidence, no suspects, no anything apparently. So, the bloke responsible could be long gone or could still be around, waiting to pounce on someone else."

Anna shivered and put her hands around her mug to warm them up. She suddenly felt very cold and would have to turn the heating up when they finished their coffee. "Goodness, I do hope not. I do so worry about Miranda ... and the rest of her walkers ... well, everyone who uses the park. It's terrifying."

"Well at least most women seem to be pretty sensible, walking in groups and not going too early or too late to the park ... and there's a new park keeper started ... he's a lot younger and keener than Freddie Fletcher and pretty burly. He could tackle someone pretty well I should think. Not many would argue with him and knowing he's around could put off our attacker trying it again through daylight hours and I doubt there will be any more ladies going to the park again in the middle of the night. Have you met him yet ... the new park keeper?"

"Bob Watkins. Yes. Can't say I warmed to him much and Miranda disliked him but I know what you mean. I should imagine he could be pretty formidable if push came to shove."

Andy smiled. "So, on a lighter note, if you need any help moving in here, I can always make myself available. I have some leave I can take and nowhere I particularly want to go."

"That's very kind of you but I think I shall be okay. The removal men will do it all. I can just make them coffee," she laughed. "And as soon as it's all done, I can go and fetch my dogs."

Andy raised an eyebrow. "Oh?"

Anna grinned and told him all about Rio and Dolly and how much she was looking forward to bringing them to the shop to live with her.

"I can't wait to fetch them here. Poor things have had such a rotten time. Sonia is going to keep them at Happylands until I can bring them home. I'm going to see them for training and walking as much as possible until then and I was hoping to bring them to the park to walk with Miranda and her gang next week. I'm a bit nervous about taking them out on my own just yet even though they responded to me very well yesterday."

"Look, I'm off this weekend, surprisingly enough ... at least I am on Sunday. How about a walk with my two ... they're both elderly and very sociable and won't react if yours are nervous and grumble or snap at them? We could walk in Peesdown ... although it's always busier at weekends so perhaps that's not a good idea ... but we could drive to somewhere quiet and walk them. There are some lovely woods over by Thorner village or we could go further afield ... up in the Dales or the Moors ... we could take a picnic for us and food and water for the dogs. We could make a real day of it, Anna," he said, warming to his theme. "I can pick you up. I have an estate car so we can put my two on the back seat and then go to Happylands and collect yours. They can go in the rear. I have a dog guard installed so they will be separated and can get used to being in each other's company before we get them out."

"What a lovely idea," she nodded with pleasure. She really liked Andy and a day out with him would be something to look forward to and in his reassuring presence, she would feel more confident in controlling the dogs. "I would like that. I'll let Sonia know. It will be so good for the dogs to have a real outing. Thank you so much, Andy."

****

74

Andy left the shop as soon as he had finished his coffee. Anna had to open and Emily had turned up so he said his goodbyes and went back outside, much happier now he had a firm date with Anna. He liked her very much and she seemed to reciprocate his feelings so he was beginning to have hopes there could be a proper relationship on the cards and where it might lead. He drove home with a smile on his face.

CHAPTER 9

William decided not to go to the park. He busied himself around the house instead, tidying, throwing clothes into the washing machine, hoovering and dusting. He could easily have afforded a cleaner but didn't want anyone nosing around and anyway, he had plenty of time and didn't mind. Funny really, he had despised helping his mother with her constant nagging to keep their home clean and tidy but here, in his own place, he felt differently and liked to keep it in order.

He was going to enjoy the garden too, which he had sadly neglected before the winter. His parents had hired someone to come twice a week to keep their grounds immaculate so he had never had an opportunity to discover what a pleasure it could be to keep it tidy and grow things. The garden here was large and was going to be a lot of work but again, he had the time. So far, of course, he hadn't had to do very much as it was late last year when he had moved in. Since returning from the cruise, he had enjoyed giving the lawn a mow, having bought a fancy lawnmower which did perfect stripes (his mother would have approved) and a blower to sort out the fallen leaves. He had found pottering about soothing to his soul and he relished pruning the roses, snapping away with his newly purchased secateurs and he found hoeing and weeding the flower beds utterly satisfying, bringing up the fresh dark earth to the light of day. Yes, he was looking forward to getting to grips with it, having bought several gardening books to study so he would know more about what he was supposed to do to keep it looking trim and beautiful for his Miranda. He could just imagine her sitting out on the lawns on a nice day, surrounded by her dogs as she sipped on tea and ate delicate cucumber sandwiches and scones covered with jam and cream. His heart filled again with love for her. He wanted so much to spoil her and look after her. She would want for nothing once she married him.

Having completed his indoor chores, he quickly showered, put on fresh clothes, ate a cheese and pickle sandwich and drank coffee in the kitchen. He stared out over the back garden. He wondered what Miranda would make of it. Would she want to make some changes? It was a massive space and a lot could be done with it. Perhaps she would like a pool. There was certainly room for one and he liked to swim and if she did too, having one installed could be most pleasurable. The only problem was that Nellie. She would more than likely jump in as she was always beetling off to the lake in the park and then emerging to shake water all over anyone standing nearby. He didn't fancy swimming in a pool full of dog hairs. Perhaps it wasn't such a good idea after all.

He looked at the clock on the wall. Time was getting on and he had to get over to Appleton Roebuck to see the house and then pop into Leeds to buy what he needed for Stephen.

He took the van, minus any advertising signs on the sides. He drove out of his gate with his bald cap, black-rimmed glasses and moustache in place in case anyone he knew saw him leave. As soon as he was clear of Peesdown, he stopped in a layby, removed his moustache, exchanged the bald cap for a blonde wig and replaced his black-rimmed glasses for a pair with gold rims. He looked in his rear-view mirror, satisfied to see he appeared exactly like a photograph on one of his fake passports in the name of John Newman, who was going to buy The Cedars with cash, which would keep the paperwork at a minimum. His other false identity, Christopher Rawlings, who had dark brown hair and wore light brown plastic glasses, would be used abroad if need be.

He had procured his false identities in the height of his raping and killing spree across Europe, thinking it prudent as a plan b or even c if things became too hot and he had to hastily leave whatever country he was in. He had also settled in Switzerland for a long period, enabling him to open a Swiss bank account. He wouldn't run short of funds if he had to scarper now as he had deposited a million pounds in each name. However, now he was back in the UK it was a damn sure thing he wouldn't be able to risk going abroad if the police were looking for him, not with all the newly installed security at airports and ferry terminals. It would be extremely foolish to try so a bolt-hole in the UK would be a sensible idea.

He was also tinkering with the idea of purchasing a motorhome. He could keep it at the new house if the garage was big enough, along with the BMW, and the van if need be, as they would all have to be kept out of sight if he had to make a bolt for it. If push came to shove, he could always escape in the motorhome, clear off to some remote part of Scotland or Wales and hide there until the heat died down and then risk heading abroad to settle. Not that any of this would be necessary of course, not once he was safely married to Miranda and leading a loving and respectable life … but there was always that nagging feeling … just in case.

He had purposefully headed over to the house early so he could have a good look around before the estate agent arrived. Having donned his new disguise and quickly affixed false number plates on the van, he drove off, easily finding the tiny track leading to the property, just off the B road to Appleton Roebuck. The name of the house, The Cedars, was on a plaque attached to wrought iron gates which were wide open but the house couldn't be seen from the road due to an abundance of thick, high shrubbery and tall conifers waving in the sharp wind that was picking up. William looked at the darkening sky. It wouldn't be long before it was pouring with rain. He had better get a move on.

He drove down the track which wound to the left and there was the house in front of him. Nothing spectacular, just an ordinary red-brick property with a black front door and UPVC windows. He parked the van and walked around the side of the house. He wasn't particularly interested in what was inside, it was the privacy aspect he was concerned with and so far, he liked what he saw.

The garden at the back was a decent size, not as big as the one in Peesdown, and surrounded by fields full of what looked like rapeseed. It was possible to see for miles and in the distance, he could just make out a few rooftops. Appleton Roebuck, obviously. So, the house was nice and private. The only disturbance would be from the farmer as he dealt with the crops in his fields and that would only be a few times every year, when he planted, sprayed, harvested and ploughed.

He could hear a car coming along the road and slowing down to turn down the track towards the house. He walked back to the front to greet the estate agent with a smile on his face. He had already made up his mind. The Cedars would do very nicely, especially when he saw the large garage which would provide adequate space to hide up to four vehicles if need be.

Having endured the tour with the estate agent who was desperate to sell the property, wasting his time as William had already made up his mind he wanted it, he was back in Peesdown an hour later, having stopped at the same spot to put on his bald wig, moustache and glasses, having agreed to buy The Cedars. The owners were now living abroad and were eager for a quick sale so the estate agent was sure *Mr. Newman* would be able to move in within a matter of weeks. He chortled to himself as he put the van away in the garage and went indoors. He had no intentions of 'moving in' to The Cedars, although he supposed he would have to visit it now and again to make it look lived in to avoid the place being burgled. He would have to put lights on timers and keep the garden up to scratch too as that would be a dead giveaway that no-one was living there permanently.

However, he should make it homely in case he had to hole up there. He wouldn't need a cooker as there was a range but he would require a microwave, fridge, freezer (which should be kept stocked up), a washing machine, a sofa, a television and a bed. That should do. He could look online to see if there was a big store which could provide the lot so everything could be delivered in one go and not in bits and pieces which would take up his precious time, which was far better spent wooing Miranda.

He hated driving into town so hired a taxi to take him into Leeds and half an hour later he was deposited near to the imposing Victorian Town Hall with the baroque clock tower and the four Portland stone lions on plinths guarding the steps to the front entrance.

He headed for the shops and spent a couple of hours purchasing new tops, trousers, jackets and shoes for Stephen. He also visited a couple of charity shops and bought a few second-hand items as it would look odd if his cousin was always in new clothes, especially walking in the park. He had tea in a nice little Italian restaurant he had frequented on another occasion, enjoying a lasagne and chips, followed by tiramisu and two cappuccinos before ringing for another taxi to return to Peesdown. He took all his packages upstairs to the first floor and into the master bedroom, which would now be allocated to Stephen. He had never liked it with just the view over the front garden because the ensuite, with its enormous frosted window, overlooked the side garden. Since moving in he had tried all the bedrooms but had finally chosen the rear bedroom for himself from which he could see No.10 on one side and the back garden and park on the other and was able to leave his curtains open at night and study the stars from his bed.

He removed all the new clothes out of their packages and hung the shirts and trousers in 'Stephen's' wardrobe and placed the sweaters in the built-in drawers, then took the old clothes he had purchased from the charity shops out of their carrier bags. They didn't smell, the shop had cleaned them before putting them on display but even so, he wouldn't want to wear them until they had been washed properly at home. William placed them in a pile by the door ready to take down to the utility room. Three dark green sweaters and a brown one … so the wearer would not be easily spotted if standing or walking in the woods. He had bought a few used t-shirts too, for the warmer weather … again in the same colours. They also went on the washing pile.

He placed the new aftershave and deodorant in the cabinet in the ensuite, along with toothpaste and a toothbrush. All different from his own. It wouldn't do for Stephen to smell like him. They had to be completely different, even if they were related.

He returned to the bedroom and looked around. He needed a few more things. The room looked uninhabited. He needed a radio, a few books, a bedside clock, a suitcase, a laptop maybe. He would have to scout around the house and bring a few things up to make it look lived in. Stephen had to be a real person, not just to others but to himself too if he was going to carry this off. He would have to get under Stephen's skin. He would have to think and act like him. He had to make this work and all he had to do now was wait impatiently until Saturday to collect the BMW and have Stephen 'arrive'.

Having thrown the clothes from the charity shop in the washing machine, he sat down at the kitchen table with a coffee and thought about collecting the car. Everything to introduce Stephen to the local populace was ready. It was just the bloody car. It was stupid to wait until Saturday. He could collect it tomorrow. The sooner the better. He picked up the phone and rang the car dealer before they closed.

CHAPTER 10

At 8.00 a.m. the following morning William left home in a taxi, the smart brown leather briefcase he had bought 'Stephen' tucked under his arm, hidden in a carrier bag. He asked to be dropped off near to the central bus station and made his way into a toilet cubicle, took the briefcase out of the carrier bag and whipped off his bald wig, moustache and glasses and placed them inside. Then he changed William's clothes for Stephen's, a brown sweater and brown corduroy trousers, which he had folded and placed carefully in the carrier bag earlier. He pulled out the small mirror and comb he had tucked into one of the compartments of the briefcase and tidied his newly dyed hair. With a thrill of excitement, he grinned at himself. 'Stephen' was ready to go. He rang a different taxi firm to hire a car to take him out to the trading estate in nearby Bradford where the BMW dealership was situated.

The car looked as good as it had on the dealer's website. A slick, smarmy salesman gave him a quick tour of what was beneath the bonnet and an explanation of the dashboard controls and then handed him the keys and the paperwork with an envious smile.

With a triumphant grin, William drove carefully onto the main road and headed for Leeds. "Now, Stephen," he muttered with pleasure. "Let's go get Miranda."

****

Veronica Anderson had just arrived at Peesdown Park. She had jogged there from Elland Street where she lived in a ground floor flat of a terraced house. She hadn't lived in Peesdown long, having recently moved to Leeds due to her new job at St. James Hospital as a Sister in the Accident and Emergency department. She had been working in London since she qualified as a nurse but wanted to move further up north to be closer to her parents who lived near Halifax. Leeds was ideal with fantastic shopping and nightlife, plus the lovely parks, and she loved her job. She liked to keep fit too and jogged every day, usually after a shift, which would help her sleep better after releasing all the tension built up during working hours … and she had decided Peesdown Park was just the place, within running distance of home and not as busy as the bigger parks such as Roundhay and Temple Newsam.

She had been on nights all week but today was her day off. She had luxuriated in bed for quite a while but now she was going to enjoy a leisurely run and following a shower, was going to spend some time shopping in the city centre as she needed a new dress for her parent's forthcoming wedding anniversary party.

She sped through the car park and down to the lake, pleased to see that there weren't many people about likely to get in her way, especially those blasted professional dog walkers with all their damned animals milling about all over the paths. A couple of times she had nearly tripped over a dog and fallen flat on her face. They were a total menace, filthy creatures, covered in mud, slobbering and shedding dog hair everywhere. All those germs! Yuk!

Then she rounded a bend and there, in front of her, was a woman she hadn't seen before. She had six dogs with her, all big bouncy things charging in and out of the lake, barking and carrying on. Veronica groaned. Bugger. She would have to head up the woodland path and she didn't like running through the woods much, always wary of tripping over tree roots but it was better than risking being bowled over by the dogs or having a row.

She headed up the path towards the top woods, keeping her eyes fixed firmly on the ground for hidden obstacles, glancing up now and again to check the way. Then she noticed the shoelace on her right trainer was loose. There was a fallen beech tree to the side of her and she stopped to sit on the log, smiling at the sound of the birds chirping merrily as she bent down to do up her trainer. Job done, she sat up, enjoying the peace and admiring the fresh new leaves of lime green on the trees and bushes around her. The woods were so beautiful at this time of the year. Then, without warning, she heard a loud crack to her right. Her first thought was of the woman who had been raped and murdered in the park a few months previously, plus a rape earlier last year. God, she had been stupid, coming up here on her own. Holding her breath, her heart thumping loudly in her chest, she stared hard into the dense trees but nothing moved. Even so, a thread of terror rippled through her. All her senses were warning her that there was someone there, watching her. She rose quickly to her feet and swiftly ran back the way she had just come, desperate to get back to the security of the open park.

****

Bob Watkins was disappointed. He had just been about to show himself and speak to her but she ran off. He was walking the woods on his own, Freddie having clocked off for an hour as he had a dental appointment. It was good to be left in charge for a while and his heart had leapt, having seen the woman in pink lycra entering the park. He had hurried around the lake in the opposite direction to her so that they would bump into each other but having seen her shoot off into the woods, he had done the same, coming across her sitting on the log, doing up her shoe. He had stood, silently, behind the vast trunk of an ancient oak tree, staring at her, licking his lips as his eyes slid over the contours of her enticing body. God, she was gorgeous. Shifting his weight, he had stupidly stood on that bloody stick and she had shot off. He had obviously put the wind up her … but there would be another time and he would get her one day. He just had to bide his time.

****

Eager to get to the park to introduce his cousin to all in sundry,

William had butterflies in his tummy. Could he pull it off? Would Miranda believe he was Stephen and not William? It was a hell of a gamble but he had to do it. She wouldn't look at him twice as William.

He had reached home, parked the car on the drive and rushed upstairs and checked his appearance for Stephen's debut into Peesdown. It was a reasonably nice day with no hint of rain but not particularly warm so the brown sweater and corduroy trousers were perfect. He smoothed down his hair, pleased with the colour, which was a remarkable improvement from the auburn, and splashed on a light aftershave. He stared at himself in the mirror. He didn't look bad. Miranda would see him warts and all for once and although there was a distinct resemblance to William, after all they were supposed to be cousins, he did look much younger, which in itself should be enough to convince her that he was Stephen.

It would be ridiculous to take the car to the park as it was such a short walk. He left the house, breathless with anxiety, his hands cold one minute and sticky with sweat the next. He was wearing a dark green padded jacket and a pair of brown leather walking shoes and he had to remember not to limp.

Miranda's empty Volvo was in the car park and he walked quickly down to the lake and peered around looking for her. She was nowhere to be seen, although the two park keepers, Freddie and Bob were walking towards him. He took a deep breath. He could try out his new identity on them and see if they recognised him. He prayed they wouldn't.

"Good morning," Freddie said, nodding at William.

William's heart missed a beat. It was now or never.

"Good morning ... you must be ... Freddie?" he queried. "I believe you know my cousin ... William Pemworthy ... he's mentioned you when he's been telling me about the park .... I'm staying with him for a while."

85

"Oh. Yes, I thought you looked vaguely familiar. How do you do?" Freddie replied with a crooked smile, his face still numb from the injection the dentist had given him before filling a back tooth.

"Very well, thank you. It's a reasonably nice day for a walk, not too cold or wet."

Bob Watkins stood silently, not even managing a smile.

William turned back to Freddie. "My cousin tells me you're retiring soon."

Freddie tried to grin. "Yes. I can't wait. Not long to go now … and this is Bob … he's my replacement," he added, glancing up at the young man beside him who was a head taller.

Bob nodded but still didn't speak. William decided it was prudent to make a move. He seemed to have fooled Freddie but didn't want to prolong the anxiety about meeting Miranda. He had to find her and get the ordeal over.

"I saw a Volvo in the car park … Four Paws, I believe? William told me to have a chat to …. Miranda … who runs the business … he said she's very nice ...have you seen her?" he asked the two men casually.

"She's just gone up into the woods, at the far end of the lake. If you walk quickly, you'll probably come across her with her pack of unruly dogs. Just be careful they don't jump all over you with their muddy paws," Freddie grimaced.

William smiled. "Right. I'll be off then. I would like to meet her. I've heard such a lot about her."

He nodded to the two men and hurried around the lake towards the first path up into the woods. It was so much easier now he didn't have to pretend to limp and could walk quickly and normally and the walking shoes he had bought from a charity shop for Stephen were extremely comfortable, having been nicely worn in by the previous owner.

He reached the end of the lake within minutes and made his way up the path, wondering which way Miranda would have gone when she reached the fork at the top of the hill. She usually walked slowly, having jokily remarked more than once that she was bringing the dogs for exercise and not herself, so she couldn't be far away now.

Then he heard the dogs, barking madly, probably at a poor squirrel up in a tree. He followed the din which became louder as he grew nearer.

Then he saw her, sitting on a massive log which had once been a towering beech tree, tears pouring down her cheeks as she tried to wipe them away with a tissue. His heart turned over. He wanted to rush up and comfort her and make whatever it was that was upsetting her better again. However, as Stephen didn't know her, there was no way he could do that.

"Hello," he said, breathing deeply, feeling the surge of butterflies in his stomach again. This was it. She had to believe he was Stephen. "Are you ... are you okay?"

"Oh!" Miranda exclaimed, staring at him in dismay, desperately dabbing at her eyes and sniffing madly. "Oh, gosh. I thought you were William for a moment ... you must be his cousin ... Stephen? He told us you were coming to stay."

"Yes, that's right," he said, relieved at her words. So far so good. "Are you okay though? You're not hurt or anything?"

Miranda tried to smile, feeling silly and stupid, having been found in such a state in the middle of the woods by a complete stranger. "No, I'm fine ... physically that is. I'm just feeling a little low and it suddenly got to me, that's all." She had been reasonably okay until Jeremy's text a few minutes ago. With grim determination, she had finally deleted and blocked his number ... and then burst into tears as the gnawing pain she had become to know so well, gripped her again. To know that she would never speak to Jeremy again, never see him again, never be held by him again was horrendous. She was utterly devastated and wrapped up in a terrible grief and to be found by a stranger when she was so low, was the final humiliation. She felt a complete idiot and stood up, shoving her tissue into her pocket.

"Well, perhaps if I keep you company, you won't have time to dwell on whatever it is and it will make you feel better. William told me to look out for you ... so if you would like to, you could walk with me and tell me all about yourself and your animals," William said, trying to look pleasantly at Nellie and Charlie as they started sniffing his legs. They weren't fooled. They knew he was William.

Miranda attempted a smile. "That's very kind. Being a professional dog walker can be a bit lonely as it's best to keep out of the main part of the park as much as possible to avoid annoying other people." She looked at her watch. "And I should be moving along. I have to finish this walk, take the dogs home and smarten myself up as I'm interviewing this afternoon."

They ambled through the woods, the dogs darting hither and thither through the trees, sometimes chasing each other and then stopping to sniff anything of interest. They ignored William now there were more enticing things in the undergrowth to find.

William gradually grew more confident as the minutes ticked by. Miranda hadn't guessed. She hadn't once looked at him funny or said anything that would make him think she thought something was wrong but he did want to find out what was upsetting her. He hated seeing her cry.

"Feeling better now?" he asked, as they neared the car park, their conversation for most of the walk being about the dogs and the park.

"Yes," she smiled. "Thank you very much for keeping me company. We've had some rather nasty things happen in the park over the last few months," she shuddered. "As a result, it's been extremely quiet this winter ... sometimes there's only been the odd professional dog walker or Freddie about and even though a few more people are venturing out now it's spring, it can be even creepier up in the woods with the trees in full leaf. When they're bare it's possible to see whose around fairly easily but now they're coming out in all their glory ... there are just so many places men can hide."

"But you have the protection of the dogs," he said reassuringly.

Miranda smiled wryly at her chocolate Labrador. "Nellie would lick anyone to death ... and did any of the dogs growl when you came upon us in the woods? No. They were just curious."

"Yes, but if I had been about to attack you, they might have reacted very differently ... especially that one," he nodded at Charlie, who was ambling along, waving his long tail casually as he warily watched the wildlife in the lake. Charlie didn't mind the moorhens too much but he disliked the swans after one had hissed at him once as he had tried to nose it. He had only wanted to say hello but the bird had made him jump out of his skin. He had kept well away from them after that encounter.

"Um. He might. Anyway, I hope I never have to find out," Miranda said. "And by the look of our new park keeper, any rapist or killer will have to be on their guard. He has the most chilling eyes ... ice-cold blue."

She shuddered and pulled up the collar of her jacket. "I hate to say this but I'm going to miss Freddie when he leaves. He's been the bane of my life ever since I started Four Paws but he's harmless enough. I'm not so sure about this other chap ... Bob ... or whatever his name is. He gives me the heebie-jeebies."

They had reached the car park and Miranda put all six dogs on the lead and opened the Volvo for them to get in.

"Thank you for your company, Stephen. It's been nice to meet you."

"It's been a pleasure and I do hope I managed to make you feel better."

Miranda shut the doors on the dogs and leaned against the car. "Yes, you have, thank you," suddenly wanting to explain to this kind man why she had fallen apart in the woods. "I had ... I had a friend ... a male friend ... Jeremy. He's in the Army ... in Germany at the moment. Well, we've had a falling out. He has another woman ... but he still keeps calling me. When you found me, I had just deleted and blocked him on my phone. It was all so ... final."

"I see," William said thoughtfully, his pulses quickening. So, that bloody Jeremy was the root of her unhappiness. Thank goodness she had told him to sling his hook. That was one major object out of the way then, although he'd certainly like to give the man a bloody nose for hurting Miranda ... but he would make it up to her. She would soon forget Jeremy!

"Look, Miranda. I need a bit of help getting to know the area. William is a bit staid and not interested in going out and about with me much. We seem to rub each other up the wrong way for some reason so it's best to keep our distance, although it's been jolly decent of him to let me stay. Luckily, the house is so big so we can keep out of each other's way quite well. However, I was wondering ... would you like to have a drink ... or a meal sometime? I'd love to hear more about your business and you can tell me all about Leeds and Yorkshire."

He had his hands in his pockets and crossed his fingers as he spoke, willing her to say yes.

"Well, I'm awfully busy," Miranda said with surprise, not having expected to be asked out. "To be honest, by the time I get home in the evening all I want to do is put my feet up and fall asleep in front of the tele."

His face fell and she felt a pang of guilt. After all, he had been so nice to her and if he wanted her company .... "I could manage it at the weekend ... perhaps lunch on Saturday ... the Red Lion only offers ordinary pub grub; you know burgers and things ... but it's well cooked and plentiful. I only have Nellie and Charlie to walk. I could do that in Roundhay ... I live not far from there ... and then come over here."

"Well, that would be lovely, if you're sure," William said, unable to prevent a relieved smile. His heart was pounding with excitement. She was going to meet him ... have a real 'date'. Oh,

God. Eager to please her, he attempted to be helpful. "Although I could always find Roundhay on my satnav in my car and come over there if that would be easier for you. We could even go further afield if there's somewhere else you would prefer. I've just bought a new car and would love to take you for a drive."

"No. The Red Lion is fine. I want to have a word with the landlord about having a little leaving do for Freddie so that will be a good opportunity. I can make it about mid-day if that's okay with you."

He nodded. "Perfect. I shall look forward to it."

He watched her drive out of the car park and waved. He had never felt so happy in his life but how he was going to get through the hours until Saturday, he had no idea.

****

Miranda drove along Peesdown High Street deep in thought. She had enjoyed Stephen's company. He was a lot like William but many years younger but it was his voice that was puzzling her. If she looked away, she could believe he was William when he spoke. How strange. She had never known anyone to sound the same as anyone else, however closely related they were.

She shrugged. Anyway, what did it matter? He had taken her mind off Jeremy and even though she had that terrible knot of hurt in the middle of her tummy which never seemed to go away, she felt a little more cheerful and it would be nice to have a lunch to look forward to on Saturday and perhaps he would be a bit more forthcoming about himself. On the walk they had only spoken about her, the dogs or the park. Nothing about him. Not that she wanted to know too much. There was no way she was going to get involved with a man again. Thank God she had her family, good friends, her business and her dogs. That was enough for her now.

CHAPTER 11

He was having lunch with Miranda on Saturday … as Stephen. The excitement had gripped him ever since she had agreed. It was the first step to a glorious and blissful future together. He couldn't ever remember being so happy. In fact, he couldn't remember when he had ever actually been happy. The nearest emotion he had experienced had been the overwhelming thrill when he had crushed the life out of his victims. However, Miranda was going to stop all of that. Their relationship was going to be on a much higher plane; real love and real trust.

He was desperate to know what Miranda had thought of his 'cousin' and as 'William', he made his way to the park at 11.00 a.m., which was around the time she usually arrived. Her Volvo wasn't there but he was interested to see that the cafe had opened up and a woman in a dark blue overall was placing a menu on the board near the entrance. This must be the Trudy Freddie had told him about. He hadn't met her before as when he came to live in Peesdown last year, the cafe had already shut for the winter. Just as he was about to make her acquaintance, Miranda's Volvo entered the car park and pulled up in front of him.

"Hello, Trudy," called Miranda, jumping out of the car. "Nice to see you back again. I'll pop in for an ice-cream after my walk."

Trudy smiled. "Lovely. Look forward to seeing you."

She went back into the cafe and William limped over to Miranda. "Hello, young lady. Fancy a bit of company?"

"Yes, please, William. Anna can't come today as she has deliveries arriving and wants to show Emily what to do."

They ambled around the lakeside path, quiet today, apart from Harry with his four black Great Danes in the distance, the Vicar and Samantha, his wife, walking their two little mongrels, two female joggers running together and an elderly couple feeding the ducks on the opposite side of the lake. There was no sign of Freddie or Bob.

It was a pleasant day. The sun kept popping out of the clouds, sending dark shadows rushing across the grass every now and again, which two of the black Labradors, Heidi and Bonnie, chased enthusiastically. The trees were now all out in their spring glory of fresh greenery, the daffodils were nodding gaily in the soft breeze and swans, ducks and moorhens glided about on the lake on the lookout for people who might have come to feed them. Peesdown Park, at that moment, was a nice place to be and William could feel the tension fly from him as he walked beside Miranda, knowing he was lunching with her on Saturday and that their relationship would progress steadily from there. He felt a surge of overwhelming pleasure and happiness and he smiled warmly down at her. She looked gorgeous this morning, even in her old working clothes. Her hair shone healthily and her skin bloomed. It was just her beautiful big brown eyes that didn't look right, sad and full, as if she was going to burst into tears at any moment ... but that would change. Stephen would soon have her smiling again.

"I hear you met my cousin, Stephen," he stated, praying she had warmed to him. "And you're having lunch."

She smiled. "Yes. He seems very nice ... just like you, William," she teased.

He grinned back, feeling the tension leaving his body. Bingo ... it was going to work!

They had reached the top part of the lake and were just turning the corner when their way was blocked by Bob Watkins and a tall female jogger in pink lycra with long dark hair swept up into a ponytail. The woman looked anxious as she ran on the spot and kept glancing up into the woods.

Bob glared at Miranda and the dogs and she quickly snapped Nellie, Heidi, Bonnie and Charlie on the lead. The remaining two, Simba and Reggie, two little Dachshunds who were no threat to man nor beast, ambled past, keen to get to nearby bushes for a good old rummage before the bigger dogs could push them out of the way.

Good morning," Miranda said as pleasantly as she could, feeling decidedly uncomfortable. What was it with the man? He had such an unsettling presence and those eyes, burning into her, as if he could see into her very soul. She shuddered, glad she had William with her. She wondered why the woman was looking so concerned. Had Bob done something or said something to worry her?

Still running on the spot, the woman turned to Miranda. "Be careful if you intend going up in the woods. I was just telling ...," she looked at Bob.

"Bob," he said quietly.

"I was just telling Bob, I thought someone was watching me up there the other day ... and just now. I hadn't intended going up there this morning, not after the last experience but I wanted to skirt around that man walking with his four big black dogs. Then I felt it again ... eyes on me ... I called out but no-one answered but I'm positive someone was hiding behind the trees and having been told there was a rape and then a murder a few months ago in the park and the chap hasn't been caught is somewhat alarming."

Miranda nodded. "It's caused a lot of panic locally and not so many people come to the park now so it's wise to be on guard. However, it's very easy to get the creeps in the woods. Believe me, it's happened to me more than once over the years," she smiled, trying to be reassuring.

"Right," said the woman, "Well, I've told you and I've told Bob so I better be off. I'm a nurse and I've been on nights and need to get to bed. Bye," she said as she ran off in the direction of the car park, keeping to the lakeside path.

Bob didn't say a word, although his eyes followed her as she sped off. Miranda gave the dog leads a slight pull. "Come on, kids. Bye, Bob," she said, keen to get out of his way.

94

He nodded and moved along the path, his eyes never leaving the woman jogger as he followed her at a walking pace.

"That man is seriously strange and why is he going that way? I would have thought he would have gone up into the woods to investigate," Miranda whispered to William. "I do wish he hadn't got the job. In fact, I'm beginning to wish old Fart Features was going to stay. I don't think Bob and I are going to get on and I certainly wouldn't want to meet him in the woods. He gives me the creeps."

"Perhaps he's just shy," William remarked. "Shy people often give off vibes that they aren't friendly."

"Um. I don't think it's that, William. He's seriously odd ... still time will tell ... and you never know, he might not like the job and leave. After all, it must be a bit boring, just walking round and round for hours on end, especially if there's no-one to talk to ... and I know how that feels but at least I have the dogs and I'm only here for an hour at a time."

They didn't encounter Bob again and there was no sign of the woman in pink lycra either as William and Miranda, with all the dogs on the lead, reached the car park.

"I'm going to go and say a proper hello to Trudy and buy an ice-cream," Miranda said, having popped the dogs back into the car. "I can see the car from inside the cafe so the dogs will be quite safe for a few minutes. Would you like to join me, William?"

"Yes. That's a nice idea. I haven't had an ice-cream since I was on the cruise," he replied, experiencing a flashing reminder of Tilly Pargeter lapping up a huge 99 after lunch one day. He grinned. She certainly wouldn't be enjoying another.

****

Bob Watkins was just leaving the toilet and saw them enter the cafe. He passed Miranda's Volvo. The four larger dogs were alert, sitting up straight, their beady eyes watching Miranda disappear. He couldn't see the two Dachshunds.

He had intended to have a coffee but decided against it. He didn't want to get into conversation with that dog walker and the old man. He would go back down to the lake and see if there were any more silly women who fancied venturing into the woods on their own.

****

A delivery van pulled up just as Miranda and William bought their ice-creams and Trudy had to busy herself seeing to it. The pair sat down at a table overlooking the car park so Miranda could keep an eye on the dogs.

"You have to be so careful," she said. "So many have been stolen out of cars and it's just not wise to leave them in there at all these days. I didn't worry once but now … it's a nightmare."

William nodded. "It must be. You certainly have a lot of responsibility … looking after so many dogs for other people." He decided to take the bull by the horns. "Stephen told me you were feeling pretty down and were upset when he bumped into you the other day. I hope you've got over whatever was troubling you."

Miranda pushed her flake down into the ice cream cone with her tongue so she could enjoy the last delicious bite of ice cream, chocolate and cone all in one. "Not really," she replied sadly. "It's Jeremy. You know, the army chap … whose father owned Anna's shop."

"Ah. Him," William's stomach knotted tightly. Christ! He remembered how before the cruise, Miranda had dated bloody Jeremy Cross. He hadn't realised the dalliance had become serious in his absence. What a damned fool he was to have thought she wouldn't continue dating the handsome army major … or that it should have become serious, as by the look on her face and her demeanour since he had returned to Peesdown, it certainly had.

96

"Well," Miranda continued. "We've been seeing each other most of the winter but not long ago I discovered there's another woman ... it seems he's probably going to marry her so I backed off ... but he's still been hassling me, constantly ringing and texting but I refuse to talk to him ... after all, there's nothing to say is there? And I flatly refuse to be his 'bit on the side'. Anyhow, I've finally deleted him from my phone, something I should have done a long while ago, so that should be the end of it." She rubbed her brow and narrowed her eyes as if in pain.

He could feel his stomach returning to normal as his spirits rose again. All was not lost. "I see. Good for you. Well, it's just as well you're having lunch with Stephen then. It will help you take your mind off ... Jeremy."

"Ummmm," Miranda uttered, leaving William not knowing whether it was because she was munching the end of the ice cream cone packed with chocolate or the thought of meeting Stephen for lunch. He prayed it was the latter.

"He's a nice chap is Stephen," William went on. "You'll like him very much once you get to know him ... and he's a lot going for him. He has a good business, plenty of money ... and a nice car. He bought it this week. A BMW series 8 ... a convertible," he added, hoping it would impress her.

"Really. That's nice," Miranda said, not taking much notice. All she could think about was Jeremy now he had been mentioned. Jeremy in his uniform, Jeremy in casual gear, walking with her, hand in hand, the dogs beside them. Oh, God. How was she ever going to get over him?

"And he's really looking forward to your lunch. You've been all he can talk about since he met you in the park."

"Oh, heavens," Miranda looked up at him, startled. "I do hope he hasn't got a thing about me. I'm quite happy to have lunch but I don't want to get involved with anyone again."

William stared at her, his heart sinking. Stephen was going to have to up his game. Miranda obviously wasn't over this Jeremy yet. Bugger the man. Bugger, bugger, bugger!

****

At the end of another busy day, Miranda went home, fed the dogs, poured a large glass of Merlot and made herself macaroni cheese with a jacket potato, heated up a tin of garden peas and sat down at the kitchen table to eat. As usual, she was exhausted and relieved Belinda was feeding the three sets of cats whose parents were away tonight so there was no need to go out again and she could relax, watch a dvd … perhaps something with Hugh Grant … she never tired of him … and finish the bottle of wine. She didn't usually drink in the evenings but tonight she was too tired and unhappy to care and when she did collapse in front of the tv, she was going to polish off that unopened box of chocolates one of her clients had given her for Christmas.

She had just begun to eat when her mobile, still in her jacket pocket began to ring. She got to her feet and went to fetch it, having made it a rule never to ignore a call as it might well be a client or a new enquiry and if she wasn't contactable, they might well go to another petsitter.

She glanced at the number but didn't recognise it. Thankful it wasn't Jeremy again, she answered it.

"Four Paws petsitting service. How may I help you?" she said smartly.

"Miranda … please … please don't put the phone down. Please speak to me. I'm going demented not knowing what I've done." Jeremy pleaded down the phone.

Her heart lurched crazily and her temperature rose rapidly. She had to sit down. She walked back into the kitchen and sank onto her chair. She didn't know what to say.

"Look, Miranda. I still don't know why you walked out of my birthday party pleading a headache … and haven't answered my calls since. It's been weeks now. Weeks of sheer agony not knowing what I've done."

Miranda took a deep breath. He sounded so sincere and just to hear his voice was making her whole body tingle. God, she loved him so much. Blast, she shouldn't be drinking wine. It was making her soft. She should have cut him off instantly but more than anything in the world she wanted the bloody Karen woman to disappear … to vanish off the face of the earth … leave Jeremy to her. She badly wanted to tell him how much she loved him. How she never wanted to be apart from him … ever. Then the image of Karen floated before her … that beautiful head of long blonde hair, the slim figure, the voice. Her heart hardened.

"Don't pretend you don't know, Jeremy. Your friend, *Karen*, made it perfectly clear at the party that you were very close and it was only a matter of time before you proposed. What the hell was I supposed to do, Jeremy? Just wait around to get hurt even more? I don't think so. I've a bit more pride than that and I certainly can't compete with the likes of her."

"Karen!" he exclaimed sharply. "So, that's it. Oh, Miranda. If you only knew."

Miranda's heart missed a beat. He sounded genuinely shocked. Gripping the phone, her eyes closed tightly, she prayed as she had never prayed before that it had all been a terrible mistake as she heard the relief in Jeremy's voice as he continued.

"Karen has been the bane of my life for the last couple of years. The damned woman formed an attachment to me as soon as we met at Sandhurst. I have never even been out with her … believe me, Miranda. It's been hard, working with her and when we're off duty she's stalked me relentlessly. She shouldn't even have been at the party. She wasn't invited but turned up anyway, knowing full well she wouldn't be thrown out."

"But … she was so convincing. She had me believing you were about to get married," Miranda exclaimed, her eyes wide with astonishment. She took a large gulp of her Merlot and then another, the intense relief engulfing her. She felt the awful pain which had repeatedly stabbed at her heart since the party gradually easing and tears of sheer joy began to run down her cheeks.

"Oh, Lord, Miranda. I am so very sorry. That damned woman has put us both through hell over the last few weeks."

"Tell me about it," Miranda muttered, dabbing at her eyes with a tissue. If bloody Karen was here now ….

"You do believe me, don't you, Miranda."

"Well, to be honest," she took another sip of her Merlot, "it's going to take a little while for it to sink in as she made me believe you were serious about each other and I was just wasting my time."

"You're not, Miranda. You really are not. Now, I need to know. Do you … do you … would you please see me again? I feel we had something really special and I don't want it to end. I have some very deep feelings for you and I'm pretty sure you feel the same."

Miranda beamed through the tears. She had wanted this so much. Every night since his blasted party she had cried herself to sleep, thinking she would never see him again … and now this. It was hard to take in, believe it was happening, that Karen was of no importance to Jeremy whatsoever.

"Miranda? Please … speak to me," he urged, his voice cracking with emotion. "Please don't hang up on me. I don't think I could bear it again."

"Of course I'm not going to hang up," she said quickly, "and I'm so sorry. I should have given you a chance to explain. It's just that I was so hurt and felt so stupid. I just wanted to get away from the party and since then …."

"I can't tell you how mad I am with Karen … putting us both through all this unnecessary misery. It's just as well I'm being posted back to London this week and won't have to work with her any longer or even see her as she's on leave for a fortnight … in Berlin … sightseeing. I don't think I could be responsible for my actions if we were to meet again."

"You're coming back to London?" she queried, her heart skipping another beat.

He laughed. "Yes. I'm supposed to be returning to the UK on Sunday but can't get up to Yorkshire until next weekend. Will you … will you have dinner with me … please? I think we need to get our relationship back on track … we've wasted a good deal of time thanks to Karen."

"Oh, yes. Oh, yes, please," she laughed with joy. "Oh, Jeremy … I'm so sorry. I really thought …,"

"I know … but it's time to move on now. Listen, I think I've a better idea than driving up to Yorkshire."

"Oh?"

"How about ... how would you like to spend a few days in Paris instead?"

"Paris," she breathed. She had never been and had always wanted to go … and to be there with him … it would be utter heaven … and soooo romantic. "But there's so much to arrange … it's Easter weekend and we're so busy … the dogs … bookings … and I need something to wear … and I haven't a clue where my passport is."

"But you want to go … with me?"

"Oh, yes. I can't think of anything I'd rather do."

"Good. We'll make it a long weekend then. If you can catch the train down to London on Thursday evening, we can fly early on Good Friday and then return on Easter Monday. Then I'll drive you back to Yorkshire."

Miranda was finding it hard to breathe. Just half an hour ago she had been as miserable as sin and now, she was going to Paris … with him … in just a few days. Things were moving so rapidly, she felt her head was going to burst with all that was going on.

"Miranda?"

"Yes ... yes, sorry. It's such a lot to take in in one go ... but yes." She thought rapidly. "My parents can have the dogs and I'll go through the bookings this evening and see what I can offload onto the girls and I'm sure I can find my passport if I look hard enough."

"So, it's all on then? I can book it?"

"Yes, please ... and Jeremy ... I am so very sorry. I should have talked to you. I shouldn't have walked out like that. I've made the last few weeks so horribly unpleasant when they needn't have been. I really am sorry."

"Stop saying you're sorry. I probably would have done exactly the same in your position but it doesn't matter now. What does is that we're okay again. I can't wait to see you next week ... but I must ring off as I have an appointment I can't get out. I have to be best man at a friend's wedding and we're meeting to discuss it. I'll ring you tomorrow and I'll email you the hotel details. Oh, Miranda. I can't wait to see you again."

"I can't either," she replied shyly.

She switched off her phone with an enormous beam on her face and danced into the lounge where Charlie and Nellie were in their baskets. She threw herself on the floor beside them and hugged them both.

"Oh, my darlings. I am sooo happy, I could burst. I'm going to Paris ... with Jeremy ... I can't believe it."

The pure joy in her voice made them thump their tails and smile back at her. Then, when the tears of relief and excitement flooded down her face, they lovingly licked them away.

CHAPTER 12

Miranda's week had been a busy and highly emotional one and when she opened her eyes at 5.00 a.m. on Saturday morning, she felt utterly shattered but deliriously happy too. For weeks she had been in the depths of despair but since *that* conversation with Jeremy, she had been in a state of euphoria and hugged herself with delight, willing the hours away until she could see him again … in Paris! Romantic, wonderful, beautiful Paris!

She pinched herself to make sure she wasn't dreaming. Last week she had sobbed into her pillow every night and every morning on waking because she was so miserable. Today she wanted to cry because she was incredibly happy. How ludicrous was that?

A light padding of eight paws coming up the stairs made her smile. It was breakfast time, and even if she wanted to, her darling dogs weren't going to allow her to remain in bed. At least she didn't have to visit cats this morning, it still being Belinda's week. It had been a good idea, and Belinda had been more than happy to comply with taking weekly turns throughout the winter, which gave them both a break from getting out and about early and not arriving home until late. However, with the summer nearly upon them, demand for their services was growing rapidly as people booked their holidays and needed their houses and cats looking after, which would require two people doing the visits … and at this rate she might well have to rope in Julie and Kate, her other two dog walkers, to do some too.

Nellie was now sitting by the bed, her eyes fixed on her owner, willing her to get up, while Charlie sat with his head on the duvet, breathing softly, his big brown eyes pleading pitifully.

"You'd think I never fed you," she laughed, kissing their soft, silky heads.

She pulled on her dressing gown and with the dogs padding eagerly in front of her, went downstairs, measured out their dry food, added a few bits of chicken and refreshed their water bowl. Within seconds all the food had disappeared.

"I don't think you even tasted that," Miranda laughed as she opened the back door and let them out into the garden for a wee. "You mustn't gobble your food like that next weekend when you're at your Granny and Grandad's. They'll think you're still hungry and give you more and you'll come back like two big tubs."

While they were sniffing and relieving themselves on the lawn, she made a coffee, filled a bowl with rice crispies and covered them with sugar and milk. The dogs wandered back indoors, wagged their tails at her and deposited themselves back into their baskets until it was time for their walk.

Miranda glanced through into the dining room where there was a huge pile of paperwork on the table begging for attention; invoices to be paid or prepared, references to send out for prospective petsitters to board the dogs, boarding agreements, dog walking forms, catsitting forms. It was going to keep her occupied most of the weekend and she didn't really have time to have lunch with Stephen but she didn't have his number to ring and cancel. She would have to go. Damn. Still, she must see the Landlord of the Red Lion about Fart Features' leaving do. The old bugger might have given her a hard time in the past few years but she was going to miss him and so would a lot of other people and he hadn't been the same since he found poor Tanya Phillips a few months ago. He had aged overnight and his usual look of pompous obstinacy had been replaced by a worried, nervous frown so it would be good to do something nice for him. He might actually smile at her then.

She looked at the clock on the kitchen wall and sighed with resignation. It would be nice to go back to bed but she wouldn't be able to rest knowing this mountain of paperwork was awaiting her attention and as she wouldn't be here next weekend, she really should get on with it. She loved her business but blimey it was growing fast and it was going to be imperative to get some help with the administration side of it soon. Still, if she applied herself for a few hours this morning, she could make a huge dent in it before the dogs needed their walk and she had to meet Stephen. Then she remembered what William had said. How Stephen hadn't been able to stop talking about her. That was worrying. She would have to make it clear today that she couldn't see him again, that Jeremy was back in her life and how she had high hopes that it was going to be a long term, permanent relationship. She sat down at her desk and started work with a broad grin on her face and butterflies in her tummy.

****

William was a bag of nerves. He had rarely smoked but craved a cigarette now. He considered having a drink but didn't want to turn up at the Red Lion tipsy and anyway he had to keep a clear head. He didn't want any slip-ups with his identity ... and he needed to impress Miranda today. She might be enamoured of this Jeremy chap but he was safely tucked up in Germany with this woman he was supposed to marry so the way was clear to make her forget all about the blasted man. Following a lovely lunch today, he would offer to take her for a drive in the BMW - perhaps tomorrow as the weather was predicted to be good. Perhaps they could have a trip to the coast or up to the Dales or Moors. He thought of bowling along with the top down, Miranda's beautiful long fair hair waving about in the breeze. She would love it. They could have lunch somewhere nice ... and maybe dinner too. There must be an upmarket hotel they could stop at somewhere. He would look some up this afternoon, after their lunch, once Miranda had decided in what direction they would go. If things went well, they might even stopover.

The excitement in the pit of his stomach made him a bit nauseous. A night away in a posh hotel with Miranda would be ... would be tremendous. He could do it with her. He knew he could.

He loved her. She wasn't like all the other women … and she would be willing and loving. She would change his life. It would never be the same again. He hurried upstairs to get ready. He wanted to make a really good impression over lunch.

****

The Red Lion was fairly busy and there were only two vacant spaces in the car park when Miranda arrived. She had no idea if Stephen was already there because he wouldn't drive when he could walk literally across the road from William's house.

As she locked the Volvo, she glanced over at the house for sale next door to William. It was so damned impressive with the sweeping drive and beautiful old Victorian facade with sash windows and huge oak door with stained glass windows. She sighed. She would have loved it.

Stephen was already in the pub's dining room. He stood up, smiling widely as she approached him and pulled a chair out for her opposite his at their table. The room was full of families, one of which had a Springer Spaniel and another, a Dalmatian, who were both behaving beautifully, resting quietly beside their owners and taking no notice of the food being brought to the tables.

"I couldn't see my Nellie and Charlie doing the same," Miranda giggled. "They're both so greedy and would let me down terribly. I could never take them into a restaurant."

Stephen smiled again. "What would you like to drink, Miranda? I'll get you something while you look at the menu … you look very nice by the way."

"Thank you," she said, thinking how charming he was and it was such a shame she was going to have to let him down. "Just a fruit juice for me please … as I'm driving."

She studied the menu as he disappeared to the bar, wondering when to mention that this would be the only time they could meet up because of her involvement with Jeremy. It was such a shame.

He looked so pleased to see her and she hoped he wouldn't be too disappointed.

She wasn't really hungry. Her usual voracious appetite had taken a battering over the last few weeks, to begin with because she was so upset about Jeremy and Karen and then because she was so elated they were going to see each other again. She felt another thrill of excitement. Next week at this time she would be in Paris ... with him ... all alone ... in a hotel. Oh, God!

Stephen returned, a glass of orange juice for her and an apple juice for himself. "The waitress will come and take our food order. What would you like?" he asked.

"Just an omelette please, Stephen. A cheese one ... with salad." That should slide down without too much of a problem she thought.

She quietly studied him. She couldn't get over how much he looked like William, which was silly, as they were closely related and wasn't at all odd ... but it was still his voice that puzzled her. If she closed her eyes while he was talking, she would think it was William speaking.

"Now, I want you to tell me all about you ... your life, your business, your likes and dislikes," Stephen said, leaning forward on the table and looking her straight in the eyes.

She shifted uncomfortably in her chair. "I would love to but before we go any further, I have to tell you that I've spoken to Jeremy a couple of days ago ... you know, the man I was crying about when you found me in the woods."

"Oh, yes," Stephen said, his voice growing cold as he abruptly sat back in his chair.

"Well, it seems we've been at cross purposes. You see, I thought he had another woman in tow but it turns out he hasn't. It was all a terrible misunderstanding." Her voice was quickening now. She wanted to get it all out as Stephen was beginning to go a bit red in the face and his lips were turning into a scowl which was slightly alarming.

107

"Anyway," she continued in a rush. "We've patched things up, our relationship is back on and we're going to Paris together next weekend," she said, squeaking the last few words, concerned by his expression. His eyes had darkened and narrowed, his lips were now pursed and he was drumming his fingers on the table.

"I am sorry, Stephen. I never would have agreed to meet you if I had known … and I couldn't cancel lunch as I didn't have your phone number."

****

He sat and stared at her without blinking, his heart sinking to his boots. He couldn't believe what he was hearing. It was all over before it had even begun. It was too cruel. How could she do this to him? He had been about to give her everything. He was going to love her as no other could. They were going to spend the rest of their lives together, have children if she wanted them, travel the world, have the most wonderful life together until they were old and grey and died. Not this. She couldn't do this. No. No. No!

He stood up abruptly. He couldn't sit here, making polite conversation. His heart was being torn out of him and his very soul was going to be lost and lonely forever. He had thought his whole life would change for the better with her by his side. Now he was looking into a dark abyss of misery, loneliness and …. and … yes, more of those bloody women when the urge became too much to ignore. He clenched his fists. She could have freed him of his terrible addiction. Now she was sending him spiralling back into it again. He was furious, acutely disappointed and desperate and couldn't remain in the restaurant for one more second.

She looked at him, startled, a flash of fright in her beautiful eyes.

"Stephen. Are you okay?" she asked.

"No. No, I'm sorry, Miranda. I have to go. I suddenly don't feel very well. I'm sorry."

He ripped a £50 note out of his wallet and virtually threw it on the table. "There. That will settle the bill. I must go. Bye."

He walked quickly, not glancing back at her, pushing past people milling at the bar, desperate to get out, feel fresh air on his face, calm himself.

He marched across the road to the house and bolted the gates firmly behind him. On opening the front door, he went inside and slid slowly to the floor, tears of rage and despair rolling down his cheeks. At that moment, he hated Miranda more than he had ever hated anyone in his entire life.

****

Miranda's omelette arrived as she was wondering whether to leave too but it looked delicious, Stephen had left plenty of money and it would save her cooking later. She ate it thoughtfully, worried she had upset him more than she had expected to. Why he had reacted so badly when they barely knew each other was certainly rather odd.

Having finished her omelette and declined pudding, she made her way to the bar to pay and have a chat with Andy, the new Landlord, about a leaving do for Fart Features. She booked it for the weekend after she and Jeremy returned from Paris thinking how lovely it would be if he was able to accompany her.

She went outside to her car and glanced over at William's house. She ought to go over and give Stephen his change. It was a lot of money and she didn't want to hang on to it but she wasn't too eager to see him again. She bit her lip, wondering what to do … but it had to be done. She walked across the road and tried to open the gate. It wouldn't budge. Then she realised it was bolted on the inside. How strange. She shrugged. She would have to keep the money with her and give it to William or Stephen when she saw either of them in the park. She got back into her car and headed home to Charlie and Nellie. She had a lot to do, finishing off that pile of paperwork and getting ready for Paris next weekend.

As usual, the dogs were pleased to see her and after a quick wee in the garden were happy to settle back down again until it was time for another walk followed by their tea.

Miranda sat down at her desk and looked at the list of things she had to do before the Paris trip. She had already rung her parents to see if they would have Charlie and Nellie and she had spoken to Belinda yesterday and they were meeting tomorrow to go through the bookings and work out who was going to do what in Miranda's absence.

Thank goodness for Belinda, who was her right-hand woman and far more flexible since finding an extra carer for her mother who was still badly disabled from her terrible stroke. Belinda had proved to be totally reliable and conscientious and all the clients and animals adored her. Julie and Kate, Miranda's other walkers, were great too but Belinda definitely had the edge.

So that was the dogs and the business organised. She just had to sort what she needed for Paris ... and her passport was the most important thing. Turning all her drawers upside down, Miranda eventually found it and sighed with relief. It still had a couple of years to run on it so she was quite safe. She then checked her wardrobe and found suitable outfits for Paris. It could still be a little chilly, being April, so she picked out a couple of pairs of jeans and sweaters and trainers for sightseeing and three outfits for dinner in the evening. There, it had been easier than she had first thought and all she had to do now was get through the next few days. Her tummy flipped over, imagining seeing Jeremy again. Then, for a split second, she remembered Stephen and his obvious disappointment at her news. She shrugged. Stephen was the least of her troubles.

****

William dashed away his tears and headed for the brandy bottle. He liked a tipple now and again but he certainly needed it now. He poured a liberal amount into a glass, downed the lot and then poured another.

He marched upstairs, glass in hand, to the most important room in the house where he prayed and worshipped Miranda. He stared at the crucifix on the wall above the white-clothed table on which stood two altar candles and his black leather bible which his parents had given him. For once he didn't feel like getting on his knees and praying. He felt too angry.

He glared at the photographs on the wall above the altar. They had previously been in another room but he had moved them all up here last week. He glared furiously at the largest, a picture he had taken of Miranda sitting on a park bench, laughing up at Anna. She had no idea it had been taken as he had been on the opposite side of the lake to her at the time and zoomed in his camera before snapping her. It was wonderful ... as were the others, all 56 of her from various walks in the park.

He could feel the anger taking over. It was sending his temperature up and the sweat was pouring off his brow. He rubbed his arm across it to wipe the moisture away. He hated Miranda, the one and only person he had ever truly loved, with a vengeance. He hated her for making him feel as he did, undesirable, useless, utterly rejected. He hated her, he hated her, he hated her! He wanted to rip the pictures off the walls, tear them to shreds in a crazy frenzy of destruction and throw them to the floor and trample on them ... but it wasn't enough. He wanted to go further. He wanted to kill. The itch was returning ... with a vengeance.

CHAPTER 13

William went to church the next morning. He had a lot to pray for and kept his head bowed for quite a while once he sat down in his favourite pew. Firstly, he prayed for Miranda, that she would quickly realise her mistake in going out with flaming Jeremy and turn to Stephen instead. Then he concentrated on asking for God's help to resist the itch which was beginning to take over again. The urge to rape and kill had been exceedingly strong last night following his disastrous encounter with Miranda but he had downed so much brandy he hadn't been able to go out anyway, collapsing on his bed fully clothed, waking up this morning stiff and cold as he had forgotten to put the heating on.

Having completed his talk with God, William sat up straight and watched people file into the church and take their seats. The young, cheerful Vicar and his attractive, kindly wife, Samantha, were popular and even though most of the churches in the vicinity were nearly empty, St. Edmunds was thriving. Between them, they ran several groups for the young and old, and organised a great many events and activities, raising thousands of pounds for various charities. As a result, the church was nearly always packed on a Sunday and many enjoyed the coffee and refreshments afterwards, providing a chance for the children to play and the adults to socialise.

Sitting where he did, near to the back on the left of the nave where he had a good view of everyone coming in at the entrance on his right, he nodded at the few people he knew, mainly people from the park. Harry, the owner of the four Great Danes, was a church warden and was always in attendance and then he recognised Mrs Smedley, sitting with a younger woman who looked very much like her, probably her daughter he surmised. Anna had told him the elderly woman had been ill with heart trouble while he was away on the cruise and then her much loved poodle, Precious, had died. She certainly didn't look too good this morning. Frail and weak and pale and pasty without the generous amount of make-up she normally wore.

Then Anna walked in. She saw him, smiled and joined him in his pew, stopping for a moment to bow her head and pray before turning to him.

"Hello, William. Nice to see you this morning. I thought as I was moving into Peesdown permanently, I should start to use the church. I like the Vicar very much ... he and his wife buy all their dog food and treats from me so I've got to know them fairly well."

"That's nice," he said. Still smarting from Miranda's rejection of Stephen, he didn't feel like talking to her best friend.

The organist began to play, the Vicar took his place before the altar, the choir shuffled into position in their pews at either side of him and all conversation was temporarily suspended as the service began.

He didn't want to stay for refreshments afterwards. Anna would probably want a little chat and the kids were getting on his nerves, making a racket in the vestry where the Sunday school teacher was telling silly jokes.

"I'm sorry, Anna. But I shall have to go. I have to see to lunch for Stephen," he said as they stood up to leave.

"Okay ... how is Stephen? Miranda told me they met for lunch yesterday but she thinks she upset him because she is back with Jeremy," she said as they left the church, shaking the Vicar's hand at the door as they filed past him with all those who didn't want to stay for refreshments.

They walked down the path towards Miller Lane.

"Stephen," William gulped, "is fine. Probably getting hungry by now. I really must go, Anna. Goodbye."

He felt her eyes boring into his back as he walked as quickly as he could back to his house, trying to remember to limp. "Back with Jeremy," she had said. The words reverberated around his head. "Back with Jeremy. Back with Jeremy." Bloody, bloody Jeremy. God, if the man was here now, he'd kill him. He hated him intensely, almost as much as Miranda. No, he didn't hate her really. He loved her. But Jeremy would have to be dealt with. He had to be expelled from Miranda's life ... for good ... but how this was going to be achieved he had no idea, especially when the blasted man was residing in Germany!

****

Elsie Makins had sat right at the back, all alone and lonely. She had thought coming to church would have made her feel better but it hadn't. The service had just reminded her of attending services with her mother and father when she was a child. The happy, laughing children had made her sadness at not being able to have one of her own even worse and the smiling Vicar, as sincere and kind as he was, did nothing to make her severe depression subside. But she had needed to come. She wanted to say prayers for Brandy in a fit and proper place before she scattered his ashes in the park.

She didn't want refreshments. No-one knew her so they wouldn't speak to her anyway. Not that she felt like talking. She just wanted to leave, get out into the fresh air, away from all the friendly, cheerful people and the mouldy old smell that always seemed to associate itself with ancient buildings. Two women smiled at her. She didn't smile back. She had nothing to smile about.

She hurried out, stopping for a brief second to shake the Vicar's hand and scurrying away before he could begin a conversation. She had something important to do. She had left home that morning, intending to drive straight to the park. Then, just as she drove down the High Street and saw all the cars outside the church, it had seemed the right place to go. To talk to God. Ask for his help. Not that she could see what he could do. He couldn't give her another job at her age. He couldn't pay the rent on her flat to stop her being evicted next month. He couldn't resurrect her beloved dog who had been put to sleep by a kindly vet last week.

114

It had been the best thing to do. Poor Brandy, whom she had rescued from Happylands twelve years ago, had been riddled with cancer. It was unfair to let him carry on but the pain was unbearable for her. He had slipped peacefully away in her arms after the vet had injected him. Somehow, she had stumbled from the surgery, bawling her eyes out as she drove home, barely able to see the road for her tears but walking into the flat and seeing his basket, his toys and his food bowl had been devastating. She had screamed with the pain of losing him. Her only friend in the world.

He had been cremated and yesterday she had returned to the vets for his ashes and this morning, brought them to Peesdown, to the park he had loved so much during his lifetime.

Leaving the churchyard, she sank heavily into her car, glancing miserably at the beautifully decorated cardboard box on the seat beside her, covered in woodland scenes from the autumn. The trees were stunning in their rich colours, as were the leaves on the ground. Her heart was breaking. As beautiful as it was, it portrayed the season was over ... just as Brandy's life was over.

She started the car and drove the few yards down the road into the car park inside the park gates. Having locked the car and carrying the box closely to her chest, feeling Brandy's presence strongly, she walked all around the lake, heading for his favourite spot, the bench at the far side of the lake where they had always sat for a while, enjoying the peace and watching the wildlife. Brandy had always been a good boy. He had never chased anything, never frightened another animal. He had been a kindly little soul and the best companion she could ever have had.

She sat, quietly talking to her Brandy, telling him how much she loved him and how much she was going to miss him. Then she stood up, opened the box and scattered the ashes amongst the bushes behind her. Then she walked away, tears streaming down her face. She had no-one and nothing in the world. There was no point in even going home. Her landlord was making her life a misery now she was two months in arrears with her rent, unable to pay it since losing her job. With little likelihood of getting another position at her age and with five years still to go before she was eligible for her state pension, she had no idea what was going to happen to her. She would probably end up in some kind of ghastly council accommodation living on benefits ... or on the streets.

She looked up at the sky, imagining Brandy up there, with her parents, with her other animals which had died over the years; two dogs, a cat and a rabbit. The clouds were black, swirling crazily. Without warning, the rain hammered down, soaking her instantly. There had been a few people in the park when she arrived. They scurried away and she was alone. She looked at the black, inky water in the lake, the rising wind and the rain making it choppy. It would be so easy to slip in. She couldn't swim. It would soon be over ... and then she would be with Brandy and all those she had loved and lost. They could meander through the clouds together ... for eternity. No more worry, no more heartache, no more tiredness and utter exhaustion. This was it. This was what she wanted. There was no point in going on. No-one wanted her. No-one cared. She stepped into the water as the rain beat down relentlessly on her head.

****

Anna drove over to Happylands after church. It was pouring with rain and her windscreen wipers had a job keeping up with the deluge. Not the kind of weather to walk dogs but she better become used to it as her two would have to go out for decent walks every day otherwise they would be a nightmare to live with.

She was excited. She and Sonia had finally decided it was time she took them out of Happylands for a walk. The dogs had formed a good bond with her now and reacted quickly to her commands but taking them out without Sonia by her side was a bit daunting and if it hadn't been for Miranda offering to come with her to Peesdown this afternoon she didn't think she could do it. It was a shame Andy couldn't take her out as they had arranged but with a couple of police officers off sick, he had been called in to do an extra shift and their walk was postponed.

She reached Happylands as the rain began to ease. Sonia greeted her with her usual enthusiasm and after a coffee and a slice of Josh's apple and cinnamon cake, they fetched Dolly and Rio. Automatically the dogs started off in the direction of the field and were surprised to find they were being led to Anna's car instead and encouraged to jump onto the back seat where she had placed a waterproof covering and blanket and fixed a dog guard between the back and front seats.

Well, that was easy," Anna laughed. "I just hope the rest of the afternoon will go as well."

"Of course it will. Just remember everything I've told you … and you will have Miranda for backup so you will be fine. Have a lovely time and I look forward to hearing all about it when you get back."

Sonia's head went up at the sight of another vehicle making its way up the lane towards the house. "Oh, good. It's John Marchant … the chap who rescued Dolly and Rio. He's keen to help with our Easter Fayre so I've invited him for afternoon tea to discuss it. He was so pleased to hear the dogs had found such a good home with you."

"That's nice. Don't forget I want to help out too and if you can give me a poster, I'll display it in the shop."

"Thanks, Anna. I will. Now, go and have a smashing time with your two new companions and give Miranda and Charlie my love."

Anna drove down the lane, waving at John, who waved back, smiling broadly as he saw the two dogs peering out of the back window of Anna's car looking so well and full of life.

****

Miranda, Nellie and Charlie were just alighting from the Volvo when Anna drove into the car park. It was still raining, not as hard as it had been earlier but enough to prevent many venturing out on a Sunday afternoon.

Miranda made a big fuss of Dolly and Rio as Anna got them out of the car and all four dogs stood and sniffed each other eagerly, tails wagging madly with curiosity and excitement.

They walked down to the lake, Anna anxious about letting Rio and Dolly off the lead.

"What about if they scarper?" she said to Miranda.

Miranda studied them. "I don't think they will. If you notice, although they are excited to be in a new place and are keen to explore, they're also watching you all the time. Thanks to Sonia's training, you've made them realise you are the alpha male in your little pack so quite honestly, Anna, I think it will be fine. Just make them sit and stay a few times, make sure they are concentrating on you and only you and then if they can do that with all these distractions," she waved an arm around the park, "you've cracked it."

Anna raised her eyebrows at Miranda and grinned. "Oh, well. Here goes."

She stood still and both dogs looked up at her, wondering what she was doing.

"Sit," she commanded.

They both sat immediately, watching her face intently.

"Stay," she said firmly, slowly dropping their leads onto the floor and backing away, her right arm stretched out in front of her with her hand upright.

Dolly shuffled a little as a demanding duck swam by, quacking furiously for food but she remained where she was, eyes still on Anna. Rio didn't move. He loved Anna, loved training and loved being told he was a good boy.

Anna waited a few moments before she went back to them, thrilled they had done as they were told in a completely new environment.

"Oh, good dogs, good dogs," she said enthusiastically, handing them a biscuit each. Nellie and Charlie were there in an instant, eager not to be left out.

"There, you see. You needn't worry. They're responding well to you. Let them off and just call them back and make them sit every now and again to remind them you are in charge," Miranda instructed.

Feeling more confident and relaxed, Anna linked arms with Miranda as the dogs started to play and dashed in and out of the lake, shutting up the noisy duck who decided, with a furious flapping of wings, that it would be more prudent to head off to another part of the lake to try his luck.

"Now," Anna said, not daring to take her eyes off her precious dogs. "Tell me all about Jeremy and this trip to Paris next weekend."

Miranda launched into an excited preamble about her hopes and dreams and the walk went well, Dolly and Rio enjoying the new company and fresh experiences.

As they approached the part of the lake where poor Tanya Philips had been found, both women's eyes automatically looked ahead and not at the water. It was impossible to forget what had happened there and their steps usually quickened past the bushes where her clothes had been found. However, Rio, who was a few yards behind, began to bark at the water, where the shrubbery was thickest at the edge of the lake. Anna called him but he remained where he was, his body taut and his ears pricked. He continued to bark, glancing first at Anna and then back at the spot where his attention was focused.

"Come on, Rio," Anna urged, unlinking arms with Miranda and walking back towards him, holding out a biscuit to encourage him, curious to see what was bothering him. Then she saw it. First, a shoe, then a foot, a coat and then … a head, face down in the water.

She gasped aloud, putting her hand to her mouth in horror. "Oh, my God, Miranda. It's another one."

Miranda dashed to her side, Dolly, Charlie and Nellie close behind. Rio ceased barking and stood quietly beside Anna now he was satisfied he had alerted her that something was wrong.

Miranda stared at the body floating in the water. "Oh, no! Christ! I'll ring the police," she said quickly, her voice trembling with shock. With shaking hands, she pulled her phone out of her pocket and pressed 999.

Anna was petrified. The woman was fully clothed so she couldn't have been raped but how had she ended up here, in the same spot as Tanya Philips, only a few months later? Had she been murdered and if so, was the murderer still lurking about somewhere … in the trees … in the shrubbery? She scanned their side of the lake quickly but could see no-one skulking about. Perhaps it wasn't murder. Perhaps it was an accident … or suicide? Whatever it was, it was earth-shattering and horrible.

"Right. We'll stay here," Miranda was saying into her phone, having told the police exactly where they were and what they had found. She switched off the phone and turned to Anna. "Come on. We'll walk to a bench further down the lake towards the car park. We can't stand here and stare at the poor soul for the next ten minutes or however long it takes for the cavalry to arrive."

White-faced and shaky, as the rain grew heavier, threatening a thunderstorm, they headed back to a bench they had passed earlier and sat down. The dogs stayed with them, remaining close to their humans without being told, realising something was badly wrong. None of them wanted to play now.

The police were there in minutes, loud sirens heralding their approach as the cars hurtled down the High Street, across Miller Lane and pulled up in the car park, an ambulance following close behind. Several police officers and two paramedics hurried towards them, Anna relieved to see Andy at the fore, his face an expression of concern.

"Anna, are you okay? I'm so sorry you've had such a dreadful experience."

Anna nodded and he turned to Miranda. "And how about you?"

"Yes. Honestly, we're fine, Andy. Just shaken up. Poor woman. I do hope it's not another murder. She's exactly where poor Tanya Philips was found."

"Well, we'll soon find out. Look, I know where you both live … and your phone numbers. The weather is appalling and you both look in need of dry clothes and a hot drink. Why don't you go home? If we need to talk to you, we'll contact you later."

"We can go back to the shop … make some tea," Anna said, glad to have permission to leave. Andy placed a hand on her arm. "I'll ring you later … to check you're okay."

He turned and disappeared along the path to join his colleagues.

****

The news spread like wildfire around Peesdown, the large police presence in the park a telling sign that there had been another serious occurrence. William could see them pouring across the park from his back-bedroom window, having been alerted by the sirens.

He pondered on going out to discover what had occurred but couldn't be bothered. Whatever it was, it had nothing to do with him.

****

Miranda and Anna took the dogs back to the shop and changed their clothes, Anna into old attire she kept for cleaning and Miranda into a spare pair of jeans and a sweater she kept in the car for emergencies. They gave the dogs fresh water and a few biscuits and Miranda took some old blankets out of the van for them to rest on while Anna made some tea, lacing both mugs with plenty of sugar. She also found a new packet of chocolate digestives and some custard creams. They sank thankfully into the garden chairs and sipped their tea, hearing more sirens rushing down the High Street.

"That's a ghastly sound. Especially when we know what it's for," remarked Miranda. "That poor woman. I can't get over it. I hope to God she's not been murdered but whatever caused her to end up in the lake must have been horrendous."

"I think I saw her this morning … in church," Anna said thoughtfully, the hot tea and sugar restoring her equilibrium. "She was sitting at the back on her own. Looked ever so miserable and when William and I left, she walked past us, got into a car and then drove into the park. The woman in the lake is about her build and her coat looks about the same."

"Oh, dear. That sounds a possibility then. I've no idea who she is, especially as she was face down in the water … and I didn't recognise her clothes. God, what a dreadful weekend," Miranda said with a scowl. "That poor woman today and that dreadful so-called lunch with Stephen yesterday … which reminds me. I need to see William … or Stephen as I have all his change … just under thirty quid and I can't keep that."

Anna looked thoughtful. "William was behaving rather oddly this morning. He didn't want to talk at all and hurried off with the excuse he had to make lunch for Stephen."

"A bit like his cousin then. He couldn't get out of the pub quickly enough once I had told him about Jeremy … and I'm beginning to think there's something a bit strange about him. He seems nice enough but it's his voice. When he speaks he sounds exactly the same as William. I've been thinking about it all night and am beginning to wonder if Stephen is William or vice versa."

Anna looked at her with a puzzled expression. "That's a strange remark. Why would they be the same person? It doesn't make sense."

"No, I know. Perhaps I'm just being silly," Miranda said, dismissing the little niggle of doubt which had been concerning her ever since she had met Stephen the day before. "Just ignore me. Now, let's try and talk about happier things for a little while. I don't want to think about what's going on in the park and if it is another murder, how I am going to feel walking there every day. I'm not quite sure if I'm going to want to ... and that woman, you know, that runner with the long hair ... says she's a nurse ... she only said the other day that she sensed someone up in the wood watching her ... twice this week. At least she can get a move on and probably outrun a would-be attacker but it would be a bit more difficult for me if one of my dogs can't move very fast and I certainly couldn't leave one behind. I think, to be on the safe side, I might just take to walking in Roundhay for a while ... or team up with Belinda. I know we're not supposed to ... as it means 12 dogs in a pack ... but if the park is going to be empty of other people, no-one will know."

"Bob Watkins and Freddie will if they see you."

"Oh, bugger them. Freddie is used to me and as he's so shaken up from that Tanya woman, will probably sympathise and as for Bob, he's not going to dictate to me and if he does, I'll get Charlie to bite his bum."

Anna grinned. Miranda grinned back. Anna started to giggle, just seeing the spectacle in her mind's eye. Miranda joined her. Within seconds they were collapsed with laughter, releasing the awful tension they had endured for most of the afternoon.

CHAPTER 14

It arrived two days later, the envelope containing a plane ticket and a beautiful brochure detailing the delights of a stay at the Hotel Napoleon in a suite overlooking the Arc de Triomphe, described as a 'front row' view of Paris. It looked simply amazing ... and expensive. Jeremy must think an awful lot of her. She prayed it was as much as she thought of him.

"Wow, Jeremy," she gasped when he rang later that evening to make sure she had received it. "I can't believe it! A whole weekend in Paris ... and staying at such a fantastic hotel but why is departure from Leeds Bradford? I thought I was meeting you in London and we would fly from there."

"Unfortunately, I can't leave Germany as soon as I thought so I will have to fly from here and meet you in Paris. I can return with you though. We'll have a fabulous time and do whatever you want," he laughed. "Dinner on a boat on the Seine, a wander around the Louvre, Montmartre, take a trip up the Eiffel tower for lunch, just see all we can in such a short space of time. I just want to make you happy."

It had been such a huge relief to get away after the trauma of discovering the body of Elsie Makins in the lake and the terrible sadness and concern that followed. By all accounts there was no sign of foul play and a little box from the pet crematorium labelled Brandy led the police to conclude the woman had either slipped into the lake by mistake or had committed suicide after scattering her pet's ashes. Either way, it was upsetting and the atmosphere in Peesdown was sombre and there were grave doubts that initial findings were correct. Whispers abounded that it was another murder and very few people were venturing into the park. Miranda had taken her dogs to Roundhay and Golden Acre all week and Belinda did likewise. Anna's customers talked of nothing else in the shop, in awe that it had been she and Miranda who had found the body. Anna told Miranda she was glad she could leave Emily to deal with the customers most of the time and crack on with preparations for moving. She wanted to have Dolly and Rio live with her as soon as possible, which would make her feel much safer, especially at night.

Miranda was glad she could escape too and was tremendously excited when Good Friday, the day of departure to Paris, finally arrived, getting up far earlier than necessary to get ready. She looked a little more sophisticated than she usually did, having had her hair cut and styled at one of the poshest hairdressers in Leeds. It had cost a bomb but was worth every penny. Her long, fair hair was now layered and rested neatly on her shoulders and it suited her, she decided. Her hair had always been long so it was a bit of a shock when looking in the mirror to see it so beautifully styled and it certainly made her face look slimmer, which wasn't a bad thing!

She dressed in a baby blue cashmere sweater, navy trousers and her leather boots and wore the cream suede coat she had bought for that first meal out with Jeremy and Anna. Belinda drove her to Leeds Bradford airport and deposited her and her new white leather suitcase at the entrance.

The plane had taken off two hours later and within a short space of time landed at Charles de Gaulle. It had seemed like an eternity getting through security but when she did, Jeremy had been there waiting for her, a huge grin on his face. He enveloped her in his arms and hugged her as if he was never going to let her go.

It was a marvellous weekend, the best Easter ever and one she would never forget. They enjoyed a whirlwind of sightseeing during the days but the nights in their lavish bedroom were the most special! Miranda had never known such joy in being with another person. They had bonded perfectly, totally in tune with each other, laughing at the same things, liking the same food, sharing the same interests. She never wanted the weekend to end. She wanted to remain in their little cocoon of love forever and never return to reality but the time flew by and then it was their last night. They dined aboard a floating restaurant on the Seine. Even though it was early April, it was snowing and wonderfully romantic, watching the white particles drifting down outside while inside they ate delicious food and drank champagne. It had been a marvellous evening but one tinged with sadness that their special time was coming to an end. When the boat finally docked, they walked back along the Seine towards the hotel, Jeremy with his arm around her. Then, without warning, he suddenly stopped, turned her so that she was facing him and took her gloved hands in his. The snow fell silently on his dark hair and his eyes were soft and loving as he spoke her name.

"Miranda. Darling Miranda. I don't want this weekend to end until I've told you how happy you have made me and how very much I love you ... I think I have done since the moment I set eyes on you outside the shop when you and Anna came to view it."

Miranda gulped. Even though they had been so close, so in tune, it was still a shock to hear him state how he felt about her. She stared up at him, knowing the powerful emotion she felt for him was exactly the same. "And I love you too," she said. "So very much ... and I can't bear the thought of us being apart again. This weekend ... it's been so wonderful ... being so close. It's going to be terribly hard to bear, not seeing you every day ... and the nights are going to be so cold without you ... even with Charlie and Nellie to keep me company," she smiled through threatening tears.

"Well, my darling girl, how about making those spoiled pooches of yours share you with me on a permanent basis? Miranda, please ... will you marry me? I realise we've only known each other for a few months but I've never felt like this in my life and I never will again. You are the one for me and I want us to share our lives together. I want to be with you forever and ever."

It took a few moments for his words to sink in but as he pulled out a little box from the inside pocket of his coat and opened it to reveal a beautiful diamond cluster engagement ring, reality kicked in.

"Miranda. Nothing would give me greater pleasure than for you to agree to be my wife and wear this ring. If you don't like it, we can always change it," he added, his eyes anxious as he waited for her answer.

"Gosh," she gasped. "It's so beautiful ... and yes, oh yes, there's nothing I want more in the world than to be married to you," she smiled, her cheeks wet with tears of joy.

With a broad smile of relief, he pulled off her glove, slipped the ring on her finger and took her face in his hands. He kissed away her tears and pressed his lips against hers. "God, Miranda, I can't tell you how much I love you ... and I'm going to leave the Army and return to the UK permanently so I can be with you far more. I've a few ideas up my sleeve. It might mean travelling occasionally but it won't be as bad as being in the army and I shall be in control of what I do ... and you might be able to come with me sometimes."

"But ... but you love the Army ... it's your life," she said with astonishment.

"I know ... but I love you more ... and from this moment on, we have an awful lot to plan for ... our future life together ... my work, your work, our wedding, where we will live ... golly, my darling, we're going to be so very busy over the next few months sorting it all out as I don't want to wait any longer than we have to."

They had hardly slept that night, drinking glass after glass of champagne while in bed, planning their future while Miranda gazed lovingly at her ring which Jeremy informed her he had purchased in Germany and brought to Paris with the firm intention of asking her to marry him. Although she didn't want the weekend to end, she couldn't wait to tell her family and Anna her news and show it to them. They were all in for a hell of a surprise!

****

The shop had been frightfully busy on Good Friday and Easter Saturday and Anna woke up on Easter Sunday, taking much pleasure in the thought that today she didn't have to go in and could enjoy it in the company of Andy and their dogs. He had rung her last night to confirm and promised to pick her up at nine o'clock, then they would drive over to Happylands to collect Dolly and Rio and then head off to the coast, deciding on Barmston and Skipsea as it would be quieter for the dogs than Bridlington or Filey.

All went to plan. Andy turned up promptly at nine, his curious elderly black Labs, Simba and Jess, poking their noses through the dog guard between the back seat and the front and gave her hand a welcoming lick as she reached out to pat them.

"They look amiable enough," she laughed.

"And so they are," Andy smiled as he pointed the car towards the Wetherby road. "They've been very well socialised all their lives with humans and animals ... as all dogs should be. Your dogs, even if they are a little nervous, will have nothing to fear from my two and they'll soon be the best of friends"

"Good," replied Anna, thinking how nice he looked in civvies. She'd only seen him in his uniform up till now but today he was wearing jeans and a deep blue sweater, the same colour as his eyes. He looked extremely handsome and she was pleased she had made a bit more of an effort with her make-up than usual and although she was also wearing jeans, she had bought a new crimson sweater and a mid-blue waterproof jacket, perfect for walking on the beach.

They arrived at Happylands twenty minutes later, Sonia walking towards them from where she had been busy in the field nearest the house, where marquees were being erected by volunteers ready for the Easter Fayre the next day.

"Hello, Anna ... Andy."

"Oh, do you two know each other?" asked Anna, raising an eyebrow.

"Oh, yes. Very well," remarked Sonia with a grin. "We've had several animals arrive here courtesy of Police Sergeant Wilkinson … and had quite a number rehomed too with his help … and a considerable amount of fundraising done too … and he's helping out tomorrow, just as you are Anna."

"Oh … you didn't say," Anna said, feeling a wave of pleasure. She was so pleased he felt the same about the welfare of animals as she did and that they would both be helping out at the Fayre.

"Well, all our conversations have been pretty brief," he grinned, "perhaps we can rectify that today."

"Coffee before you go or are you in a hurry to get off?" Sonia asked.

"Thanks, but we'll head off once we have the dogs on board if that's okay. It seems we have a lot to say to each other so we best make the most of every minute," Andy grinned, throwing an arm around Anna's shoulder and squeezing it.

She felt a thrill of pleasure ripple through her at the prospect of a day in his company … and his arm around her felt so natural. It was the first time a man had touched her since Gerald had died and it felt good. She pushed away the deep sadness at the memory of Gerald. She wanted to enjoy today with Andy. She would be silly to spoil what promised to be a lovely day in the company of a lovely man … and the dogs, of course. She was looking forward to having them with her all day.

Dolly and Rio greeted Anna with joyful enthusiasm and couldn't wait to get out of their kennels to join her, surprised to find that they were not going to the field but were being taken to the front of the old farmhouse and encouraged to jump up into a strange man's car. However, they clambered in quite readily, eager to meet Simba and Jess and to see where they were going.

"What a difference a few weeks make," Anna remarked. "They looked so wary and thin when I first saw them and now look. You've done wonders with them, Sonia."

"Well, my dear. You and me both. They love and trust you now. Go and have a fabulous day out and when you get back this evening, I'll have a nice bottle of wine waiting for you … and supper if you would like. I believe Josh is trying out a new recipe and if you can make it back by around 8pm, you are both very welcome to join us."

"That would be a delightful end to our day," Andy said, holding out the passenger door for Anna. "We'll certainly take you up on that, won't we, Anna."

Anna got into the car. "Yes, Sonia. We'll look forward to it. Thank you."

They headed back onto the Wetherby road and turned towards Leeds so they could join the York road which would take them to the coast. Anna kept turning round to make sure Dolly and Rio weren't stressed but both dogs seemed more than happy and were busy making the acquaintance of Simba and Jess through the dog guard which separated them.

And that was how their day went … pleasant, companionable and thoroughly enjoyable. The weather was chilly but dry and bright. The dogs, having made friends in the car, were pleased to mix properly once they could get onto the beach and allowed off the lead.

They walked quite a way, stopping now and again on a grassy dune to give the dogs a rest and just enjoy the scenery. They talked non-stop about anything and everything and Anna had no objections when Andy took her hand and held it while they were walking. It just seemed right and even though she still grieved for Gerald, she knew he wouldn't want her to be without another man in her life. She also knew he would have liked Andy.

Halfway through their walk they found a path which led up to a welcoming pub offering lunches with a water bowl for the dogs outside and a notice advising that they could offer special doggy meals too. They put the dogs on leads and sat down on a bench outside which had a spectacular view of the beach. Surprisingly enough, considering it was Easter Sunday, the pub wasn't that busy.

"It's been closed for a couple of years. The owners bought it a few months ago, have done it up and only just reopened. Believe me, with their food, I don't think it will be quiet for long, not once word gets around," Andy said, handing Anna a menu.

"You've been here before then?"

"Once or twice ... me and the dogs ... but it's much nicer with you and yours and it would be lovely if we could do it again sometime."

He smiled and Anna smiled back. There was nothing she would like more.

****

William was frustrated. He had promised to help the Vicar at the fete this afternoon in the park but really didn't want to and it would probably be a complete waste of time as more than likely there wouldn't be many turn up as most people were panicking about the latest dead body to be found and even though it had been confirmed that this death was either an accident or suicide, there were very real fears amongst the local populace that the murderer of Tanya Philips had been at it again. He could have told them otherwise.

He wished he hadn't promised to assist today ... it was a damned nuisance ... but then, he had nothing else to do ... and Miranda was away ... gone to Paris with that bloody Jeremy so Anna had told him ... for the whole weekend! He had seethed for hours when he had found out. God, how he detested Jeremy Cross. It was a damned pity the country wasn't at war so the Major could be placed in the line of fire. The man was a damned nuisance and something was definitely going to have to be done about him and pretty soon by the look of it. Miranda was getting far too friendly with him. Paris! How dare she? She should be going with him. It was a damned sure thing that unlike him, darling Jeremy wouldn't have millions stashed away and be able to take Miranda absolutely anywhere she wanted to go. God, he was so angry, so jealous, so hurt ... but she would want for nothing once she finally realised it was him she needed to be with for the rest of her life ... and that had to happen soon or otherwise he would go crazy.

He went to church. He liked the Easter morning service, full of hope for the future. Feeling a little less aggrieved about Miranda and Jeremy afterwards, he made his way to the park where preparations were being finalised for the fete. In front of the lake, small individual marquees had been erected for the stalls which included bric-a-brac, books, cakes, various charities, a fortune teller and a male author whom William had never heard of who wrote books about dogs and was going to donate a portion of his profit from his sales today to whatever charity the fete was in aid of. Then there was a ringed-off area in readiness for the dog show, a band and games for the children and a refreshment tent which was offering tea, coffee, juice, sandwiches and cakes.

He bought some sandwiches and a coffee and stood watching the few people who had already arrived milling around. The sun was rising in the sky and it was going to be a pleasant afternoon. He made his way to the book stall, which the Vicar had asked him to be in charge of. He wondered what Miranda was doing. God, he wished she was here now, with him. He needed her ... badly!

CHAPTER 15

They parted at Charles de Gaulle airport, Miranda for her flight to Leeds Bradford and Jeremy to Germany. Desperately sad their romantic weekend was over, leaving her new fiancé was the hardest thing Miranda had ever had to do, although she was looking forward to telling her family and Anna the tremendous news that she and Jeremy were engaged. However, she did have one concern she wanted to get off her chest.

"I'm terribly nervous about meeting your friends and colleagues again. I spoke very little to them at your party at Daphne's before I walked out and I'm sure they'll think I'm completely batty and totally unsuitable for you," she said as they lingered over a coffee while waiting for their flights to be announced.

"Don't be. They'll all love you."

"But I don't talk posh and I haven't a degree or anything … they'll all think I'm some kind of ignoramus and wonder why on earth you want to settle down with me."

Jeremy smiled and put a reassuring hand on hers. "Miranda, you really must stop having this downer on yourself. You're very special and it doesn't matter a jot about not having a degree, or talking with a plum in your mouth. You daft thing … you have a special gift and you're using it. You have a natural rapport with animals which has allowed you to build a solid business, your clients trust and respect you, the animals adore you. You have a kind and lovely heart and believe me, in this troubled and sometimes exceedingly cruel world, that's priceless and worth far more than a blasted degree and speaking like the Queen."

She smiled and squeezed his hand. "You're so lovely. You do wonders for my confidence."

He sighed. "I just wish I didn't have to go back to Germany … I've always loved the Army and never minded the restrictions but now I want to be free of it and spend as much time with you as I can. I have to do one more year and it's going to be tough, although it won't be so bad being stationed in London ... and I should be back there permanently by the end of this month so I can pop up to Yorkshire far more frequently to see you."

Miranda smiled at him, her eyes shining. "And just think of all those lovely reunions."

Jeremy laughed. "Yes, they'll be very special, although I can't wait for us to settle down ... talking of which, I want to set a date ... how about in the summer ... August? I can have three weeks leave and if you can find someone to look after Charlie and Nellie, we can head off somewhere special ... is there anywhere you would particularly like to go?"

"Gosh," Miranda gasped, her eyes widening with surprise. "August! Blimey, Jeremy, that's a bit soon ... there's so much to arrange ... and apart from Christmas, that's my busiest month ... so many people are away then and want their dogs boarded or their cats looking after. I'm usually run off my feet."

"Sooner then? July ... June ... May?"

Miranda giggled. "Now you're going from the sublime to the ridiculous. It's April now ... there's no time to arrange anything."

"Do you want a big wedding?"

"Gosh, no. Can't be doing with all that palaver again. I had it with Barrie ... you know the Beastly Bastard ... so a quiet one in a Registry Office will be fine."

"Well, it doesn't have to be a registry office these days. How about a posh hotel ... or a stately home? I believe Temple Newsam offers weddings ... how about there?"

Miranda laughed. Jeremy was certainly full of the most wonderful surprises. Life was certainly going to be fun with him! "That, my darling, would be fabulous. It's so grand and ... old but it will cost a fortune. I can't ask Mum and Dad to pay again and I might have a thriving business but I'm not sure I would be able to afford even half of it."

Jeremy squeezed her hand. "Don't you worry about a thing. If it's a stately home you want, a stately home you will have. When you get home, ring Temple Newsam ... and don't worry about the expense. Honestly, Miranda, I have plenty put by. I've managed to save a decent amount in the Army and invested it wisely and don't forget Dad had a tidy sum and selling his house and business and splitting the proceeds between me and my beloved sister has left us very well off. We, that is, you and I, my darling, can have the wedding we want and have a military guard of honour too," he grinned.

Miranda felt a warm rush of excitement. Her, getting married in Temple Newsam. "Wow, my parents will be bowled over."

Jeremy laughed. "It will be spectacular and just think of the photographs we will have to show our children and grandchildren. So, if we're now in agreement as to where we're going to be married, you get on to it as soon as possible. I don't want to wait any longer than we have to, darling. So, that's it, then. We book the wedding; you buy a nice dress and bob's your uncle. Then we just have to decide on where to go for a honeymoon ... and buy somewhere to live, of course."

"Well, you can just move in with me," Miranda smiled, imagining them curled up in her bed and Charlie and Nellie waking them up every morning.

Jeremy paused before he spoke. "Well, I can do but your house, as lovely as it is, isn't that big if you want to expand your business ... and I shall need an office too ... and then there will be our children ... who will require a good deal of space. No, darling. We need a much bigger house. What would you like, a new build with all the mod cons or something old with plenty of character?"

"Oh, old. I'm not keen on new builds. Actually," Miranda said thoughtfully, "If you want something big ... and with character ... there's the most gorgeous house along Miller Lane, next to William's, which is for sale. It's Victorian." She laughed. "Anna and I were being nosy last week and had a look at the details online. It has two big reception rooms and an enormous kitchen and dining room downstairs and then six bedrooms and two bathrooms on the two upper floors. Then there is the huge garden of course … and it would be so handy for me … being so near to the park … and I could home board quite a few dogs there with all that space."

Even as she said it, she knew she was wishing for the moon. Jeremy might be financially comfortable and she was earning a decent amount now the business was doing so well but even so, she doubted they could afford such a property.

"It sounds ideal, darling. You can get cracking on that too. Arrange a viewing, take loads of photos and send them to me. Then, if it's suitable, we can put an offer in. Don't leave it too long though as we don't want anyone else snapping it up."

"What … are you serious?" Was there no end to the shocks he had in store for her? "It's not exactly cheap."

"As I said, don't you worry about that. I can raise enough, I'm sure, so if that's the house you want, do as you're told, woman," he grinned. "Get on to the estate agents first thing."

Her flight was being called and they stood up, Miranda grasping the handle of her suitcase and throwing her bag over her shoulder. Suddenly she felt sick. This was it. She wouldn't see him again for days. How was she going to bear it?

Jeremy threw his arm around her, "I know. I feel the same but we're both busy and the time will pass quickly. Before you know it, I shall be back in Leeds. Now you must get on your plane and I'll ring you as soon as I get back to barracks this evening and don't forget ...I love you very, very much."

She felt utterly bereft as he kissed her lips, gave her a final hug and as his flight was also being called, walked off in the opposite direction.

****

Miranda felt quite lightheaded once she was back in Leeds, on familiar territory, as if the weekend had been an exciting, wonderful dream but the twinkling diamond ring on her finger told her otherwise. Jeremy really did love her and he wanted to spend the rest of his life with her. She felt crazy with happiness and couldn't wait to tell her parents the news as she bowled along in a taxi from the airport to their ex-council house in Seacroft, where they had lived all their married lives and purchased when Maggie Thatcher allowed the sale of such properties.

Charlie and Nellie greeted her at the door. They had been curled up together on the sofa beside the front room window and had seen the taxi pull up outside and howled with delight when they realised their mistress was home. The reunion was wet and hairy, both dogs knocking her against the door with their enthusiastic greeting as she shut it behind her.

"Calm down, calm down," Miranda giggled, trying to cuddle them both at the same time, having her face washed repeatedly. "'I'm not that dirty," she cried, "I have had a shower this morning!"

Her mother had followed the dogs into the hall and laughed at the sight of her daughter on the floor being pounced on. Then she noticed the ring sparkling in the sunlight from the open door.

"Miranda!" she shrieked. "That's an engagement ring!"

Miranda laughed and dangled her hand in front of her. "Isn't it gorgeous?"

"What's all the racket about?" asked Miranda's father, poking his head around the kitchen door.

"George! Miranda has become engaged," her mother exclaimed, pointing at the sparkling ring on her daughter's finger.

"Well, well, well, Sheila. We've got rid of her again ...only our Tricia to go now," he laughed, giving Miranda a big hug and admiring the ring. "Congratulations, love. I think this calls for a drink," he said, winking at his daughter.

"It's a bit early, George," Sheila said, looking anxiously at the clock.

"Yes, but this is a special occasion. It's not every day one of our precious offspring becomes engaged … but goodness knows what we've got in. As you know, Miranda, your mother and I only have a drink on a Saturday night when we have a takeaway and watch Casualty and a dvd."

Miranda's father, recently retired from his job as a train driver, hurried over to the old-fashioned cocktail cabinet in the lounge and brought out a bottle of Harvey's Bristol Cream. He looked at Miranda ruefully.

"I'm so sorry, love. This is all we have in … left over from Christmas … your mother must have finished the Bailey's Irish Cream last week … but we'll make up for it as soon as your Jeremy is in Leeds. We'll push the boat out with all the family … your sisters are going to be so happy for you. We'll have a good nosh somewhere posh … and we'll have champagne. Can't say I like the stuff but it's the right thing to do."

"Jeremy sends his apologies, Dad. He would have liked to have asked your permission first but it's taken us a bit by surprise … and it just seemed so right … getting engaged in Paris of all places."

"Don't let him worry about that. As long as you're both happy, that's all I care about," George said, pouring them all a small sherry. He held up his glass. "And here's to you both and may you have a long and happy life together."

"Thanks, Dad," Miranda said, sipping her sherry. She liked it but usually only drank it before lunch on Christmas Day. "I presume Tricia is at work," she stated. Her younger sister was employed at Tesco's but her shifts alternated from week to week and Miranda could never remember where she was supposed to be.

"Yes. She's working until late today," Sheila said, "but she'll be thrilled with your news. She'll want to be a bridesmaid again, you know ... although you won't be able to be married in church again so where will you have it?"

Miranda gulped. "Jeremy suggested Temple Newsam ... but you don't need to worry, he's going to pay," she said quickly, concerned at the look of horror on her father's face. He had spent a vast amount on her wedding to Barrie and there was no way she expected him to fork out again.

Her father gulped too. "That's good of him ... but I ...."

"Look, Dad. Jeremy is pretty well off and he wants to do it so don't worry ... in fact ... in fact ... he wants us to have a big house ... there's one for sale ... a large Victorian property along Miller Lane. I'm going to try and view it this week and if it's suitable, we could end up there."

Sheila gasped. "Oh, Miranda. It certainly looks as if you've landed on your feet now, my girl. I can't wait to meet this young man."

Miranda was pleased to see her father was smiling with relief. She knew he had a bit put by and his pension but her mother had just finished her working life and although they had enough for a nice, comfortable retirement they certainly couldn't afford to splash out on a second wedding for her. They had spent a fortune on a posh wedding for Griselda, Miranda's older sister, last year ... and then there would be Tricia at some point. She hadn't found anyone she wanted to settle down with yet but when she did, Dad would want to shell out for that too.

"So, if your Jeremy is so well off, perhaps you could afford to give up work once you're married ... I do so worry about you, Miranda. Going into empty houses when people are on holiday and walking in the parks ... especially Peesdown with all that has been going on. I can't sleep at night, worrying about you in the woods all alone with a rapist and murderer on the loose."

Miranda touched her mother's arm reassuringly. "I do have six dogs with me ... and some of them are pretty quick off the mark

... and anyway, I haven't been to Peesdown for a little while. Belinda and I have been walking elsewhere."

"Good ... and make sure you keep it that way until this evil person is caught. The last thing I want to hear is that he's done anything horrible to you, my girl," George stated firmly.

****

Miranda took an excited Charlie and Nellie home later in the day. Her mother had walked them so once they had been fed, were curled up in their baskets and she had thrown her dirty washing in the machine and made a banana sandwich and a coffee, she stretched out on the sofa and opened her laptop. She had sent Belinda a text to say she was home and had one in return to say there had been no problems while she was in Paris so it was possible to concentrate on her personal life for the evening. There was a lot to do and she wanted to be able to tell Jeremy what she found out when he rang later in the evening.

The estate agents who were selling No.10 were easy to find on the internet and the details took her breath away now she knew that there was a very real possibility the beautiful residence was going to be her future home. It was so big, so old, so perfect ... and so posh. Eeeek! She jotted down the telephone number of the estate agents. They would be the first people she spoke to in the morning.

Anna rang to find out how the Paris trip had gone just as Miranda was about to have a look at the Temple Newsam site and their wedding package. She had great delight in relaying the incredible events of the weekend and the plans for the wedding and their home.

Anna was as flabbergasted as Miranda as to the speed which Jeremy wanted to go.

"I can't believe it," Anna breathed. "Gosh. Engaged, marrying at Temple Newsam *and* buying No. 10 Miller Lane! Boy,

Miranda, you don't do things by halves," she laughed. "Can I come with you when you view the house, please?"

"Naturally. I was going to ask you anyway as I need someone with me who will have a sensible head on. You know me, I could get quite carried away. I'm going to ring the estate agents first thing in the morning to book a viewing."

"Great. Just let me know when it is and I'll squeeze it in. Thank goodness I have Emily as I suspect I'm going to be pretty busy for the next few weeks packing up for my move."

"Yes, but won't it be lovely when you're settled and we'll only be up the road from you too. Oh, Anna, I'm so excited. It will be ideal up in Miller Lane, peaceful and quiet and I don't expect William will be disturbing us with loud music and riotous parties," she giggled.

Anna grinned. "I shouldn't think so. He'll probably turn out to be the perfect neighbour."

****

William was watching what was occurring next door from his attic bedroom. He had been up and down all morning, spying on all the activity. A removal lorry had turned up around 7.30 a.m. and two men brought out furniture and packed it carefully and neatly in the van before they drove off just before lunch. Then, a few minutes later, a second van turned up and now that one was being packed too.

He was sad in a way. His neighbours had given him no trouble. They were so quiet, he hadn't even really been aware they were there. He did hope the next occupants would be the same. He certainly didn't want nosey people threatening any of his plans.

He went downstairs to look at his scrapbook and check his trophies. He had something to add ... something of Miranda's ... not that she knew of course. It was only a toggle off the hood of her duffle coat ... but it belonged to her and was something to be treasured. He had watched it come adrift when they were walking last week and stopped to pick it up. She hadn't noticed. She had kept walking and talking to Anna. He had slipped it into his pocket with great satisfaction.

CHAPTER 16

It was a perfect spring day as far as Miranda was concerned when she rose the next morning and shot off to do cat visits, Belinda having done them while she was in Paris and dropped the keys through her letterbox last night.

Driving along the Leeds ring road, the trees were mostly in leaf and the islands in the middle of all the roundabouts looked a picture with the spring bedding the council gardeners had planted. Her spirits were high and soared even higher with the sight of such delights and she just knew her day was going to be a good one.

She was late this morning. She normally commenced cat feeding between 5.00 and 6.00 a.m. but today she had overslept and it was now 6.30 a.m. and beginning to get busy with people going to work. Thankfully, she only had three sets of cats to visit, all in north Leeds, not far from home. Two were quick and easy as the houses had cat flaps so there was no need for litter trays and it was just a matter of feeding the furries, who were always delighted to see her, and checking the house was secure, turning off the lights Belinda had left on for the night and drawing back the curtains.

Miranda took the matter of house security just as seriously as caring for the cats and every room was checked on every visit to make sure nothing was amiss. She was often amazed at how some people just upped and left their houses; piles of dirty washing-up in the sink, unmade beds, laptops, printers, televisions and dvd players left on standby, often on carpets or beds, which was a real fire risk. Then she had entered a house on one occasion to find a lamp the owners had left on a landing had been tipped over by the cats and could very well have set fire to the carpet within hours. She had turned it off immediately and made a mental note to put it in her terms and conditions that lamps were not to be put on timers if cats could get anywhere near them. Other people had left windows open, taps on, showers running, fridge doors ajar. Some had even left handbags on view and keys in patio and French doors. These were all removed out of sight immediately. Then there was the other extreme when she arrived for a first visit on an afternoon and discovered all the curtains were closed and bins out on the drive when it wasn't the right day ... a burglar's delight. Needless to say, she took the bins back in and kept the curtains open throughout the day.

Being in charge of someone's house and pets while they were absent was a huge responsibility and one she enjoyed but it did come with its worries, especially entering a house in the dark. She always tried to get visits done before then, not only for her own safety but to make sure the houses were well lit during the night to deter burglars, illuminating upstairs as well as down, and leaving curtains not fully closed at the top to let through a chink of light. However, occasionally she was late in the winter when it was dark early and twice she had been horrified when the fuses had blown during her visits and she had to feel her way around to find the fuse box with only the aid of the torch on her mobile, a most unnerving experience.

However, all was well at the three properties this morning and having opened them up, as she called it, and made sure the cats were all present and looking fit and well, she left them to enjoy their day, glad that Tiger and Fluff, who lived together in a lovely old cottage not far from Roundhay Park, hadn't decided to bring her a present during the night. She had discovered numerous dead birds and mice in the past and even found a rat on the patio one morning. Luckily the owners had left a spade in the garden and she had scooped it up and chucked it in the black bin. Not a nice task.

She was home by 7.30 a.m. Charlie and Nellie were tucked up in their baskets having had their breakfasts and relieved themselves in the garden before she went out. They thumped their tails in acknowledgement of her arrival and then went back to sleep.

144

Miranda sat down with a coffee and a pile of paperwork to while away the time until she could ring the estate agents and make an appointment to view No. 10 Miller Lane later that afternoon. She was told the house was now vacant and the estate agent was going to show Miranda around.

"It's a splendid property ... bags of character," said the girl at the other end of the phone. "Although there will be no furniture so it won't look very welcoming."

"Good," Miranda remarked. "I shall be able to see exactly what space is on offer without a lot of clutter ... anyhow I shall be there at 3.30 p.m. sharp ..., oh, and I shall be bringing a friend with me. Will that be okay?"

"Yes, Miss Denton. That's fine."

Miranda sent a text to Anna to confirm the appointment, messaged Jeremy to say she would ring him later to tell him all about it, then printed out the particulars for No. 10, reading and re-reading them. She couldn't wait to get inside and have a really good look around.

Throwing all caution to the winds, she decided to walk in Peesdown today. She wanted to drive along Miller Lane and sit outside what could be her new home to get a feel for the place. She wondered what William would say when he discovered she and Jeremy were thinking of buying it. She hoped he wouldn't mind as there might be a bit of barking from the dogs and she didn't want to annoy anyone or give any cause for complaints.

Her next task was to ring Temple Newsam to make enquiries about the wedding. Overnight, Miranda had given a lot of thought to exactly when it should take place. Whatever Jeremy said, it couldn't be in the summer. The business was booked solid until late September with dog boarding and cat sitting and it wasn't fair on her staff if she was to swan off on honeymoon at the busiest time of the year. She sent Jeremy a text to explain how she felt and asked what he thought about early October when things were slightly quieter. Generously he had replied that he quite understood and although he hated the thought of waiting for so long, he was more than happy for her to book whichever date she wanted … as long as she booked it!

Light-headed and light-hearted, with Charlie and Nellie on the back seat of the Volvo, she set off to collect her pack of dogs. For some absurd reason, she sang 'Some Enchanted Evening' over and over again until they reached the park and she virtually skipped all the way down to the lake with the dogs. She grinned. Fart Features and Bob Watkins were walking towards her.

Nothing could make her miserable today and undeterred by their expressionless faces, she virtually sang her greeting. "Good morning, gentlemen … and isn't it just a glorious one and isn't this just a glorious place to be?" she beamed.

Freddie pointed at Sammy who was in the throes of depositing his waste on the grass just yards behind Miranda. "It would be, if you collected your dog's poo," he muttered darkly.

****

Having suffered from a niggling toothache all night as a result of a loose filling, William had rung the dentist and the only appointment was at 11.30 a.m., which annoyed him immensely as he knew Miranda was back to work today and he desperately wanted to see her but with the pain increasing, he had no choice in the matter.

Peesdown didn't have the luxury of a dentist and the nearest was in Crossgates, a nearby suburb of Leeds, so he took a taxi. He didn't want to drive 'Stephen's' BMW and he kept the van, used mainly for his sorties, out of sight in the garage.

Filling fixed, he returned home and was astonished but delighted to see Miranda's Volvo parked opposite No. 10. What was she doing? Was she waiting for him? Had she finally seen the light and realised it was Stephen she wanted? His heart skipped a beat. He felt almost faint with desire. She was waiting for him. He just knew it.

His steps quickened and he approached the car. The engine was switched off and Miranda was staring intently at No.10. The gates were open, there were no cars or removal vans in the drive. It looked deserted.

"Miranda?" William said, approaching the Volvo and ignoring the six dogs in the back. Most of them wagged their tails but one mongrel he didn't recognise gave a ferocious growl. "Are you ok?"

"Just looking, William. Just dreaming," she said, not taking her eyes off No.10.

"Oh," he said, following her gaze. "I see my neighbours have finally gone … I keep wondering who is going to move in."

"Me … if you're lucky … that is, me … and Jeremy," Miranda grinned.

"What?" he exclaimed, staring at her incredulously. No. She hadn't just said that. No. No. No!

"Don't look so shocked," Miranda giggled, "Jeremy and I are engaged, look."

She held out her left hand to show him her ring, the diamonds twinkling brightly as they caught the sun. "We've decided to marry in October but we need somewhere to live and No. 10, quite frankly, is perfect for us. I've a viewing this afternoon."

"Goodness," William gulped, letting this new and disturbing information feed into his brain, which felt as if it was going to explode. The last thing he had expected was for her to return to Peesdown *engaged* to bloody Jeremy … *and* talk about moving in next door. Not if he could help it. He wanted her in his house and without that damned man. Miranda was his and his alone. 'Darling' Jeremy really would have to be dealt with and very, very soon.

"Well, I hope you still think it's wonderful after we've moved in," she was saying. "The dogs might bark a bit, although I'll do my best to keep them quiet. They're pretty good most of the time as they have such a lot of exercise and sleep when they're at home but to begin with, all the new smells and things in a new garden might set them off."

"Don't you worry about that," William said automatically, doing his best to keep his expression pleasant and normal. "It won't trouble me at all. I just can't think who I would rather have as my neighbour, Miranda, I really can't."

"That's nice, William. Thank you," she said, turning the key to start the Volvo. "Anyhow, I must be off … get the dogs back to their homes. Bye."

William stood and watched her turn the car around and drive off. He couldn't tell anyone how tormented he felt at that particular moment. Miranda was home but waving that ring about had hurt him to the core. He wanted to cry. He wanted to hit something. He wanted to kill something. If Jeremy had been anywhere near him at that moment, he would have struck him dead without hesitation.

* * * * * * * * * *

Miranda drove away with the nagging sense of unease she had begun to feel in William's presence. It was the odd remark and the odd look he gave her occasionally … and now he had just said 'neighbour' and not 'neighbours', as if Jeremy didn't exist. His smile hadn't looked genuine either, with his lip beginning to curl, and she was sharply reminded of Stephen's expression when she had mentioned that she was having a relationship with Jeremy.

Suddenly feeling uncomfortable, she had wanted nothing more than to get away from William and was glad when she had turned the car around and could drive along Miller Lane to turn right into the High Street. She looked in the rear-view mirror to see him standing exactly where she had left him, staring after her. For

148

some reason she shivered and twiddled the knob on the dashboard to turn up the heating.

Was she being silly ... was she just imagining William could be a threat? She would have to mention it to Anna and see if she had any similar concerns. She had never said anything so probably not. Oh, dear, stop it, she told herself. You have far more important things to concern yourself with ... what with a forthcoming wedding *and* buying a house.

She smiled, spotting Charlie and Nellie on the back seat in the rear-view mirror. They were curling up tight, tired after their walk and it wouldn't be long before they were snoring and breathing heavily. The others, in the rear, had all settled down now the car was moving, none sitting up and looking out of the window as they did on the way to the park. She felt a wave of satisfaction. She had given them all a good time and they were happy ... and she was happy ... and yes, she was being daft about William. He was just a nice man ... and probably a lonely one. When she and Jeremy moved into No. 10, they could invite him over for supper occasionally. Jeremy wouldn't mind. In fact, they could have a housewarming party and dinner parties. She giggled. Her, entertaining in a grand Victorian house. What a laugh!

CHAPTER 17

Anna was already outside No. 10 when Miranda arrived.

"It's awfully grand," she grinned, waving at the house as Miranda locked the Volvo. "You'll have to learn how to be a lady living here."

Miranda laughed. "I know. I can't quite believe I'm going to view something like this. Never, in my wildest dreams, did I think I would live in such splendour. I thought my little terrace would be the best I could wish for."

"This must be the estate agent," Anna nodded as an older woman with permed grey hair pulled up behind Miranda's Volvo in a smart silver Mercedes. She scrambled out, carrying a large black leather handbag and a green folder with No. 10 Miller Lane in big letters printed on the front. She walked towards them, smiling and holding out her hand.

"Good afternoon ... I'm Christine Timmins from Cherryfield Estate Agents and you must be ...,"

"Hi, I'm Miranda Denton ... and this is Anna, my friend, who will be viewing with me," Miranda said, shaking Christine's hand.

The three women walked up the gravelled path to the front door of No. 10, Miranda taking note that the roof looked in good order, as did the windows and front door, so no immediate layout there then. The garden looked a picture too. Flourishing rhododendron bushes possessed a vast number of big fat buds, heralding a magnificent display in a month or so and the tulips, in a variety of colours, looked lovely. There were masses of early bluebells, several white and pink camellias and much lily of the valley. Miranda also noted the witch hazel, japonica and forsythia as well as healthy looking rose bushes dotted around the lawns in their own private flower beds.

"It's certainly all neat and tidy and well cared for," Miranda remarked happily. "I trust the rear garden is the same, although I know it's much larger. Jeremy, my fiancé," she explained to

Christine, "did say there was probably room for a swimming pool. Can't say I'm too keen on the idea though," she laughed. "Nellie, my daft Labrador, would be straight in there and I have absolutely no intention of swimming around in a load of dog hair. I might love my dog but there are limits!"

Christine chuckled, unlocked the front door and they all stepped into the well-proportioned hall with the stairs in the centre. As the girl from the estate agents had explained, the house was empty of furniture and their footsteps echoed on the highly polished wooden floors.

"The previous owners had to leave earlier than intended," Christine explained. "The husband has been very unwell and is now living in a care home in Dorset and the wife is with her sister nearby. It's all very sad. They had lived here for forty-odd years, ever since they married apparently, and were devastated to leave but the wife couldn't manage the place any longer and he couldn't cope with the stairs so it seemed the best solution for them."

"That's very sad," Anna said as Miranda nodded in agreement and ventured into the drawing-room on their right, with its double aspect.

"Wow. This room is fabulous and so light," she sighed with pleasure, staring out of the enormous sash windows, one overlooking the front garden and the other, the side garden and laurel hedge, separating No. 10 from the property next door.

Turning her gaze upwards, she noticed the beautiful crystal chandelier still in situ. She grinned. A chandelier … her mother would be impressed!

"This is a 'wow' factor fireplace," Anna grinned behind her, touching the top of the marble with reverence. Miranda turned to look and agreed. It was quite splendid and she could just imagine it festooned with Christmas decorations next winter.

"That," Christine pointed to the door beside the fireplace, "leads to the sitting room with a fabulous view of the back garden but let's have a look at the dining room first. At least, the owners used it as a dining room but as it's identical to this room, you could change them about if you so wished. Either will fit either function."

The dining room, on the opposite side of the spacious hall to the drawing-room, again with a double aspect, was just as imposing, with a slightly different but no less awesome chandelier and another marble fireplace. It overlooked the front garden with the side window facing William's property, although only the upper floor of his house could be seen as the laurel hedge between the houses was so high.

"Gosh, William can see straight in here if he's upstairs," Miranda remarked, feeling a little disconcerted. "In fact, I think I can see him now, looking out of the upper window. Yes, it is him. Look he's waving," she added, putting up a hand in acknowledgement.

"You know the neighbour? That's nice." Christine remarked.

"Yes. We see him walking in the park … pleasant old boy … quite charming," Anna said helpfully, wondering why Miranda was frowning. "If it bothers you, Miranda, you could always put nets up but it's only William. I don't suppose he'll be spending his time spying on you."

"And you would have the same problem in the drawing-room with the house on the other side," Christine said. "But nets … or pretty blinds could be the solution for the side windows."

"That's true," Miranda said thoughtfully, wondering why, even though she had been able to see the top of the neighbour's house from the drawing-room, it hadn't seemed important. She knew the owners. A dentist and his wife and their three children, plus two gorgeous black flat-coated Retrievers she had home-boarded once. Lovely dogs and lovely people. She would look forward to having them as neighbours.

Still puzzling as to why she felt qualms about William, she followed Anna and Christine through to the cosy sitting room at the rear, which she fell in love with instantly. She could see herself and Jeremy curled up on a squashy sofa with the dogs in their baskets in front of a blazing log fire in the slightly less grand fireplace with a solid oak mantel and pretty flowered tiles.

"Except for the bathrooms, all the main rooms possess a double aspect," Christine remarked.

Miranda walked to the massive rear window and gazed outside with awe. "Yes. I like a lot of light. I say, Anna, just look at this garden. It's a whopper. The dogs will have a super time out there. I'll never get them in, especially with the park the other side of the laurel hedge at the bottom," she laughed.

Anna joined her and nodded. "Gosh, yes. It is big ... and just look at what's out there ... apple trees, an oak by the look of it, a weeping willow and silver birch. How lovely ... and there are loads of shrubs too. It's going to look amazing in the summer. Blimey, Miranda. I'm so envious. I know I have a lovely garden down at the shop but this is something else."

Miranda clapped with delight. "Oh, I love this room ... and so will Jeremy."

Christine smiled, walked out of the sitting room, across the hall and into the kitchen, Miranda and Anna following her. Miranda's eyes darted straight to the window facing her on William's side. Again, he would be able to see straight in. She wondered about blocking it up and putting more cupboards in place of it but Jeremy would think she was mad.

"This is simply gorgeous," Anna said, eyeing the kitchen with admiration.

"Yes, it is," Miranda replied, turning her attention to the remainder of the room.

The rear doors, next to the window, were French, the frames made of wood and painted cream. The units were all in solid light oak with cream granite worktops and the floor tiles were cream to match.

"When I came to do the valuation, the owners had a large table in front of the window," Christine said. "It certainly has an attractive view if you don't want to eat in the formality of the dining room."

"Does that lead to the cellar or is it just a cupboard under the stairs?" Anna asked, waving a finger at a door to their right.

"Cellar," Christine answered. "Used mainly as a utility room but there's masses of storage space down there … and all the meters, of course. I don't do cellars, and certainly not in these," she added, staring woefully at her five-inch heels. "But you two go on down. I'll wait here for you."

They weren't long. Miranda didn't particularly like cellars either, horrid things happened in them in films and she had a vivid imagination. However, she'd have to get over it if she had a washing machine and tumble dryer down here. There was a small window, eye level with the lawn, so it wasn't as claustrophobic as it might have been without one … and she could always bring the dogs down here with her if she was feeling nervy. She would soon get used to it.

"Now, for upstairs," Christine said once they were safely back in the kitchen. "As you know, there are six bedrooms over two floors plus a bathroom on each and the master bedroom has an ensuite."

"Which side of the house is the master?" Miranda couldn't help asking, praying it wasn't going to be William's side, as they trooped back into the hall and then up the honey-coloured oak staircase. Christine confirmed her worst fears. Oh God, how was she going to be able to relax, knowing William could see into their room. She would have to have the curtains drawn on that side of the house the whole time at this rate … but perhaps she could persuade Jeremy it would be nicer to use one of the remaining bedrooms, after all, there were six! She was sure he would agree, even though he would probably think she was crazy.

The master, at the front of the house, was on the next floor and Miranda had to admit it was a nice room with plenty of built-in cupboard space and wardrobes but the ensuite was a definite no-

no. The window was floor to ceiling in the centre, with a bath and shower cubicle to the right and a toilet and wash hand basin on the left of it.

"Oh, gosh. I don't like this," Miranda said, shaking her head with a look of dismay. "There's very little privacy in here with that window, even though it's frosted glass."

"You could have a huge roller blind," Anna suggested. "The last owners must have had something up here. Look, the brackets are still there so they must have done."

"Of course," Miranda said with relief. "However, I still don't like it very much. It will all need replacing and rethinking," she said, eyeing up the well-worn bath and shower cubicle.

"You could always use the family bathroom until this is sorted," Christine suggested.

They moved along the landing. There was another large bedroom opposite the master and at the rear, on William's side, was another. Facing that was a bathroom.

"Oh, wow, just look at this!" Miranda exclaimed with delight. A fresh white suite had been recently installed, with a jacuzzi big enough for three or four people, there were white and turquoise tiles on the walls and the floor and, to top it all, there was a fabulous view of the rear garden and the trees and shrubbery of the park.

She opened the window and breathed in the fresh air. It would be lovely in here, having a bath in the summer with the window open. No-one would be able to see her but she would be able to watch the tops of the trees waving about and listen to the birds. It would be so relaxing. She loved it.

They ventured onto the top floor where there were three more bedrooms and another bathroom.

"Jeremy and I need an office each but we're going to be spoilt for choice as to which rooms we will use," Miranda laughed, although she guessed she would end up with the one at the top front, away from William.

155

Oh, blimey, she was being silly, becoming paranoid about William watching her. Why? He had never given her any real cause for concern ... just that weird feeling occasionally. He was such a nice old boy, everyone said so. No, she was being utterly foolish.

"Do you mind if I wander around and take some photographs for my fiancé?" she asked Christine. "Then I can send them straight to him and hopefully he can get back here in the next few days for a viewing and we can place a firm offer ... because as far as I'm concerned, we definitely want it and I can't for the life of me see anything Jeremy would disapprove of," she added.

"No. Carry on. I'll go and mooch around that lovely back garden while I'm waiting. I've plenty of time ... no more viewings today, so there's no need to rush."

Christine stepped out of the French windows, down a short flight of steps and into the garden where she made herself comfortable on a wooden bench in the sunshine.

"Are you sure about this?" Anna asked.

"Yes ... oh yes, Anna. It's so lovely and I know Jeremy is just going to love it too," Miranda replied, clicking away madly with her phone as they moved from room to room.

"And the master bedroom and the ensuite hasn't put you off?"

"No. I've been thinking. If Jeremy and I have the other room, opposite it, we can have a door knocked through into the family bathroom and have that as our ensuite and then the master can be the main guest room."

"Well, that sounds like a good idea. I'm so envious. This is such a beautiful house and you will have that fabulous garden to enjoy ... and backing onto the park. You are just sooo lucky," she sighed.

"Well, that's if Jeremy likes it," Miranda murmured, concentrating on taking more photographs as they meandered outside to join Christine.

"Oh," Anna laughed. "What's not to like?"

She glanced up at William's top windows and was surprised to see him still there, looking down on them. She smiled and put up a hand. He did the same.

****

William watched them leave; the estate agent, Anna and Miranda. From the expression on Miranda's face, she was obviously enraptured with the house and was shaking the estate agent's hand enthusiastically, beaming and laughing at Anna.

He clenched his hands. He didn't want her buying No. 10. He wanted her in here ... with him. Damn and blast that bloody Jeremy. He would have it coming when he put in an appearance ... whenever that would be. He would have to ask Miranda the next time he saw her ... in the park tomorrow ... and then he could decide exactly how to dispense with *Jeremy* and once he was well and truly out of the way, the path would be clear to push Stephen's cause.

As the three women drove away, he gazed at No. 10. It wouldn't be a bad idea to get a clear idea of the layout of the place. It was probably the same as his inside as it was out, but it wouldn't be a bad idea to have a good look and the way was clear ... but he couldn't venture on to Miller Lane to get in as someone might see him and he wanted to avoid that at all costs.

He looked at the laurel hedge separating the two residences and, having an idea, headed outside to his garage for a pair of shears. They wouldn't make as much noise as his electric hedge cutters. He wandered along the hedge, finally deciding it was best to make a hole right at the end, which would be less noticeable if the leaves died off. He knelt down and started clipping. He only needed a big enough opening for him to wriggle through. It only took a few minutes. He had only cut the top of the square, the right-hand side and the bottom so he could pull it all out and then push it back when he had been through. With a bit of luck, it

157

wouldn't die off too badly and look odd if anyone was at the end of either garden.

Satisfied with his handiwork, he dashed upstairs and checked the street from the top window. All was quiet so there was little chance he would be noticed in No.10's garden.

He shot back outside, crawled through the hedge, stood up and headed straight towards the French doors of the kitchen. He knew the last occupants had hired a cleaning lady twice every week as he had watched her come and go from upstairs, wheeling her bicycle around to the back and taking a key from beneath a pot containing a hydrangea. Hopefully, it wouldn't have been removed.

Bingo. It hadn't. He picked it up with a grin. If Miranda didn't change the locks, he would have access to her home at all times of the day and night.

Careful to keep away from the windows, he crept around the house, interested to discover that while the layout of the ground floor was the same, the upper floors were a little different with the bathrooms on the opposite side of the house to his. Pleased with his recce, which would be useful if he had to walk about in the house in the dark at some point, he locked up, crawled back through the hedge, replaced the foliage carefully and went indoors for tea.

CHAPTER 18

"I'm being posted back to London on Friday but can't get up to Yorkshire until late. I need to see Daphne so will stay there for the night but spend the remainder of the weekend with you," Jeremy announced when Miranda rang him that evening. "I've had a good look at the photos you sent through and the house looks great. Was there anything you didn't like about it?"

"The master bedroom," Miranda said without hesitation. She pulled a face. "The ensuite is simply awful and I was thinking we could use the opposite bedroom and knock through to the newly installed bathroom on the other side. It will be so much nicer and we can wallow in the gigantic jacuzzi and look out over the treetops in the park," she giggled.

He laughed. "Sounds good to me. So, if that's all, I can't see any reason why we can't put in an offer straight away."

"But you haven't seen it yet."

"No, but I trust your judgement and it all looks perfect from what I've seen and read about it … and we don't want to mess about and lose it. I'll ring this Christine woman, offer the full asking price and if it's accepted, which it should be, it will set the wheels in motion and you can show me around on Saturday morning if you're free."

Miranda's head was in a whirl. Everything was going so fast. 'Marry in haste, repent in leisure.' Was that what she was doing? Was she heading for another disastrous marriage? Should she put the brakes on? She loved Jeremy with every fibre of her being but there was a niggle of doubt that he wouldn't find her good enough at some point and if he fell out of love with her when he discovered all her imperfections, that would be the end of that. She would be back to where she had been two years ago when she and Barrie had split up but even more heartbroken as she certainly hadn't felt so intensely for her first husband as she did for Jeremy. He was her world now and more than anything she wanted to be his wife and settle down in No. 10 with him. She took a deep breath. Nothing was going to go wrong. They loved each other. They were going to be married, settle down and live life to the full with their businesses (whatever Jeremy's was going to be), their children and their animals. It would be simply wonderful.

"I'm free," she grinned, mimicking Mr Humphries from 'Are You Being Served.'

The offer for the house was accepted and Jeremy picked her up as promised on Saturday morning and they drove straight to Christine's office.

"As you're first-time buyers, it should only take about six weeks for completion and then these will be yours," Christine smiled, as she handed them a bunch of keys. "If the office is shut when you return them later, just pop them through the letterbox. They slide into a secure bin so no-one can fish them out."

They explored what was to be their new home like two big kids, giggling and larking about as they went from room to room, deciding on what furniture they were going to buy, joking about having a large family and loads of animals and how homely it would all be.

"It will be too big for you to manage, especially as you're so busy with your business, so we'll have to have a cleaner, a gardener and probably a nanny," Jeremy remarked.

"A nanny? Goodness, that's going a bit far."

"Well, I don't suppose you'll want to give up Four Paws and it looks like I'm going to be pretty busy too, making enough money to keep you in the style to which you want to become accustomed," he laughed. "Someone is going to have to look after the kids occasionally."

Having explored every nook and cranny in the house, they strolled around the rear garden admiring the trees and shrubs and sat down on the bench at the far end.

They could hear people in the distance in the park; kids yelling, adults chatting, the odd dog bark.

160

"Will noises from the park bother you?" asked Miranda, leaning her head against his shoulder and staring happily up at the house. The windows glinted in the sunlight as if they were winking at her.

"Not at all … and it's certainly a lot nicer than listening to guns and grenades on nearby army ranges," he smiled. "I've informed my Commanding Officer that I want to leave. I can't for a year, you know that, and it can't go quick enough. I desperately want to be here with you, although I'll remain at the London barracks until I can be discharged so I shan't be so far away."

"So, what exactly are you going to do with yourself when you leave? I'm intrigued," Miranda quizzed.

"Well, I've a friend, Perry … he's going to be best man at our wedding but you'll meet him before then. We went through Sandhurst together but he obtained his discharge last year and set up a security business … looking after celebrities and minor royalty and the like … mainly in Europe but in America and Canada too. He's made a tremendous success of it and needs a partner to expand even further, I happened to mention I was leaving the army and he made it clear he wanted me to join him … and after a great deal of discussion, I've agreed."

"Oh … that sounds great but if it's looking after people in other countries, won't that mean you're still going to be away a lot?" She looked at him anxiously.

"Occasionally but it will be rare for me to carry out security duties, other guys are employed for that. I shall be finding and managing future contracts, much of which can be achieved from a home office and Perry, who is single, is happy to do most of the travelling so it will only be now and again … and as I said before, you can probably come with me."

"Whew. That's a relief then," she grinned. "I didn't want us to buy this house and have to live in it myself for most of the time."

"There's no chance of that, my dear," he grinned, his eyes scanning the garden. "You know, this is simply perfect for

161

children and animals. It's so big we can split it in two, one area for the dogs and the other for us and the children. As much as I love Charlie and Nellie, I don't want to sit where they frequently wee and poo and if you're going to board hundreds more it could be a bit grim," he grinned. "Come on, my darling, let's have lunch before our appointment at Temple Newsam this afternoon."

He pulled her to her feet and started walking towards the house, surprised when she let go of his hand and stood still, a strange expression on her face.

"Miranda?"

She sensed William was watching them. She turned her head slowly to her right and there he was, standing at a window on the top floor of his house. He didn't smile and nor did she.

"Miranda?" Jeremy touched her arm and turned her to face him. "What's the matter?"

She shivered. "I don't know. I just feel a bit cold all of a sudden."

"Come on. Let's get over to the Red Lion. You need a hot coffee and some lunch. The sun might be out but it's not that hot yet and the house was chilly with no heating on."

They lingered over lunch, ordering a steak and kidney pie for Jeremy and a cheese and onion quiche for Miranda, both accompanied by a generous helping of mashed potatoes, swede, carrots and broccoli. It was all piping hot and along with the coffee, warmed Miranda quickly, Jeremy relieved to see the colour return to her cheeks. She had looked strangely white in the garden.

Miranda did her best to push the sight of William up at the window away from her mind and concentrate on Jeremy enthusing about the house and how they were going to decorate it and which firm was best to carry out the work of knocking into the bathroom from the bedroom but as she looked around the restaurant, she was sharply reminded of the last time she was there … with Stephen … and how strangely he had behaved. She hadn't set eyes on him since that day so perhaps he was out and about sorting out his business. She was glad. She didn't particularly want to see him again.

Lunch over, they drove up to Temple Newsam for an appointment with an efficient young lady who gave them a tour of the areas they could use for the wedding; the grandeur of the Great Hall which could cater for up to one hundred guests, the downstairs rooms and the magnificent central courtyard which was the main entrance to the house. Use of the South Terrace with fabulous views over the parkland was also included and would provide opportunities for some stunning photography. Jeremy signed the booking form and paid a deposit. Miranda was handed a stunning brochure and another appointment was made for her to discuss the finer details of their special day the following week.

Miranda felt slightly dazed as they drove along the tree-lined drive back to the main road. She hadn't planned on a big second wedding but suddenly it was going to be much larger and grander than she could ever have envisaged. Her parents and her sisters were going to be thrilled. She was thrilled. She looked at Jeremy. From the expression on his face, he was thrilled too.

"I think we'd better collect Charlie and Nellie, go for a long walk and come back down to earth a bit," she laughed. "I can't quite take all of this in. Getting married in Temple Newsam, which was once classed as the Hampton Court of the North … and going to live in Miller Lane in that beautiful, incredible wonderful old house … and with you … Gosh, I think I must be the luckiest girl alive at this moment in time."

He grabbed her hand and squeezed it. "God, I love you, Miranda," he said huskily. "You're the very best thing that's ever happened to me … nothing and no-one will ever be as important to me as you are."

He lifted her hand to his mouth and kissed it and Miranda's heart filled with pure joy.

****

William couldn't help himself and followed them once they left the Red Lion. He had watched them leave No. 10 and walk across to the pub. Knowing they would be in there for a while, he drove the van out of the garage, leaving it on the drive and unlocked his gates so that as soon as they made a move, he could be after them in a flash, which he had, having kept watch from his bedroom window.

The Jaguar headed out of Peesdown, towards Crossgates, straight past the shopping centre, up to the roundabout at the top of the road and then indicated right towards Leeds city centre. The traffic was heavy and slow so William managed to keep two cars behind without difficulty. Then, to his surprise, the Jaguar turned left onto the tiny road towards Temple Newsam, entered the estate and parked in front of the house. Puzzled as to why they were there without any dogs, he pulled up next to a 4x4 which shielded most of the van from their view but didn't prevent him from seeing what they were up to.

He watched them go inside the house. Perhaps they were just being tourists. After all, the mansion was a huge attraction, around 500 years old, he believed.

He kept his eyes glued on the doorway through which they had disappeared. They emerged an hour later and his heart plummeted when he saw the wedding brochure Miranda was waving about and how they were laughing and hugging each other as they walked back to the car. It was hard to suppress the urge to rush over and prise them apart, knock bloody *Jeremy* to the ground and whisk Miranda off in his van and ravish her. He glared at them, wanting to spit, clenching and unclenching his fists. He punched the steering wheel. He wished it was Jeremy's face.

The Jaguar headed back to Miranda's house, William and his van a short distance behind. Miranda dashed indoors, came out with Charlie and Nellie and they all got into the Volvo. William sneered. *Jeremy* probably didn't want dog hairs in his precious Jaguar. Miranda was driving now and headed towards Peesdown Park. They were obviously going for a walk.

He followed, slowing down along the High Street to allow them time to get into the car park before he drove along Miller Lane to turn up his drive and hide the van back in the garage. He limped to the park and stood still for a moment, scanning the landscape. Then he saw them, down by the lake, arm in arm, Charlie and Nellie trotting beside them.

His stomach was churning madly. There was a searing pain in his chest as if his heart was breaking. He wanted to yell at *Jeremy* and command him to leave Miranda alone. She was his. His, his, his! The pain was unbearable. Miranda was looking so happy. They were talking quickly, smiling broadly at each other. Miranda reached up and touched *Jeremy's* face. God, he wanted to vomit. His head was pounding. He rubbed his brow but the sharp ache increased. He had never felt so angry, so helpless, so out of control in all his life. It had to be dealt with. He couldn't live like this. The blasted man would have to be dispensed with, despatched into another life. There was no room for him in this one any longer.

He turned away, unable to witness the sight of them so happy in each other's company. He wanted to think, to plan, to take action. He walked in the opposite direction, pondering hard on the best method of doing away with his adversary. He didn't want to attack him physically. Jeremy was fit and trained to kill. He would win any fight easily. No. It had to be by stealth, done sneakily, when the man was least expecting it.

He was back at the car park. He eyed up Jeremy's smart Jaguar standing a few feet away. Now there was a thought!

****

Jeremy and Miranda were enjoying their stroll, discussing their future and relaxing after their exciting day. Deep in conversation, they didn't see William until they were virtually on top of him as they entered the car park.

"Hello, Miranda ... Jeremy," he said, standing directly in front of them, leaning heavily on his stick.

Jeremy nodded but Miranda jumped and gripped his arm more tightly.

"Oh, William. You startled me. Hello."

"I hear congratulations are in order," William stared at Jeremy. His lips were smiling but Miranda was startled to see his eyes, behind those black-rimmed glasses, looked cold and menacing.

Jeremy appeared not to notice and grinned happily at William and then at Miranda. "Yes, thank you. We've just booked the wedding and we're buying No.10 Miller Lane. I believe you live next door so we shall be neighbours."

"Well, I can't think of anyone nicer," William looked at Miranda. "I'm sure we will get along just fine ... so, when is the wedding?"

"October," Jeremy replied. We would have liked it earlier but Miranda is extremely busy throughout the summer and as we're planning a long honeymoon, it was better to wait until then. However, the house won't take so long. As there's no chain, we should have the keys in a few weeks ... and when we do, we will have to have a little housewarming party and you will certainly be invited, William."

"Anyway," Miranda said, looking pointedly at her watch, decidedly uncomfortable in William's presence. What the hell was wrong with her? Why did she feel like this around him now? "We have to go as I've cats to feed before dark."

"Well, it was nice to see you. Perhaps we'll bump into each other tomorrow or the day after and can have a longer chat," William said, on a fishing trip to find out when Jeremy was leaving Leeds.

"Probably not," Jeremy replied, "We're spending tomorrow with Miranda's family as I haven't met them yet and I have to be back in London by 9.00 a.m. on Monday and will be leaving Leeds at the crack of dawn."

William could have shouted for joy. It had been completely effortless to find out what he wanted to know. As soon as he arrived home, he would go up to Miranda's room, kneel at his little altar and send up a prayer of thanks to God who must have been instrumental in providing this golden opportunity.

"Well, enjoy the rest of your weekend," William smiled easily now he knew the one person who stood between him and Miranda would soon cease to exist. "And you," Miranda murmured automatically.

"Thank you. Anyway, I must be off too. I have to buy one or two things for Stephen's dinner tonight. By the way, Miranda, he sends his regards," he added, looking her straight in the eye.

****

William couldn't stop grinning, his heart much lighter than it had been on entering the park a while ago. He limped home, thinking hard and chortled as he unlocked his gates, entered his grounds and locked them again. He imagined Miranda, in her grief, naturally turning to him ... and Anna ... and her family ... but it was to him she would give herself, wholly and completely, in the not-too-distant future. Of that, he was certain.

However, he had to think about the practicalities of sending *Jeremy* to meet his maker, such as where the Jaguar would be parked tomorrow night. Would it be outside Miranda's or in Headingley where Jeremy's sister lived? It would be easier to do what was necessary there as the house was nice and private with that long drive. Miranda's would be far more difficult as her tarmacked parking space had once been the front garden, just off the road.

He certainly had some serious planning to do but luckily had a day and a half to do it in. He would think through every step carefully as this was the best chance he could ever have to finally get rid of the one person who stood between him and complete happiness. He went straight upstairs to Miranda's room, sank down at his little altar, fixed his gaze on the crucifix on the wall in front of him and prayed for help to do what had to be done.

****

Miranda and Jeremy spent the evening at her house, curled up on the sofa, idly watching Casualty on tv, eating crisps and drinking Merlot. They went to bed early, made love and slept like babes until Nellie and Charlie woke them in the morning demanding breakfast.

Most of Sunday was taken up with visiting relatives. Not wanting to go out in Miranda's doggy smelling Volvo, they placed waterproof sheeting and a blanket on the back seat of the Jaguar for Charlie and Nellie and drove to Miranda's parents for lunch. It went well. Jeremy was an instant hit, presenting Sheila with a beautifully wrapped bottle of Chanel No.5 and a bottle of Krug and over a glass of beer with George, discovering a mutual interest in rugby.

Tricia struggled downstairs nursing a hangover following a party the night before, keen to see who her big sister had caught this time. Anyone would be an improvement on Barrie. As soon as she set eyes on Jeremy, she was smitten and forgot all about her hangover.

Griselda and Paul, Miranda's older sister and her husband, arrived in their new white BMW and were taken with Jeremy almost instantly, Griselda by his looks and charm and Paul, because he was another keen supporter of rugby.

After a traditional Sunday lunch, cooked to perfection by Sheila, the men took the dogs for a stroll and the women cleared up, their conversation mainly about Miranda's forthcoming wedding and how impressed they were with her second choice of husband.

Miranda and Jeremy left just after tea as they had promised to drop in on Daphne and Nigel and hopefully see the twins before they went to bed.

"Look forward to seeing you again, young man," George said, shaking Jeremy's hand as they all said goodbye on the doorstep. "It's been a real pleasure meeting you and I'm really pleased you're going to join the family."

Jeremy smiled. "It's been lovely meeting you all too and thank you for such a fabulous lunch," he said, turning his gaze on to Sheila. "The beef was cooked to perfection. You're a brilliant cook."

Sheila flushed as he bent down and kissed her cheek.

Waving at Tricia, Griselda and Paul, they returned to the Jaguar, tucked Charlie and Nellie on the back seat and departed for Headingley.

"They all love you," Miranda grinned. "You were a real hit."

"They're a nice bunch. It will be nice to see a lot of them when we're finally settled, especially now your father, Paul and I have a mutual interest in rugby. I don't think you'll be seeing much of us next season." "Twickenham, here we come," he laughed.

Daphne and Nigel were delighted about the engagement, having been telephoned by Jeremy on his return to Germany from Paris but this was the first time they had seen Miranda since the happy event.

Daphne, drenched in expensive French perfume, hugged Miranda tightly and welcomed her into the family and Nigel, slightly more reticent, kissed her cheek. The twins were in their playpen, surrounded by toys, in the snug adjacent to the kitchen. Their little, chubby faces lit up with joy when they saw their Uncle Jeremy, who always made a fuss of them and brought lovely presents. Fred and Merry, snuffling and slobbering, jumped all over Miranda, assuming she had turned up to take them for a walk.

They only stayed for an hour. Daphne and Nigel had work to do as they were both in court in the morning and as it was the nanny's night off, had to bath the children and put them to bed.

After such a pleasurable day, they returned to Miranda's house, Jeremy parked the Jaguar next to the Volvo and with a bottle of wine, and the dogs relaxing in their beds beside them, they cuddled up on the sofa for the evening, their conversation naturally turning to what was going to happen in the next few months.

"I'll have a week with you during August," Jeremy stated, running his hand up and down her arm as she nestled into him, "but I'm going to save most of my leave for the honeymoon. We will be away for three weeks and I flatly refuse to tell you where we are going. It's a secret … but, my darling, you are going to enjoy every single second. Just make sure you pack plenty of sunscreen, a bikini or two and some sensible walking shoes."

She was intrigued but no matter how many questions she asked, how much she badgered him, he wouldn't tell her where they were going and happy and laughing, they went to bed.

****

William made his move at 1.00 a.m. Dressed all in black, with a balaclava to pull over his head when he reached his destination, he drove the van to Miranda's house first, hoping Jeremy would have returned to his sister's home in Headingley but no, the Jaguar was parked right beside the Volvo in Roundhay.

The house was in darkness. William glanced up at the bedroom window, his stomach turned over and he felt a wave of nausea, thinking of the woman he loved being pawed over by that man … but it would be the last time. Tomorrow morning it would all end, all be in the past and he would never have to think of them together again … and in her pain, Miranda would turn to him, he would help her see that it was him she truly loved and all would be well.

He drove past, checking there were no lights on in the houses to either side of him. There weren't. All the occupants were in bed. He parked farthest away from street lights and houses that might have cctv. He got out of the van and listened intently for signs of someone up and about. Nothing stirred, apart from a slight breeze in the tall conifers in a nearby garden. It was now or never.

Already wearing rubber gloves, he pulled on the balaclava and with the wire cutters in his jacket pocket, he walked quickly and silently in his black leather trainers towards Miranda's house, keeping as close to trees and bushes as he could. His heart was beating wildly as he shot into her drive and knelt silently behind a thick evergreen bush, waiting for Charlie and Nellie to sense his presence and begin barking. They didn't. Breathing heavily, he reached for the wire cutters and slid beneath the Jaguar.

CHAPTER 19

Having committed his act of sabotage, William crept back to his van, keen to dispose of the wire cutters and rubber gloves as fast as possible. He returned to Peesdown, leaving the van in a nearby street in case anyone was awake in Miller Lane and would wonder why he was out in the middle of the night. He would collect it in the morning.

He walked to the park. There was a half-moon which gave a soft glow and enabled him to see his way down to the lake. He stood beside a bench, listening to make sure he was alone but all he could hear was the gentle lapping of the water. He pulled the wire cutters from his pocket and threw them, as far and as hard as he could, into the lake. He heard the plop. He had been told it was particularly deep in that area so the chances of them being found were exceedingly slim and there was no reason at all, if they were, why they should be connected with him. He had cleaned them carefully before he left home to remove his fingerprints and had only handled them with gloves ever since.

There was a bin next to the bench. He rummaged in his jacket pocket for a poo bag. He had bought a packet from Anna a while ago and always carried them in the park in case Miranda ran out and he could save the day for her. He tore off his rubber gloves and pushed them into the poo bag, tied it up and threw it in the bin. The likelihood of anyone ripping open the bag and discovering the gloves was negligible and rubbish collectors always turned up on a Monday morning so the evidence would soon disappear for good.

He sat on the bench, allowing the soothing sounds of the night to relax him, the pent-up tension leaving his body. He sighed with relief as his breathing and heart rate gradually returned to normal. The solitude was calming after his nerves had been stretched to breaking point for the last hour, worrying whether someone would catch him in the act at Miranda's and report him to the police.

He thought about the consequences of what he had just done. He checked his phone. It was just after 2.00 a.m. Very soon Jeremy would be off to London, to join the busy traffic on the M1. On a Monday morning there would be numerous heavy lorries and hundreds of cars and vans all jostling for space at high speed. Sometimes it was necessary to brake sharply when someone did something stupid and in all that traffic there would surely be a few idiots and having no brakes in that lot was a recipe for disaster.

He walked home, imagining the scene; the look on Jeremy's face when he realised the brakes were useless, the crash, the paramedics pronouncing Jeremy dead, Miranda's face when she was told and finally, how he would comfort her, give her a shoulder to lean on, make her aware of how much he loved her and would always be there for her in her hour of need.

He went to bed but after several failed attempts to sleep, he went downstairs and made coffee, taking it through to the lounge where he drew back the curtains, curled up on the sofa beneath an old tartan blanket and waited impatiently for dawn.

He must have nodded off as he awoke to the sounds of the birds shouting their pleasure at being alive for another day. His heart leapt. Jeremy would be leaving Miranda's very soon, if he hadn't already. God, he wished he could be a fly on the wall but he was going to have to be patient for a little while longer. Miranda would be informed sometime this morning which meant she wouldn't be in the park as she would be consumed with grief. However, she would probably tell Anna and she would tell him if he made an appearance in the shop. He would go around lunchtime and feign much sadness and sorrow at the news. Then he would buy Miranda a huge bouquet and take it round to her house and make her aware that he was there for her whenever she needed him. However, he had a decision to make. Who should he go as, William or Stephen?

The alarm went off at 4.30 a.m. Miranda groaned. She was cocooned in Jeremy's arms, cosy and warm and wanted to remain as they were forever. She was dreading the beginning of the day, watching him leave and for the first time since starting her business, not wanting to concentrate on it, although remaining busy was the key to keeping her mind occupied so she didn't miss him quite so much.

Jeremy was awake and hugged her tighter, kissed her neck and then turned to get out of bed. "I'm sorry, my darling but I have to go. Stay there. I'll let the dogs out and make you a cup of tea."

Without him beside her, she felt bereft, even though he was still in the house. She wanted to cry but didn't want him to see how upset she was at the thought of him leaving her for weeks on end.

He brought the tea, having dressed and showered, and stroked her cheek tenderly before he kissed her. "I'll ring you later, probably lunchtime as I'll have to go straight into a meeting when I get to London. Although I'll text you to let you know I've arrived safely."

She gulped and nodded, wanting to cling to him but that was pathetic and weak. She had to pull herself together and be the big brave girl she usually was.

She listened to him going downstairs, opening and locking the front door and posting her key back inside. She heard him start his car, turn out of the drive and as the noise of the engine quietened and eventually disappeared as he headed away from the house, she buried her head in her pillows and cried.

All the traffic lights were on green, enabling Jeremy to sail along at a steady 30 mph, occasionally a little faster when the speed limit allowed, heading for the M1 and London. There was very little traffic about, just the odd lorry or van. He switched on his radio to Classic FM. He recognised Mozart's Eine Kleine Nachtmusik, which he loved. It set him to thinking about the music for the wedding. He would let Miranda choose it but he might make a few suggestions.

The slip road for the M1 was empty and he was able to enter the light flow of traffic easily. He put his foot down, upping his speed to 70mph. It was tempting to go faster but the last thing he needed was a speeding ticket or worse. He eased off the accelerator and let the car cruise at the legal speed. Traffic began to increase. More salons, estate cars and hatchbacks joined the motorway as more slip roads were passed.

He groaned and eased off the accelerator when he saw the flashing red motorway signs advising there were roadworks ahead, reducing the speed limit to 50 mph. It was lowered to 30 mph when the construction works were within sight. Jeremy took his foot off the throttle again, allowing the car to slow to the required speed.

He saw the motorway lorry in the distance, easing out into the single lane in front of him and taking a while to gain momentum. He braked gently but the pedal shot loosely to the floor and stayed there. In desperation, he slammed his foot down again and again but to no avail. The brakes were utterly useless. He was still cruising at 30mph and the vehicle in front could only be doing half that and he was approaching it much faster than he would have liked. He stamped on the pedal, praying it would move, knowing if he crashed headlong into the lorry, the chances of escaping with minor injuries were pretty slim. Then, to his horror, he realised they had reached a steep incline and his car was gaining speed at an alarming rate and if he didn't take drastic action immediately, he wasn't going to come out of this alive. He pushed down the panic, trying to keep a cool head as his military training came to the fore.

He glanced at the vehicle ahead and the bollards and heavy machinery all around him, both on the hard shoulder and the middle lane. He had no choice, he had to do something pretty quickly. He changed down through the gears. The car jerked and shuddered and the engine shrieked in protest. He gripped the steering wheel tightly, his knuckles turning white. The car had slowed a fraction but due to the sharp incline in the road, the decrease in speed was not enough to prevent it hurtling into the back of the lumbering lorry. There was nothing else for it. Jeremy pulled on the handbrake. It was a similar experience to being on a fairground ride but without the pleasurable thrill and utterly terrifying as the back brakes locked and the Jaguar spun crazily around, smashing into the bollards and motorway diggers, the sound of metal on metal excruciatingly loud as the car was ripped apart. Finally, it smashed headlong into a digger and he lost consciousness as the airbag shot open. He didn't see or hear the cars behind him as they thudded into each other, their tyres screeching on the tarmac as their drivers fought to avoid him.

****

Miranda received the call an hour later. She had just showered and dressed, fed the dogs and was about to set off to feed four sets of cats. She didn't recognise the number and couldn't quite take in what the girl at the other end was telling her.

"Jeremy Cross," the nurse repeated, "he's asked me to ring you. He's been in a car accident and he's in St. James' Hospital in Leeds."

"Oh, my God," Miranda gasped. "How … what?"

"Don't panic. He's been lucky. It looks like he has a broken leg and a few bruised ribs. He's in X-ray at the moment and will ring you later but he wanted me to let you know in case you heard via another source."

"Does his sister, Daphne, know?"

"I'm just about to ring her. He wanted me to contact you first."

"When can I see him?" she asked breathlessly, her heart thudding wildly.

"Well, his injuries aren't life-threatening but we will be keeping him in overnight as a precaution so any time between 12 noon and 8.00 p.m., which are our normal visiting times."

Miranda slumped onto her sofa, not knowing whether to laugh or cry. Thank God he was okay and back in Leeds, where he would probably have to remain for a while now as he couldn't return to duties if he was injured. Every cloud certainly had a silver lining!

She hurried to feed all the cats and rang Belinda to ask her to walk her pack of dogs today as she wanted to be at the hospital as soon as visiting hours commenced at noon. She walked Charlie and Nellie in Roundhay and tried to concentrate on paperwork, watching the hands of the clock move annoyingly slowly. She just wanted to be at the hospital with Jeremy. She wanted to make sure for herself that he was really okay.

She rang Anna as soon as the shop was open but she couldn't chat long as it was busy and Emily had the morning off. Then, just as she finished the call, Daphne rang.

"Miranda. Are you okay? I've only just heard from the hospital. I had my phone switched off as I was in court … and then I had to talk to my client who has got himself into a right pickle. I gather Jeremy only has a few bruised ribs and a broken leg so it might be damned painful but at least it's not serious."

"Yes, Daphne. I'm shocked but okay. I'm going to the hospital soon so I can be there as soon as visiting commences."

"Good. I can't get there until later. Now, he will have to come home to us when he leaves hospital. He obviously won't be able to manage stairs and we have a spare guest room with an ensuite on the ground floor so he can have that until he is well again … and you are welcome to turn up at any time to see him."

"Thank you, Daphne. It would be difficult to have him here as the bathroom is upstairs so I'm so pleased you have a sensible solution."

"Good. As long as you're okay with that. I'll probably see you at the hospital later then."

Daphne clicked off and Miranda breathed a sigh of relief when she saw the time was now 11.30 a.m. and she could make a move for the hospital. She couldn't get out of the house and into the car quickly enough.

****

William left it until lunchtime before he pottered down the High Street and entered Pampered Pets. Anna, who was scribbling in a notebook behind the counter, looked up and smiled.

"Good morning, William. How are you?"

"Fine," he replied, disconcerted to see her so cheerful. Surely, she should be sobbing into her handkerchief by now. "I was just doing a bit of shopping when I realised I hadn't seen you for a few days ... or Miranda come to that, so I thought I'd just check all was okay with you both."

Anna snapped her notebook shut and looked at him. "Well, Miranda has had some unsettling news."

"Oh?" He tried not to look too eager to hear about Jeremy's demise.

"Poor Jeremy had a car accident this morning and is in hospital ... at St. James."

"Oh, no," he exclaimed, doing his best to sound concerned. What the hell was the man doing in hospital? He should be in the bloody morgue!

"He's reasonably okay. Just has a few bruised ribs and a broken leg and should be able to go home tomorrow."

William had no idea how he managed not to slam the counter in rage or show Anna in any way that he was aghast. He stumbled over his words as he proffered his hopes that Jeremy would recover quickly and made his get-away quickly, making the excuse that he had a dental appointment.

By the time he entered his garden and bolted the gates behind him, he couldn't even remember walking up the street, he had been so traumatised and deep in thought.

He'd thought he'd cracked it, got rid of the one major problem standing between him and Miranda and their future together ... and it hadn't worked. He was furious. He was more than furious. He was ... he didn't know what he was. He slammed the front door behind him, ripped off his disguise, threw his walking stick in the corner and marched straight to the drinks cabinet and poured a huge brandy. He downed it in one and poured another. It steadied him but the anger wasn't evaporating. It was as intense as ever. The bloody man was still alive and even worse, injured, and Miranda would be all over him, pandering to his wishes, making sure he regained his health. Bugger, bugger, bugger! He had blown it. Utterly blown it. What the hell was he going to do now?

****

Miranda was shocked when she set eyes on Jeremy, resting in bed, his leg in plaster and a nasty gash on his left hand.

"I'll live," he smiled ruefully.

"Oh, Jeremy. Whatever happened? Thank God you're okay. I don't know what I would have done if ...."

She sat on the bed and took his right hand in hers. It was warm and dry and just touching him, realising he was still with her, was sheer joy. All morning she had been imagining what it would have been like to lose him and the mere thought was unbearable.

"To be honest, I'm not sure," he winced as he shifted position. "The brakes failed."

"But they were okay yesterday when we were whizzing about Leeds," she said with a puzzled expression. "Why would they suddenly go like that?"

"I don't know. The car had a full service a couple of weeks ago and the brakes were new so I've no idea but the garage is reputable so I can't imagine it's the fault of the mechanic. Anyway, it's a write-off now so I'll have to get another, which is a shame. I liked that car. By the way, there's a coffee machine over there," he waved a hand at the top of the ward "and I don't know about you but I'd love one."

Miranda smiled and did as she was told, surprised to see Andy in his police uniform walking down the ward towards Jeremy as she returned.

"Hello, Andy. I didn't expect to see you here," she said, placing the two coffees on Jeremy's bedside table.

He nodded. "Miranda, Jeremy. I'm sorry to see you in here. You were damned lucky ... by the looks of it someone meant you to suffer a lot more than you have."

"Whatever do you mean?" Jeremy asked, raising an eyebrow.

Rigid with fear, Miranda stared wide-eyed at Andy.

"The motorway police," Andy went on, "have been in touch. They've examined your car and it didn't take them long to discover the brake cables have been cut. Have you any idea who would do such a thing? Have you upset anyone lately?"

Miranda gasped and put her hand to her mouth. Jeremy laid back on his pillows, his expression incredulous. "No. No, of course not. I've been in Germany for months and then London until this weekend."

"When was the last time you drove the car?"

"Yesterday. We were in it on and off all day and it was fine."

"Where did you park it last night?"

"Outside Miranda's house. Next to her Volvo."

"And has that been okay today, Miranda?" Andy asked her.

"Fine," she looked at him aghast. "But you don't think someone did it outside my house?"

"Well, it looks more than probable. Do you have cctv by any chance?"

"No … and I don't think any of my neighbours do either."

"Well, we'll do a door to door and make sure. You never know. Someone might have it. In the meantime, Miranda, don't take your vehicle off your drive unless you've checked the brakes are working properly."

CHAPTER 20

Jeremy resided with Daphne while he was recovering from his injuries, Miranda visiting him every day at different times depending on the duties she had to carry out for Four Paws. Two weeks after the accident, with his ribs feeling better and he was able to move around easily with crutches, it was decided he could return to his desk job at his London barracks. Miranda wanted to drive him down but the weather was superb and it seemed like the whole of Leeds wanted to go on holiday and leave their pets in her care and she simply didn't have the time, although she finally gave up on the paperwork. Gail, the mother of one of her dog walking clients had masses of secretarial experience. She was newly retired but bored and was more than willing to work on a Monday and Wednesday every week, which meant Miranda could concentrate fully on pet care and expanding the business.

Daphne had friends in London whom she wanted to see so she drove her brother back down, Miranda waving them off tearfully. She consoled herself with the fact that she had more than enough to keep her occupied with the business, planning the wedding, selling her house and moving into No. 10 and she wouldn't have time to mope about Jeremy not being with her. It was complete madness, doing everything in the middle of her busiest months but with the help of Gail, Belinda, Katie, Julie and her parents and sisters, she was able to achieve all she needed to but she still missed Jeremy terribly. He had wanted to return to Leeds at weekends but with the plaster cast and crutches, it was difficult so it was decided he would stay in London until he could drive again and purchase a new car.

The police had come up with nothing in the search for whoever cut the brakes on the Jaguar. There was no motive from what they could make out, no evidence and no-one in the immediate vicinity had cctv. Jeremy and Miranda were told to be careful but there was nothing else that could be done although the case would remain open.

Miranda diligently checked her brakes several times each morning before leaving her house and even though she had loved living there, was now desperate to move. She wasn't sleeping, paranoid about someone creeping about outside. Several times during the night she rose from her bed to peer out of the window to check her car and the street but there was never anything to be alarmed about, only people returning from an evening out and walking straight past her house, taking no interest in her vehicle.

It played on her mind, not knowing who had tried to kill Jeremy and why. He had no enemies. Everyone liked him. He was affable, kind and considerate. Who could wish him harm? It was bizarre and terrifying and even though she was well occupied, she thought about it frequently and there was a sick feeling in the pit of her stomach all the time.

Jeremy was concerned for her, as were her parents, who urged her to stay with them and Anna had offered her a room in her flat above the shop. However, with such early starts and late nights now there were so many cats, rabbits and guinea pigs to visit, she didn't want to disrupt the lives of others and then there was Charlie and Nellie and the odd dog she boarded when all her home boarders were booked so until she could finally move into No.10, she had to stay where she was and just be ultra-careful.

****

Following a tearful farewell to her house, Anna moved into the flat above her shop in the middle of May and Dolly and Rio came to live with her two days later, soon settling into their new home and new routine and seeing Andy, Simba and Jess regularly for long walks. Time and his duties permitting, Andy who liked to eat out, treated Anna to dinner and on two occasions, the theatre, where they saw Phantom of the Opera and Grease.

Anna was happier than she had been since before Gerald died. Sometimes she felt a tiny pang of guilt but brushed it away. Gerald wouldn't have wanted her to be sad and miserable for the rest of her life. He would have been happy for her.

Not only was she content in her personal life but her business was improving day by day. The shop was becoming well known and was increasingly busy. The garden room was up and running by the beginning of June and proving popular, especially on warmer days when Anna opened the French doors and allowed customers, often accompanied by their dogs, to sit and relax with their drinks and snacks on the benches outside.

She had employed more staff. Becky, a middle-aged woman, who was a friend of Sonia's and passionate about animal welfare, was now running the kitchen and producing the most delicious home-made savouries and cakes to eat in or take away which were so popular, it was rare anything was left at the end of the day. Two students from Leeds University did the waitressing, Geraldine in the mornings and Lois in the afternoons. Both girls were keen animal lovers and never missed an opportunity to point out Sonia's information sheets of animals needing a home. Thanks to their efforts, quite a few found their forever parents. Emily was happy to do more hours and Anna managed to work the rota so that when any of her ladies had a day off, she undertook their duties. So, all was well with Anna and Pampered Pets.

****

No-one in Peesdown knew William's purchase of The Cedars, his bolthole near Appleton Roebuck, had gone through.

He was elated when he had finally been given the keys and could set about making it comfortable in case he had to hide up in a hurry. He ordered a sofa, table and chairs, television, dvd player and laptop for the lounge, white goods for the kitchen and a decent bed, wardrobe and a couple of chest of drawers for one of the bedrooms. He filled the kitchen pantry with dry goods and two chest freezers with frozen meals and vegetables. If push came to shove and it became impossible to flee abroad, he could make himself very comfortable and wouldn't have to step outdoors for months if he didn't want to … and it was a good place to keep anyone away from the public eye too. In fact, once Miranda was in his clutches, because she was going to be eventually, it might be a good idea to take her there for a while. Get her used to the idea of living with him away from Peesdown. If he blindfolded her, tied her up in the van and drove around for an hour or so before coming here, she would have no idea where she was. It was certainly a thought and one that kept him sane in the weeks and months following Jeremy's '*accident*'.

He also purchased a motorhome in case he had to go on the road for any length of time and once Miranda fell in love with him and wasn't a flight risk any longer, she might very well like to go travelling too. They could meander through the glens and around the lochs of Scotland and explore the Lake District thoroughly. He had been there once with his parents many years ago and had fallen in love with the tranquillity of the place. He began to grow quite excited at the thought of wandering around the country, Miranda by his side.

****

The day finally arrived when Miranda could collect the keys for No.10. With Nellie and Charlie in the car, she was at the estate agents the moment they opened at 9.00 a.m. Christine handed her the keys and wished her well. She drove straight to the house, wanting to have a good look around and check everything was as it should be before her furniture was delivered by the removal men the next day.

"This, my darlings, is your new home … and we are going to be extremely happy here … with Jeremy," she smiled, parking on the gravel near to the front door.

The two dogs thumped their tails hard on the leather seating in answer and made wet nose marks on the windows as they looked with interest at the front garden.

Miranda automatically looked up at William's upper windows. There was no-one there and she shrugged away any unsettling feelings about having William and Stephen next door. She had to get a grip. William was a harmless old man and Stephen had kept his distance from her since she had given him the heave-ho. She had seen him in the park once or twice and acknowledged him but he made no attempt to chat, for which she was thankful and even though William had made an odd remark or two, he had been extremely pleasant when she had bumped into him and made her wariness seem somewhat ridiculous and childish.

Anyway, she couldn't allow herself to have silly thoughts as she had to face a few months living at No. 10 on her own. Jeremy wouldn't be leaving the army until next year so would only be at home for an occasional weekend until then or when on leave, even after they were married. At least, she had the dogs so she wouldn't be totally alone and although Nellie had a tendency to be lazy on the guarding front, Charlie was on the ball and barked loudly if anyone was about, which was strange, thinking about it. He hadn't made a sound the night Jeremy's car was tampered with. Stop it, she told herself, pushing away the fear.

Anyway, she could start home boarding fairly soon and fill the place with dogs. She would be able to have more here than in her little terrace and as she had tons of enquiries every week, it wouldn't be hard to find more dogs who needed the love and security of home boarding. The council needed to check the place first and she had made an appointment for one of the inspectors to visit next week but she couldn't see any problems with such a large house and garden.

Then Gail would be here working in the office two days a week and friends and family would visit frequently so she wouldn't be that lonely and Tricia had offered to come and stay with her when Jeremy was away, which was kind of her ... and Anna, Dolly and Rio were only down the road now, which was a comforting thought. So, she just had to be a big girl and get on with it ... after all, she wanted this house so badly. She had fallen utterly in love with it and was thrilled it was going to be her family home forever and ever, although the first thing she was going to have installed was security lighting everywhere, especially over the garage, the doors of which would have heavy-duty locks. She had a security guy coming the day after tomorrow to discuss her requirements and she would be jolly relieved when the work was done. Until then, she had to rely on her beloved dogs.

"Come on, children," she grinned, opening the car for the dogs to get out. "Come and explore your new home ... you are so going to love it here."

****

William heard the car and guessed it was Miranda as he knew she would have the keys today, having heard her mention it to Anna when they were all in the park. He made his way upstairs to the top bedroom overlooking No.10. Miranda was letting the dogs out of the Volvo and then she walked up the front steps, unlocked the door and called the dogs to follow her. They all disappeared inside and William could feel the excitement in the pit of his stomach. She was finally there. Next door. Close, really close at last ... and without her dratted fiancé anywhere to be seen.

Knowing she was more or less going to be living on her own for the next few months had mollified him after the '*accident*' went so badly wrong. Furious that Jeremy survived, he had read every mention of it he could find in the local newspapers so he knew exactly where and when it had occurred and what had actually happened. The bloody man had been tremendously lucky the incident had been at a slow speed in amongst roadworks. If he had braked in the outside lane in fast traffic, he would have gone to meet his maker. ... but he hadn't. He was still alive. He was still going to move in next door. He was still going to marry Miranda ... or at least, he thought he was!

William's first reaction on hearing the news of Jeremy's survival had been to find another way to do away with him but that would have been utterly crazy. He had avoided any attention from the police so far and that was the way he wanted it to stay and now Miranda was next door, he could take his time ingratiating himself ... although he didn't want to wait too long to make her his. He wanted her too badly ... and it was going to be hard to take when Jeremy was here and in bed with her. No. He couldn't bear too much of that!

This weekend was going to be particularly difficult. Miranda's intended was returning to Peesdown for a couple of days and they were going to have a little housewarming party, to which he and Stephen had been invited. He was definitely going to attend but had proffered the excuse that Stephen had returned to the south of England to see to his business down there for a while. He didn't want to be in company pretending to be Stephen in case there were awkward questions he couldn't answer. No, it was safer to attend as William.

It would be an interesting evening. Having access to No. 10 with all the furniture in situ would help him get the feel of the place if he ventured in after dark to kidnap Miranda. He was gradually preparing for that day ... or night. He checked his garden regularly and was satisfied that the hedge where he had cut the foliage was still intact and didn't look noticeable to anyone standing near to it. He had crawled through it three times now, at night, creeping into No.10 when the moon was clear and he could make his way about with the fraction of light shining through the massive windows. He enjoyed his nocturnal visits, especially spending a bit of time in the master bedroom and imagining Miranda having a bath or showering in the ensuite. He had a lovely bathroom in his house and would enjoy seeing her in there too, stripped of her clothing and just waiting for him to join her.

God, he couldn't wait! It had been agonising listening to Miranda and Anna talking about Jeremy and the wedding for the last few weeks when he had joined them on their walks but very soon, once Jeremy had returned to London, Stephen would start to work seriously on Miranda again and if she didn't begin to fall in love with him and play ball, well then, he would just have to abduct her and keep her captive until she saw sense.

CHAPTER 21

Miranda's moving day went well. The two men from Carter's of Leeds were quick and efficient and by mid-afternoon all her furniture was where she wanted it. Tricia had the day off from Tesco and turned up with Sheila and George to help with the unpacking, insisting the most important things were making the bed and finding the kettle.

Belinda, who had taken Charlie and Nellie for a few hours to keep them out of the way, brought them home at tea time and stayed to help open a few more packing boxes. In the early evening, Anna arrived with Rio and Dolly and two bottles of Moet Chandon, six generous portions of fish and chips and a black forest gateau made by Becky that afternoon in the Pampered Pets kitchen. It was a lovely evening and they all sat in the back garden devouring Anna's offerings, George and Sheila on the bench and the younger members of the party on the lawn around them. Jeremy rang to make sure it had all gone smoothly and delivered the news that he had bought a new car and would be driving back to Leeds on Friday evening.

Miranda waved everyone off around ten thirty, all of them offering to stay the night if she was nervous.

"I'm absolutely fine," she insisted. "I'm so damned tired, I shall just die when I eventually get into bed."

"Ring me if you do get worried," Anna said, hugging her. "I can be up here with the dogs in a couple of minutes."

She watched them go, her parents and Tricia in the Ford Escort, Belinda in her van and Anna walking briskly towards the High Street with Rio and Dolly walking beautifully by her side on the lead.

Letting Charlie and Nellie out of the house for a last wee, she turned her attention to securing the property for the night. As a precaution and taking a leaf out of William's book, she had bought a hefty chain and padlock the day before for the wrought iron gates

190

which were twice her height and looked as if they had rested where they were for years. They creaked and groaned with protest as she hauled them together.

"Why the hell didn't I ask someone to help me do this before they cleared off?" she hissed at Charlie who was watching her with interest as she panted from the exertion, threaded the chain through the gaps in the wrought iron and clicked the padlock. "Where's Nellie?" she asked him, peering around the garden, with only light from the street lamp outside the gates to aid her. The sooner the security lights around the house were up, the better. Trying to see a chocolate-coloured dog in deep shrubbery with little illumination was not easy. A good deal of snuffling coming from Miranda's right alerted her to Nellie's whereabouts. Quite partial to a bit of fox or squirrel poo, she was naturally hunting for anything tasty.

"Oh, she is naughty," Miranda grinned at Charlie. "Thank goodness you're a good boy."

He licked her hand and she bent down to cuddle his solid, warm body, breathing in his lovely doggie smell with pleasure. "Come on, darling boy, we're as secure as we can be. Let's go to bed," she said "and if someone tries to move the gates, hopefully it will make enough racket to wake you two up. You've both got to go to sleep with one ear cocked … do you hear me?" she smiled as Nellie joined them, licking her lips and her breath smelling vile. "And you, madam, are simply disgusting."

She walked across to the garage and gave the padlock a hefty tug but it didn't open. Satisfied the Volvo was reasonably secure and with the dogs at her heels, she went indoors, shot the bolts across the front door and after turning the key, removed it. She did the same for the kitchen door and dropped both keys out of sight of the kitchen windows into a pretty little pot covered in red roses on the worktop. She checked all the downstairs windows were shut tight and called the dogs, who were beginning to settle in their beds in the kitchen and looked surprised that she wanted them to go upstairs with her. Unbeknown to them, she had purchased two new baskets from Anna which were now in the bedroom. They would sleep with her when she was alone. Charlie and Nellie didn't mind a bit and settled down without hesitation, quite content to be upstairs with their mistress.

She had a quick shower in the bathroom, looking forward to the following week when a local building firm would be arriving to knock through from the bedroom, which would make a huge difference. She had checked out the master bedroom again just in case she wanted to change her mind about using it but she hadn't. That big window in the ensuite made her feel totally vulnerable. Even with a blind, she wouldn't be able to relax in there knowing William … and Stephen … could be looking down at the room, imagining her naked. She had shuddered and shut the door.

Nellie was already asleep but Charlie smiled and wagged his tail as Miranda flopped into her comfy old double bed absolutely exhausted. Jeremy had expressed a wish to buy a king-size but she would miss her old bed which was going to be moved into one of the guest bedrooms. She grinned. When he was away, she could sneak back into it. She turned off the light and, in a few minutes, all three occupants of the bedroom were fast asleep.

****

The weekend housewarming party was a success. Miranda and Jeremy had only intended to have a small gathering but somehow it expanded. All of Miranda's family arrived laden with gifts, Daphne and Nigel turned up in their new Porsche and made everyone green with envy, Anna was accompanied by Andy and their dogs and Sonia and Josh came in their tatty old van along with John Marchant who was eager to see how Rio and Dolly were settling into their new home with Anna. They were thrilled to see him, their saviour, and Sonia and Josh were also given a thorough licking. The dogs hadn't forgotten who had rescued them and given them a second chance.

The Vicar brought his wife, the smiling Samantha, and all the staff turned up; Belinda, Julie, Kate and Gail from Four Paws and Emily, Becky, Lois and Geraldine from Pampered Pets, those who hadn't already been inside keen to have a tour of Miranda's posh new abode.

It was a beautiful evening and after dispensing drinks and showing the house to those who hadn't seen it, Miranda at the fore of the group and Jeremy at the rear, they wandered outside to the back garden, which looked particularly pretty with the fairy lights Jeremy had fixed up that afternoon. Anna and Miranda's family were guarding the sumptuous finger buffet Miranda and Becky had prepared earlier from the dogs, who were more than a little interested in the delicious aroma of turkey, beef and salmon.

"Well, I must say, brother dear," Daphne smiled, linking her arm through Jeremy's, "it's a very nice house indeed. Not as nice as ours, of course ...," she laughed. Jeremy grinned. "And what do you think, Nigel?" he asked his brother-in-law who was eyeing up the roses, for which he had a penchant.

"Not bad. Not bad at all," he said in his best barrister voice. "And I do believe you have a couple of rare species here. It looks very much like the last occupants had exceptionally good taste."

"Oh, dear," Miranda giggled. "I don't think they're going to last long with the dogs cocking their legs."

Nigel looked aghast and Miranda did her best not to laugh aloud. "We'll move them," she said, trying to hold back her mirth. "We'll put them in the front garden. The dogs won't be allowed to roam out there because of the road ... I don't want any of them getting run over or stolen."

"I think that was the doorbell," Anna called. "Would you like me to go?"

"I will," Jeremy said, letting go of Miranda's hand. "Who else is there to come? I thought everyone was here."

Without waiting for her answer, he made his way to the front door and was surprised to see William on the doorstep holding a big bouquet, a box of chocolates and a bottle of Moet Chandon.

"I'm so sorry I'm a bit late," William said, nearly choking over the words. He had expected Miranda to answer the door, not bloody *Jeremy*.

"No problems, William. Please … come through and meet the others … although I expect you know most people from the park … and thank you for the presents. That's really kind of you," he added, taking them from William, "but before we do that, would you like a quick tour of the house? We've shown everyone else … although I suspect it's pretty much the same as yours."

William beamed. "I'd love to see it … if you don't mind."

"Hello, William," Miranda said pleasantly, appearing from the kitchen. "I was wondering who was missing."

William smiled. "Yes, it's only me. It's a shame Stephen couldn't come but as you know, he's temporarily returned to Bath to see to his business but he sends his best wishes and hopes you will be very happy in your new abode, as I do too."

"That's very kind," Jeremy said, handing Miranda William's gifts. "I'm just going to give William the tour. We won't be long."

Miranda stood in the hall and watched the two men head up the stairs. William turned and smiled broadly at her. She automatically smiled back but a shudder of apprehension ran through her body. Not again! What the hell was the matter with her?

****

Jeremy returned to London and Miranda had no time to worry about William as she was rushed off her feet. Not only were there the usual cat visits, dog walking and boarding to do but there were now other animals to care for too. She had four lots of chickens to let out and put away at night and then one client was going away

194

for a month who owned pigs, goats, sheep, ducks, geese and dozens of chickens as well as an elderly Border Collie. Being such a big job, it couldn't be managed with visits alone so Kate had kindly offered to housesit, just popping out to do a group dog walk in Roundhay Park in the mornings. The clients were so grateful they told Kate and Miranda to take as many eggs as they liked for themselves and their family and friends. Miranda made full use of hers, whipping up the most enormous omelettes with the duck and goose eggs and even managed to find time to bake a cake and put it in the freezer for when Jeremy returned the following weekend.

The builder arrived and made a splendid job of knocking through the wall between the bedroom and bathroom. The king-sized bed was delivered and the delivery men were most obliging and with much puffing and panting placed her old double in the guest room above. They had been surprised she didn't want it in either the original master or the back bedroom on the first floor but knowing she would use it on occasions, Miranda couldn't bear the thought of it being in either room which overlooked William's house.

The new bed took a bit of getting used to on her own but she discovered she was sleeping better, probably because she was so tired and the dogs, her guardian angels, were in her room. Tricia repeated her offer to stay on the nights she wasn't working but Miranda declined. Even though the house could be a bit creepy, if she flooded it with light (bugger the electricity bill), she didn't feel particularly nervous, especially since Jeremy had paid for a security firm to install a burglar alarm and motion sensor lights on all sides of the property and over the garage. It would be exceedingly difficult for anyone to gain access to the house or garage now without being seen and if they did and tampered with the windows, the dogs would hear it and cause a right ruckus.

Feeling far more at ease and relaxed in her new home, although she would be extremely glad when Jeremy finally left the army and was with her for most of the time, she began to prepare for her wedding and the honeymoon. She still had no idea of where they were going but guessed it would be somewhere romantic. She questioned Jeremy repeatedly during their long phone calls but he just laughed and refused to give anything away.

"Just do as I say and pack plenty of sunscreen and a bikini or two," he said, and with that, she had to be content.

****

William was deliriously happy to have Miranda living next door and be able to watch her every day. He placed a net curtain over the window in 'Miranda's' room which overlooked No. 10 so he could gaze upon her without her knowing he was there, although he had been disappointed to be told by Jeremy on the tour that they wouldn't be using the master bedroom. It would have been quite titillating to know Miranda was having a bath or shower when the lights went on in the ensuite but then it wouldn't be long before she was in his house anyway and he could do what he liked with her.

However, he didn't want to make his move too soon. She wasn't marrying until October, not that she would of course because she would be living with him by then, either here in Peesdown or at The Cedars or even travelling the country in the mobile home.

In the meantime, he made himself as amenable as possible so that she was used to him being around and could be taken by surprise when he did finally act. Whenever he heard her car return in the afternoons, he would make an appearance, either just to say hello and have a little chat or sometimes taking a meal he had made, saying he was worried she was so busy she wouldn't have time to make herself anything. He also provided plenty of treats for the dogs such as sausages and cuts of meat and juicy bones. Needless to say, Charlie and Nellie loved him and as soon as they saw him their tails wagged furiously.

"You must stop spoiling them," Miranda had scolded when she got out of the Volvo yesterday. "And me as well, William. I do have plenty of food in the freezer and it doesn't take much time to pop something in the microwave."

"Yes, but that's not the same as home-cooked, as well you know, Miranda," he had said firmly. "And I don't mind. I really don't. I love having you as a neighbour and I want to make sure you are well looked after while your Jeremy is away."

"Well, that's very kind of you … but there really is no need," she had remarked politely. "I must go indoors, William. I need to sit down. My feet are killing me and I want nothing more than to remove my walking boots."

"Oh, and I've decided," he smiled, as he walked away. "Once you and Jeremy have managed to settle in and have a bit more time, you must come round for dinner."

Miranda didn't answer. That bothered him.

CHAPTER 22

A month went by and William began to grow impatient. He had done everything he could think of to make Miranda like him and want to be with him but while friendly enough, she wasn't as warm towards him as she used to be and it was bugging him. He wanted her to love him ... as he loved her.

He spent a lot of time in 'her room' upstairs, kneeling at the altar for an hour at a time, praying for guidance on how to make her love him. He sat on the bed and stared at all the photographs he had sneakily taken of her in the park and just lately, in the garden of No.10 with his zoom lens. He itched to have her in his own house. He itched to have her in his bed. He just itched ... and if she didn't show some signs of responding to him soon, he was going to have to take drastic action. He had to scratch his itch.

Then, one Thursday afternoon in September, he could bear it no more. He knew Jeremy was coming home for the weekend and the very thought of knowing they would be in bed together again was crucifying. He couldn't bear it. No, he couldn't do it again. He wasn't going to. It had to stop. Miranda had to be his ... and now. He couldn't delay any longer.

He waited until she went to work. He watched her load Charlie and Nellie into the car and drive out of the gates, heading off to collect her pack of dogs to walk. He needed to get into No.10 to find out if she had made any changes to the layout and to open the window in the basement so he could get in after dark. He had a few hours to play with as she wouldn't be back until around 3.00 p.m.

He walked down to the bottom of his garden and glanced at where there were now a couple of concealed openings, the first through the hedge into the grounds of No.10 and the second, which he had worked on later, in the adjoining hedge overlooking the park. They were both unnoticeable if one didn't know they were there.

He turned to the first, moved the foliage so he could crawl through to Miranda's lawn and then walked smartly to the back door. He guessed she bolted it at night but hoped she wouldn't bother through the day. She hadn't. He let himself in with the key which he had never put back under the plant pot by the back door, removed his shoes so he wouldn't leave any footprints and padded through the rooms, downstairs first and then upstairs to the bedrooms.

He had to admit his darling girl had made the place nice with decent furniture and decorated it well with subtle colours. He liked it. He would give her carte blanche to do similar in his house … in their house, he corrected himself.

He went into the bedroom she shared with Jeremy and suddenly felt a wave of seething anger as he stared at the enormous bed and then at the photograph of Jeremy in his uniform on the table beside it. He grabbed it and hurled it at the wall. The glass shattered into tiny pieces. He ripped out the picture, tore it into shreds and threw it on the floor beside the frame and the broken glass. God, how he hated that man. He should have died on the motorway … but he was going to be hurt, perhaps not physically but definitely emotionally, which, when he thought about it, might be even better. William's rage began to dissipate. Jeremy was going to be devastated when Miranda was taken away from him and that thought gave him immense satisfaction. He would have the last laugh in the end.

Having meandered around the remainder of the rooms, he ventured down to the basement. It was an ideal hiding place. He had heard Miranda tell Anna that she didn't like coming down here unless it was absolutely necessary, although she had to at least a couple of times a week because the washing machine and tumble dryer were in situ.

He looked at the window. It was big enough for him to get in and out of and he could leave it ajar. It was pretty doubtful Miranda would check it regularly, naturally assuming it was always locked. There was a tiny key on top of the electricity meter in the corner. He guessed it was for the window. He was right. He unlocked it and opened it a fraction. Hopefully, she wouldn't come down here this evening, notice it wasn't shut properly and secure it as he would have to postpone his plans if he couldn't get in. He pocketed the key and went home.

The rest of the day passed in agonising suspense. He couldn't wait for it to get dark so he could put his plan into action. He saw Miranda return home just after 3.00 p.m. and then go out again at 5.00 p.m., no doubt to feed cats. He heard her car just after 7.30 pm., shot upstairs and from behind his net curtain, watched her drive the Volvo into the garage, lock the door and then head indoors with the dogs. Now all he had to do was wait until she went to bed. She usually did so around 10.00 p.m., at least that was when all the lights went off. He had sat there, night after night, to get some idea of when she retired. He couldn't see any reason why tonight should be any different as she had no visitors and was probably exhausted after another gruelling day.

He remained in her room, on the bed he was going to tie her to, running the rope through his hands again and again and then he knelt at the altar and prayed for a successful outcome to what he intended to do in a few hours.

****

By 9.30 p.m. Miranda was shattered and desperate to get into bed but badly needed a shower. She had been too tired to bother when arriving home, needing to satisfy her hunger first. Then she fell asleep on the sofa. Charlie had woken her up, poking her with his nose, telling her it was time for bed and he wanted a wee. She let both dogs into the rear garden and checked all the windows and the front door were secure. They came in and she locked the back door and threw the bolts across. She didn't set the alarm as she was going to come back down and make a hot, milky drink after her shower.

She forced her tired legs to carry her upstairs, followed by the dogs who, having been out with her all day, were as tired as she was and settled straight into their baskets with deep sighs.

She went straight into the ensuite without bothering to turn on the light in the bedroom or draw the curtains. Showering was quicker but the huge jacuzzi looked particularly inviting and she could feel her body cry out for a battering with the jets and a good soak in her favourite Norfolk Lavender bath foam which would ensure a good night. It didn't take long to fill and after allowing the jets to do their job, she turned them off and luxuriated for half an hour, nearly falling asleep in the warm, soapy water. It began to go cold and she hauled herself out and used a big fluffy turquoise towel to get dry. Deeply relaxed and with her eyelids drooping, she turned off the light in the ensuite and crossed the bedroom floor to draw the curtains.

"Bugger!" she exclaimed loudly when she stepped on something sharp. She touched her foot. It was wet. Hobbling over to the window, she pulled the curtains across and turned on the light. Her heel was bleeding. She looked at the carpet and saw the shards of glass, the broken frame and Jeremy's photo, ripped to shreds.

She didn't know how long she sat there in total shock, the blood from her wound dripping onto the pale blue carpet. Someone had been in the room. Someone had smashed Jeremy's photo frame and torn his picture up. Who? Why? How the hell did they get in? Were they here now? She was so scared she couldn't move. The dogs were looking at her lazily, both bordering on going to sleep, seemingly unaware she was quivering with fear.

She considered ringing someone. The police? No. They would think her crazy and they were so busy, she didn't like to bother them. Her parents would be going to bed and she didn't want to worry them. Tricia was at work. Anna was out with Andy this evening and it wouldn't be fair to contact him as he was off duty. She certainly wasn't going to ring Jeremy. He would worry himself sick.

She jammed a piece of tissue onto the wound which had stopped bleeding, pushed her feet into her slippers and pulled on her nightdress. All thought of sleep had fled. She was wide awake now. The sight of the destroyed photo was shocking. Someone had deliberately stood in her room and done that. Was it the same person who had sabotaged Jeremy's car?

The fear became panic. Someone had it in for Jeremy and they had gained access to the house. She was being stupid and had to ring the police. She dashed back into the ensuite where she had left her mobile phone. She pressed 999.

****

He saw the police arrive. Their sirens were quiet but the flashing blue lights came quickly along Miller Lane and stopped outside No.10. He saw a fully dressed Miranda run down the path and open the gates to let them in. Two uniformed officers got out of the car and walked indoors with her. She was speaking quickly and gesticulating with her hands.

William sank back onto the bed behind him. Why had she called the police? She should be in bed by now and falling asleep. What the hell had she seen or heard to make her suspicious?

He suddenly realised what he had to do and how easy she had made it for him. He rushed down to the kitchen and took out the small phial of Rohypnol he had purchased last week. It had been relatively easy to get hold of. He had taken the van, with false number plates attached, into a dodgy part of Leeds and after watching one particular rough-looking individual whom several equally unkempt people approached and then cleared off quickly after exchanging something, he presumed money and drugs, decided to try his luck. The bloke had been highly suspicious at first but when William waved a good deal of money under his nose, he agreed to have what was required available the following evening and William now had that precious liquid here … to aid him with Miranda.

He shoved it into his jacket pocket and headed quickly down his path and up hers. The door was ajar. He knocked on it loudly, hearing voices in the hall, Miranda's high-pitched and shaky. A police officer poked his head outside.

"Yes. Can we help you?"

"I'm William Pemworthy. I live next door. I saw your car and as I know Miranda is on her own and she's a friend, I just wanted to make sure she's ok."

"You'd better come in, Mr Pemworthy, so we can ask you a few questions."

The officer held open the door and William stepped inside. The second officer and Miranda were facing him, Miranda looking pale and worried and nibbling her lower lip.

"Miranda?" he asked. "Whatever's wrong? Can I help in any way?"

She smiled nervously and shook her head. "Someone's been in the house. These officers are going to carry out a search to make sure they've gone."

"I don't suppose you've seen anything suspicious today?" asked the blonde-haired officer who had let him in. "No-one lurking about outside?"

William shook his head, trying to look as if he was thinking hard. "No. Nothing … and I've been around for most of the day. I only popped down the High Street for a pint of milk earlier."

"Okay. Would you mind sitting with Miss Denton while we check the house and garden?"

"Of course not. Miranda … should we go into your drawing room and should I get you a brandy?" William asked.

She nodded and let him guide her to the sofa, the dogs, puzzled as to all the activity in the middle of the night, following behind.

"I don't think there can be anyone here now," said the officer, "especially as your dogs aren't disturbed … but we'll make sure."

The two men disappeared, one to go out of the kitchen door to check the garden and the other made his way upstairs.

"Where do you keep the brandy, Miranda," asked William.

"In there," she replied, pointing to a polished oak cabinet in the corner which had belonged to Jeremy's father.

He found a bottle of Hennessy and poured a little into a brandy balloon and handed it to her.

"So, what makes you think you've had an intruder?" William asked, suddenly remembering smashing the photograph earlier. Oh, Christ! That must be what she had found. Seeing it must have terrified her. What a stupid move on his part that had been. He should have removed it. She would still have thought it odd but not see a wanton act of destruction. Still, there was nothing he could do about it now.

Her words confirmed his recollection. "A photo of Jeremy … it's been ruined," she whispered, her bottom lip trembling.

The dogs, unhappy she was so distressed, were sitting on either side of her. Nellie licked Miranda's hands and Charlie placed his head on her lap and fixed his gaze on her face.

"Oh, no. How awful," William replied, conscious that the policeman who had gone outside was now back in and opening and closing doors in the kitchen and then he heard his footsteps going down to the basement. He began to get fidgety and rolled the phial in his pocket round and round with his fingers. He wished they would hurry up and leave so he could get on with what he had to do. Miranda had drunk the brandy slowly and was now staring into space, with no inclination to make small talk and he didn't know what to say to her anyway.

On returning to the drawing-room, the blonde-haired officer looked grimly at Miranda.

"Everything seems in order, apart from your basement window, which was ajar and was probably the entry point. I've shut it but it's not locked as I couldn't see a key."

Miranda gasped and clapped her hand over her mouth. "Oh, good heavens. I haven't been down there today and I know it was locked yesterday as I checked ... and I leave the key on top of the electricity meter ... did you look there?"

"Yes, but didn't see it. I suggest you have all the locks changed tomorrow, just in case whoever it was has taken any keys for the main doors."

"Oh, hell. That's reassuring," Miranda groaned.

"I presume you didn't put the alarm on today when you went out?"

"No. I was in such a rush. I had so much to do ... I just forgot," she replied woefully. "I make sure it's on at night though."

"Well, put it on again after we leave and you should be safe ... especially with the dogs ... but I'd certainly think about changing the locks."

"It's all very strange," Miranda said. "What did they want? As far as I can see nothing is missing and the only way I knew anything was wrong was because of Jeremy's photo being so viciously destroyed. Who would do such a thing? Why come in and attack that and just leave? It all seems so odd."

"Um ... unless they were disturbed and scarpered. Oh, and you did mention on the telephone that your fiancé had the brakes tampered with on his car and he had a nasty accident. I don't want to alarm you Miss Denton but I'd have a good think about who has it in for him as it might not just be a would-be burglar you're dealing with. Now, we've secured the basement window and inspected everywhere, including all the cupboards and wardrobes and beneath the beds and we're completely satisfied there isn't anyone hiding. So, would you like us to contact a friend or a member of the family for you?"

"I'll stay as long as you need me," William stated quickly.

"Thank you ... that's very kind," Miranda whispered, ignoring William and looking up at the policeman. "I'll ring my friend, Anna. She lives down at Pampered Pets, you know the pet shop in the High Street. She'll come and keep me company. She'll bring her dogs too."

"Right. We'll leave you now as you're obviously quite safe with Mr Pemworthy until your friend arrives ... but don't hesitate to contact us if you feel threatened again."

Miranda walked with them into the hall and William headed back to the oak cabinet. He poured her another small brandy and added a couple of drops of the Rohypnol.

Miranda had waited until the police car had turned out of the drive before she shut the front door and then returned to the drawing-room.

"I'll ring Anna now," she said to William. "Oh, damn. My phone is in the bedroom and I haven't put her number in the home phone."

She started to turn towards the stairs but William put out a restraining hand. "Just drink this, my dear," offering her the glass of brandy. "It will make you feel better and let me ring Anna for you. I have her number in my phone," he said, removing it from his jacket pocket.

"Thank you," Miranda sighed, sinking back down onto the sofa with the glass in her hand. She was so tired and shaky, she would have accepted help from the devil himself at that point.

William pressed a number on his phone and waited a few minutes. "Anna," he said. "It's William."

Miranda had no idea he was talking into thin air.

****

William's heart was racing and his breathing was erratic. The dogs were getting in his way, milling around, sniffing and licking Miranda who was out cold on the sofa. He strode through to the kitchen and opened the fridge. Cheese. All dogs loved cheese, especially Charlie and Nellie. He knew because he had given them plenty in the park before now. He grabbed an open packet of shredded cheddar.

Hearing the fridge open, their attention was diverted from their mistress. They were behind him, alert and keen to take whatever he offered. William opened the basement door and slung the packet of cheese down the steps. They galloped after it. He slammed the door shut behind them.

He went to the kitchen door and unbolted it. The police had locked it with the key. He undid it and left it ajar. He returned to Miranda. Her blonde hair was strewn across the arm of the sofa, her beautiful eyes were shut and she was breathing softly. She looked divine and his heart filled with love for her. Her eyes were flickering and she moaned. He had to get on with it.

He picked her up and carried her through to the kitchen, down the outside steps and to the hedge at the bottom of the garden. He laid her on the grass, pulled the foliage aside, shuffled through and then dragged her by her shoulders through into his garden, whereupon he picked her up again and carried her quickly across his lawn, up the steps and into his kitchen. He kicked the door shut, panting with the exertion and excitement. Miranda was slim but to carry her such a long way and negotiate steps wasn't an easy task. He waited for a few moments, getting his breath back, the thrill of having her in his arms filling him with tenderness. Her soft hair brushed against his cheek, her eyelids flickered, she smelled of lavender. God, he felt such deep love and desire for her. He had never felt like this before. It completely consumed him. He slowly carried her upstairs to what was *her* bedroom and tied her hands to the brass railings of the bed with the blue rope. He covered her with a duvet. The heating was on but he didn't want her to get chilly.

He looked around the room with satisfaction. When she came round, she would see all the pictures of her on the walls. She would be delighted he had taken such an interest in her ... and then there was the crucifix and the altar. She would see he was a devout and good person and he would ask her to pray with him. She would like that.

Locking the door behind him, he slipped stealthily back to No.10. He didn't like the idea of the dogs being shut up in the basement all night. He let them out into the garden for a wee and gave them a bowl of dog food and fresh water in case no-one turned up to look for Miranda the next day. He certainly didn't want them to be hungry or uncomfortable. After all, he was a kind and considerate person. He locked the kitchen door and went home to Miranda.

CHAPTER 23

Miranda stirred and opened her eyes a couple of times throughout the night to discover she had the most appalling hangover, an awareness that something was badly wrong and excruciatingly painful arms but within seconds, drifted back into a deep sleep.

But now it was daylight and although she was properly awake, she felt dreadful. Her head was pounding, there was a sharp pain in her stomach and she wanted to be sick. Her whole body felt cold and clammy, even though she was covered up by a heavily patterned duvet which reeked of mothballs. She hated that smell.

Her arms were going numb. She couldn't understand why until she looked up and saw her hands tied to either side of the bed with blue nylon rope which was chafing her wrists and making them sore. Thankfully, her legs were free. She began to think she was dreaming. Where was she? Why was she tied up? Why did she feel as if she had been on a bender last night? She couldn't remember going out … couldn't remember much about last night at all apart from having her tea and falling asleep on the sofa. Did she have a bath? Did she go to bed? Where were the dogs? So many questions and she had no answers.

Her eyes weren't focusing very well and she blinked a few times to clear her vision and trying not to move her head in case it made the headache worse, looked around the room. She didn't recognise it although it seemed familiar. It was bizarre, like being in her own house in a room she had never been in. The size and period of the room and the style of the windows were the same but the walls were a grim grey. She disliked that shade and would never have used such a depressing colour.

Then she began to feel a terrible, chilling fear when she saw the wall exactly opposite her. The top half was covered from one side to the other with pictures of her … in the park … some with, some without the dogs. In all of them, she was laughing. She didn't feel like laughing now.

Her fear turned to terror when, beneath the photos, she saw the gold crucifix on the wall and three large white candles and a bible resting on a small altar. She started to shake. This sort of thing happened in films ... to other women. She must be dreaming. She must!

****

William looked at his watch. It was 9.00 a.m. and nothing was stirring at No.10. It was exactly as he had left it. He hoped the dogs were ok. He had considered going to let them out for a wee but that secretary woman might turn up at any minute so he wouldn't risk it and anyway, he had important things to attend to here.

He headed up to 'Miranda's' room. He had popped in a couple of times during the night to check on her but she had been dead to the world and he had resisted the urge to touch her, to stroke her face and play with her hair as he watched her breathing in the light from the landing.

However, she was more than likely awake by now and probably hungry. Oh, he was so pleased to have her here, under his very own roof. He felt a rush of pleasure as he reached her room and opened the door.

The duvet had slipped off the bed and he gulped. She was still fully clothed in what she had thrown on to greet the police last night, a pale blue sweater and navy leggings. He had thought about undressing her to begin with but that would have stirred up the itch and he really didn't want to stoop to raping her. She was too precious.

"Hello, Miranda," he said softly, pleased to see she was awake although she was staring at him with shock and horror. "How are you feeling? I'm so sorry to do this to you but you'll soon see, it's for the best."

"You!" she hissed, her eyes wide with fear and loathing. "I might have known. I've had a bad feeling about you for a while now. How dare you do this to me. Damn well untie me and let me go. You'll regret it if you don't. Jeremy will kill you!"

"Now, now, my darling. Don't be like that. I had to do it. I had to get you away from him so that you could learn to love me as I do you."

Miranda closed her eyes tightly and he noticed her whole body was shaking. He walked towards her. "Are you cold, my love? Here, let me make you warmer."

Her eyes shot open again but he was making no attempt to touch her, just pulling up the duvet until it reached her neck. The smell of mothballs was overpowering.

"I've such plans for us, Miranda. You will learn to love me, I promise you, and then we can have a wonderful life together. I've bought a camper van. We can take off in it. Go wherever you like … all your favourite places. We can have wonderful adventures together, just you and me. It will be fantastic, I promise you."

She shut her eyes again. He looked down at her, feeling the itch. He badly wanted to rape her there and then but for once he had to control himself. He wanted her to love him. He wanted her to want it as much as he did, not struggle and scream like the others … then all would be well. No, he had to be patient and in a few days it would happen. He just knew it would. He sighed with contentment. She was his now and she wasn't going anywhere.

"I'll get you something to eat," he said. "I've made some porridge and there's toast and marmalade and coffee. You'll feel much better then."

"I want the loo," she muttered.

"Okay. I'll untie you and take you across the landing to the bathroom." He knew she couldn't get out. He had boarded up the window … and anyway, they were on the top floor and she'd break her neck if she jumped from there. He had considered boarding up the window in this room but hated thinking of her remaining in permanent darkness so he had left it alone, even though it overlooked No.10. However, he had taken the precaution of adding extra locks so it was impossible for her to open it.

He untied her. She sat on the bed and rubbed her wrists and arms. They were stiff and sore and it took a little time for them to come back to life. "This won't work, William. You can't keep me here?" she said through gritted teeth.

"Miranda," he said softly. "I love you. I've always loved you, right from the moment I set eyes on you in the park. I want to marry you and have you live here with me. We're going to be so happy, my darling. Believe me. Once you've got your head around this, you'll see it's the right thing to do and you won't regret it, I promise you."

Her brain was beginning to wake up, the fog was beginning to lift. She looked at him with realisation. "Christ! You didn't limp when you crossed the room." She paused, staring at him with shock. "You're not just William, you're pretending to be flaming Stephen as well," she gasped, a great shudder running through her body as he grinned back at her. "I knew there was something odd about you ... about Stephen. I'm right, aren't I?"

In answer, he whipped off the bald wig, glasses and moustache, having put them on this morning in case the police came calling again.

She gasped. "Oh, God!"

"Now there's another thing ... please don't blaspheme, Miranda. I don't like that. I gather you've seen my little altar. I pray there every day, mainly that you will be here with me ... and God has answered. So, perhaps we should both kneel and say a prayer of thanks."

"I need the flaming loo," she cried. "If I kneel down, I'm going to bloody pee myself and I don't think you or God will like that very much!"

212

The complaints began around 1.00 p.m. Belinda was walking her pack of dogs in Roundhay park when her mobile rang twice with quick succession. Both clients wanted to know why Miranda hadn't picked up their dogs. She apologised profusely and promised to find out what was going on as this was most unlike her boss who was adamant that no client should ever be let down.

Puzzled but not particularly alarmed, she rang Miranda. There was no answer, which was strange as Miranda never ignored her just in case there was something wrong. Not sure if Gail was working today, Belinda tried No.10's house phone. Gail had just arrived, having had the morning off, surprised to see a restless Nellie and Charlie home in the middle of the day with no sign of Miranda.

With growing trepidation, Belinda rang Anna. She had no knowledge of Miranda's whereabouts either.

"Is her car in the garage?" Anna asked, growing concerned.

"I'll get Gail to check," Belinda replied.

Gail found the key and had a look. The Volvo was there. As a precaution she ran through the house, concerned Miranda might have fallen upstairs or was ill in bed. She wasn't. She rang Belinda. Belinda rang Anna.

"Perhaps something has happened to her parents. Perhaps she's at the hospital with them," Anna said.

"But she would have contacted me to see to all the dogs … and there are quite a few cats which needed feeding this morning. She wouldn't have abandoned all of them," Belinda replied.

"I know. It's exceedingly strange and not like her at all," Anna agreed. Where on earth could Miranda be? "I'll ring her parents. Just in case. I don't want to worry them but if something has happened there, at least we'll know."

"And if it hasn't?"

"I think it's a matter for the police."

Within half an hour they were all at the house, including the police. Anna arrived first, running up the road and charging straight into No. 10 to join Gail who had discovered the broken glass and ripped up picture of Jeremy.

"Come and look at this, Anna," she said, hurrying her up the stairs.

Anna felt sick. Something seriously bad must have happened to Miranda because this certainly wasn't her handiwork.

Miranda's parents arrived next in their dark blue Ford Escort, Sheila white and wringing her hands anxiously, George looking drawn and uncertain what to say or do.

Behind Miranda's parents were Andy and a young constable by the name of John Dixon in a police car. They had been informed by their colleagues that a call had been made from No.10 the night before and what had occurred and they relayed it to the concerned group.

"It seems whoever broke in obviously came back, although Miranda did have William from next door with her when our colleagues left her. We'd better speak to him," Andy said, patting Anna on the shoulder and striding off down the path.

Belinda shot up the drive in her white van and into the house to collect the keys for the cats and dogs Miranda hadn't seen to. "Julie, Kate and I are going to split it all between us … I'll take Charlie and Nellie too. Keep me informed of progress," she yelled as she and the dogs dashed to her van.

Anna walked into the kitchen, a cold feeling in the pit of her stomach. Gail was trying to be useful, making cups of tea and piling in the sugar. Miranda's parents were slumped at the table, holding hands, Sheila trying hard not to cry. Anna sat down beside her and took her other hand.

****

William was in the room next to Miranda's and had seen it all from the windows which overlooked No.10 and Miller Lane. He knew she couldn't hear all the activity as he had put sleeping tablets in her breakfast and when he had checked a few minutes ago, she was out for the count. She looked so uncomfortable with her hands tied up again, he had relented and undid them. She wasn't going anywhere now she was fast asleep.

He debated about moving her to The Cedars tonight, when it was dark, where it would be far safer to keep her. He could easily carry her out to the van as the garage couldn't be seen from No.10. Driving past her family, friends and the police with her comatose in his vehicle would certainly be a triumph.

They could remain at The Cedars. She wouldn't have to be doped up as no-one would hear her if she yelled, only the birds and rabbits in the fields surrounding the house. He could have taken her there last night, immediately after abducting her, but had wanted to watch the goings-on next door and didn't want to miss the sainted Jeremy coming home. He wanted to witness his anguish ... see him hurting. That would give him the utmost pleasure.

He saw the policeman, that Andy somebody or other, Anna's boyfriend, head for the gates. Taking a deep breath, William ran down the stairs, strode out of the house, down the garden path and shot back the bolts.

"You need one of those gate entry systems," Andy said, "how did you know I was here?"

"Funnily enough, Sergeant, I've ordered one and it should be installed in the next week or so ... and I saw you. I was in the bedroom and couldn't help but notice all the hubbub next door and was about to come round to ask if everything was okay, especially after the events of last night ... and then I saw you heading in my direction."

Andy cleared his throat. "I'm afraid Miranda has gone missing and according to my colleagues, they left her with you at around

10.00 pm. Apparently, she was intending to ring Anna. Do you know if she tried to as Anna says she didn't hear from her?"

"She changed her mind and said she wanted to go to bed instead so I left a few minutes after the two policemen. I heard her bolt the front door after me ... but isn't she out and about feeding cats or walking dogs?"

"No. Her car is still in the garage and none of the animals have been seen to."

"Oh, dear," William said, wringing his hands. "Whatever could have happened to her? Poor girl. She was so scared last night ... if only she had let me stay or contacted a family member ... or Anna. I do hope she's alright."

"Yes, so do we. Thank you, William. If you've nothing further to tell us we'll start making other enquiries but we might want to speak to you again."

William nodded as Andy walked back to No.10. He re-bolted the gates and kept his expression serious in case anyone was watching him from the windows next door. He entered the house, shut the door and beamed widely. It had worked. They simply had no idea Miranda was only yards away, safe and sound and sleeping like a baby.

****

Having been alerted to Miranda's disappearance by Anna, Jeremy was on his way home, speeding up the motorway in his new black Range Rover as fast as he dared. He was terrified for Miranda and furious with himself. He should have never left her alone in the house. Even if he couldn't have been there, he should have made sure Tricia or her parents or even Anna or Belinda ... was with her after what had happened to him. Who the hell had it in for them? Who wanted to hurt them, kill him and abduct Miranda? Because that was what had happened. She wouldn't have gone off on her own, without her car, money or her dogs and she loved her parents too much to worry them and then there was the business. She was meticulously conscientious and would never have abandoned the animals. So, there was only one explanation. Someone had taken her ... but why? What were they going to do with her? Rape her? Kill her? Oh, God, he felt so sick, so frightened for her. He loved her so much and if something happened to her .... He put his foot down even harder, uncaring if he was breaking the speed limit. The sooner he hit Leeds and helped with the search the better.

****

Detective Inspector Philips and Detective Sergeant Williams arrived. They questioned everyone in the house, asking numerous questions about Miranda and her usual movements. They wanted to know about her previous mental health and her present state of mind. They walked around the house, they listened to Miranda's messages on the home phone and her mobile, they spent a lot of time in the basement and requested forensic samples from the window and the remnants of Jeremy's photo and frame. Uniformed police went from door to door along Miller Lane, with the exception of William's house as Andy reported he had already talked to him. A team of constables were sent to search the park but by the time Jeremy arrived, two hours later, no-one was the wiser as to where Miranda could be.

Jeremy was distraught and kept running his hand through his hair repeatedly. He hugged Anna, shook Miranda's father's hand and kissed her mother on the cheek. He looked at the two detectives.

"Where the hell is she? Who could have done this? I'm positive it has to be the same person who cut the brakes on my car. Miranda has no enemies. Everyone loves her ... so it has to be connected. It has to be something to do with me," he said helplessly, suddenly overwhelmed by tiredness and intense anxiety and sinking into a chair at the kitchen table.

Gail made him a strong tea and then Inspector Williams took him through to the drawing-room to question him alone, going over and over what had occurred with the Jaguar, trying to find a reason for Miranda to be abducted. He came up with nothing.

"The only hope is that we will receive a ransom note or a phone call very soon."

"But we're not rich," Jeremy exploded. "Okay, we're comfortable but not exactly loaded. We've bought this house with my inheritance and savings but after I've paid for the wedding and the honeymoon and invested in my new business, all we have is my army salary until I leave next year and Miranda's business … oh, and any proceeds from the sale of her house, which is due to go through soon … but that aside, why would they have tried to kill me?"

"I don't know, sir. It's all very puzzling."

"Oh, God! I can't stand this. I'm going out to look for her," Jeremy said angrily.

"Where?"

"Oh, I don't know. Anywhere. I can't sit here like this, doing nothing. I've got to find her. Miranda is the most important person in my life. I just have to."

With that, he marched out of the house, down the drive and into the park. He could see uniformed policemen dotted around, talking to walkers, joggers and cyclists and that new park keeper, Bob Watkins, but they all seemed to be shaking their heads, indicating they hadn't seen her. Jeremy's heart sank even further. Her car was in the garage, the bed wasn't slept in, she wasn't in the park, she hadn't been to feed the cats this morning. Where the hell was she?

****

William was thoroughly enjoying himself watching the goings-on next door. He saw the detectives arrive and then he witnessed Jeremy driving through the gates, looking dishevelled and upset. Then he saw him a while later, hurrying out and turning left towards the entrance to the park.

William shot to the rear window in 'Miranda's' room. She moaned and flung an arm out but didn't wake.

He scanned the park. In the distance, he could make out a policeman talking to Harry with his four Great Danes. Another was in conversation with the Vicar and Samantha. Two more were walking around the lake, scouring the water and heading up the path towards the woods. Then he saw Jeremy. He was standing still, staring around the park with his hand shielding his eyes. William grinned broadly. No doubt the poor man was in tumult. No doubt he was feeling sick and worried, full of fear for Miranda, not knowing what was happening and whether he would ever see her again. William's grin grew even broader as he turned to look at her.

****

Anna returned to Pampered Pets to collect Rio and Dolly mid-afternoon and to make sure all was well with the shop. Emily, Becky and Lois assured her that it was and they would lock up so she could concentrate on Miranda's dilemma.

Anna gave the dogs a brief walk in the park, noting how the police presence had increased, which reassured and alarmed her at the same time. It was good they were being so diligent but so far with no luck and time was ticking on. She took the dogs back to No.10 where despair was rife.

Gail left for home at 5.00 p.m., having made sandwiches and pots of tea for everyone and dealing with everything that needed doing for Four Paws as regards paperwork and telephone calls from the office on the top floor.

"I'll return in the morning, even though it's not one of my days but please ring me before then if there's any news," she said to Anna. "I've only known Miranda a short time but she seems a strong and determined young woman and I'm sure she will be dealing admirably with whatever she has to and will be home soon."

"Thank you," Anna said tearfully. She gave Gail a hug and watched her walk down the drive towards Miller Lane.

An exhausted looking Belinda brought Charlie and Nellie home a few minutes later. "Kate and Julie have been marvellous," she reported. "Between us, we managed to walk all the dogs, even though some were going out really late and were desperate, poor things, and we're now sharing the cats. I'll just check the bookings to see if there are any extras in the morning and if there are, I'll take the keys for them too. I presume there's no news?"

Anna shook her head miserably. Belinda grimaced and continued upstairs to the office.

Miranda's parents weren't going anywhere, waiting anxiously, not knowing what else to do. Tricia had finished her shift at Tesco's and had joined them, frequently bursting into tears and not helping anyone at all. Griselda and Paul were on a break in the Lake District but had been informed and were on their way home.

Jeremy returned from the park and frequently checked his phone in case Miranda was trying to contact him as he paced up and down the garden. He strode back out into Miller Lane and to the High Street, praying Miranda would suddenly appear. He walked to the church, which was open, sat down in the nearest pew and pleaded with God for her safe return. He talked to everyone that was entering or leaving the park. He paced the High street, looking in all the shops. He returned to No 10, hoping she would have turned up in his absence.

The police had contacted all the hospitals in and around Leeds to no avail. Reporters started turning up at the gates, taking pictures of the comings and goings. The police gave them a statement and a picture of Miranda. It was in the evening papers.

'Miranda Denton', owner of Four Paws petsitting service, is missing from her home in Peesdown. She was last seen around 10.00 p.m. last night. There is considerable concern for her safety and if anyone can provide any information as to her whereabouts, please contact your local police station as a matter of urgency.' There was more about the business, her engagement to Jeremy and the forthcoming wedding.

Sheila, George and Tricia decided to stay the night and Anna made up beds for them in the guest rooms, guessing that even if they did venture upstairs, they would get little sleep. She kept glancing out of the windows, wishing she could see Miranda playing with the dogs in the garden and grinning up at her, telling her it was all some crazy joke. It didn't happen. Where was she? What on earth had occurred? Why hadn't she managed to get to a phone and ring someone?

It was nearly dark as Anna finished making the last bed and she glanced across at William's house. It was strange he had put in an appearance last night … and stayed with Miranda. Why, if she was frightened and upset about the damaged picture of Jeremy, hadn't she rung her? She would have hurtled down here with the dogs and they could have stayed the night. Why depend on William, especially as Miranda had voiced how she had been a bit uneasy about him.

Anna was on the top floor of No.10 in the front bedroom opposite the office. She narrowed her eyes and looked across at William's house, bit her lip and thought about him. He had always seemed harmless enough but Miranda had been wary of him lately and then there was the Stephen episode which was all a bit strange with Miranda thinking he and William not only looked very similar but sounded the same, which Anna had to admit was a trifle odd. She knew two sets of identical twins and even though they looked alike, their voices weren't exactly the same. With a jolt, she realised that although Stephen was supposed to live somewhere near Bath, he didn't speak with a west country accent. It sounded more Liverpudlian ... just like William. With her hand to her mouth, Anna experienced a flashback from when she and William were leaving church, remembering seeing him begin to stride down Miller Lane and then start to limp, as if he suddenly remembered to do it.

Anna sat down on the bed and thought hard. Was William to be trusted? After all, they knew little about him as they only chatted to him in the park or when he popped into Pampered Pets. He had attended the housewarming party and been generous with his presents but he hadn't stayed long after his tour of the house.

By all accounts, William had only been living in Peesdown for a short time although she wasn't exactly sure how long because he was here before her. He was pleasant enough and helpful. After all, look how he had assisted when she moved into Pampered Pets and the interest he took in the shop even though he hadn't a pet of his own.

Anna tried hard to recall things Miranda had said about William and Stephen, remembering the comment about how the two men were never seen together and there was always an excuse as to why not. That was strange in itself. Could they be the same man? Could William or Stephen or whoever he was, have an ulterior motive in their friendship with Miranda? What had happened here after the police had left last night? Had William departed to go home as he told them he had or had he remained here and done something to Miranda?

It was odd that he hadn't set foot in the grounds of No.10 all day today? She knew Andy had spoken to him at lunchtime but even so, why hadn't he come round since to see if there was any news? The people next door had popped in and asked if there was anything they could do, as had the Vicar and Samantha, who brought sandwiches and cake. Andy and Liz from the Red Lion had also rung and offered to carry out another search of the park, along with some of their clientele and despite the police being confident Miranda wasn't and hadn't been in the park since yesterday, a crowd from the pub set out around 7.00 pm to scour the park and woods again. So far nothing of interest had been found. Someone, Anna couldn't remember who, had suggested sending down divers into the lake but the police ruled it out as it was apparent Miranda, much in love with her fiancé with a wedding in the offing, a home she was thrilled to move into and a thriving business, had no suicidal tendencies.

However, in all this activity and concern for Miranda's welfare, there had been no sign of William, who was always so keen to talk to her in the park, lighting up as soon as she made an appearance and hanging on to her every word.

Anna ran her fingers through her hair and tugged it with anguish. Was she being overly suspicious? Was she making a mountain out of a molehill? God, she was so tired now, she could barely think straight. She needed to be with the others. She needed a cup of tea.

They were all exhausted now. The detectives had left to do whatever detectives did in cases like this, leaving a woman police constable called Wendy as family liaison officer. She remained in the kitchen most of the time, taking over from Gail and making endless cups of tea and sitting beside Miranda's mum, trying to make conversation.

"I've made up beds for everyone. Would you like me to stay too?" Anna asked Jeremy who was slumped over the kitchen table, his head in his hands. He looked up tearfully at Anna.

"God, Anna. I don't know what to do. I feel so bloody useless."

She sat down beside him and put a hand on his shoulder. "I know. I feel the same. I hope to God nothing really bad has happened to her."

They stared at each other with tears in their eyes and a deep feeling of dread in their hearts.

Jeremy's voice broke. "Who could have done this, Anna? Who?"

CHAPTER 24

Miranda slept solidly all day. Already exhausted from working so hard for months, her body did little to resist the slumber, even though her mind wanted it to. When she did wake, it was in semi-darkness and she had no idea if it was early morning or late evening or how long she had been kept captive. William or Stephen, or whoever the hell he was, must have given her something strong to keep her quiet but while she was out for the count she wasn't scared. She certainly was now, remembering clearly what he had shown her after he spoon-fed her a breakfast of sickeningly sweet porridge and skimmed milk, which she loathed. She had forced it down, knowing she had to keep her strength up if there was any chance of getting away but it was what came after she had finished the last drop of the ghastly well-sugared coffee he gave her, that the real horror began.

"Let me show you your pictures properly. You probably can't see them too well from the bed," he said, pulling her upright and propelling her over to the wall of photos.

"Do you remember this ... and this ... and I love this one," he pointed to individual pictures of her, his voice cracking with emotion. "I have a larger version of that beside my bed."

There was a hard knot of fear in her stomach which was growing more intense as she stared at the images of herself, having been totally unaware he was hiding away in bushes and behind trees, clicking away with his blasted camera for months, all the while pretending to be her friend.

He had taken her back to the bed, made her sit and then took out a big box and a scrapbook from a chest of drawers in the corner of the room. "Now these, you will be interested in," he gloated. "But there will be no more of this, Miranda. Now that I have you, I shan't need to find any more whores."

He showed her the photos in the scrapbook of various girls, naming them all. He then produced locks of hair for each one and then the jewellery, the earrings, the necklaces, the bracelets. "I raped and strangled them all," he said proudly. "I sent them off to heaven so they could be pardoned for their sins and I'm sure they must be looking down on me, thanking me for sending them off in such a spectacular fashion before they could sin again. And here are another two ladies," he added, producing a photo of a smiling chubby woman on what looked like a Caribbean beach and then handed her another. "And you probably knew this one ... Tanya Philips."

Miranda stifled a cry as she saw lovely Tanya floating in Peesdown Park lake.

"Oh yes," William smiled, "that was me too. Crazy woman wanted to walk around the lake at night. Only women of the gutter do that sort of thing. She had to be saved," he sniggered.

Miranda had often thought the phrase 'blood turning to water,' was a bit weird but she knew what it meant now. She began to panic, she wanted to scream, she wanted, more than anything, to escape before this mad man did something equally as awful to her as those poor women he had violated and murdered, no matter that he insisted he loved her. He was crazy, totally insane and as she looked down at the blue rope around her wrists, she knew she was in terrible danger.

"Don't you like my trophies, Miranda?" he said, running his fingers down her cheek.

She shook her head. "Not much," she said with a croak.

"But I have one of yours ... look."

He pulled out the toggle from her duffle coat and she had to force her stomach to behave before the hated porridge ended up in his lap.

"It came off your coat and I managed to grab it before you saw it. It's been one of my favourite possessions, Miranda, because it belongs to you ... but now, I have all of you ... what could be better, my darling?"

226

He then told her about his last victim … and his parents … and finally left her, shaking so violently she could hear her knees knocking, re-tying her to the bed and covering her up with the disgusting duvet. She must have passed out so the semi-darkness must mean it was probably evening. She had no real idea. She had totally lost track of time.

Physically, she was stiff and sore and sick to the stomach of smelling mothballs. She could vaguely remember him untying her wrists but unless it was a dream, they were wrapped in the blue rope again and her arms were protesting madly with an ache so intense she could have screamed.

God, she had to get out of here! He had left the box of his precious trophies and the scrapbook on the little altar. She thought about all those poor women he had made suffer so terribly, especially poor Tanya. She had been such a lovely person, living quite happily with her cat, Marmite, and if she wanted to walk around the park at night, as daft as it was, she had been quite entitled to do so without ending up as she did.

Then there was that poor woman on the cruise.

"Tilly was besotted with me," he had grinned. "And asked for it. She thought I was going to fall in love with her and marry her. Daft female. She soon found out different," he gloated, relaying exactly what he had done to her, drowning her in the sea on a deserted island and pretending it had been an accident because she couldn't swim.

Miranda had swiftly concluded that William was totally cold-blooded but it was his last confession which had been even more appalling, if that was possible.

"It all started with these two," William murmured, handing her a photograph of a middle-aged couple. "They are my parents. I strangled them too. Oh, don't upset yourself, Miranda," he said, seeing the tears welling up in her eyes. "They deserved it and they loved God so much, they would have been pleased to be with him earlier than they had expected. You might even remember the case, although it was in Liverpool, where we lived at the time. There was a right hullabaloo. The police were convinced it was me but I had an alibi. I had been to the pictures, I had the ticket and someone I knew saw me outside, so I got away with it … and inherited all the businesses, the house and loads and loads of lovely money. Oh, Miranda. I had such a wonderful time in Europe afterwards … I was completely free, with plenty of cash to do as I wanted … and all those women … but that all stops now, Miranda … thanks to you."

She could vaguely remember his parents being murdered. She recognised them from the photo. It had been on news bulletins for days. Christ, what a truly evil man he was … and she was completely at his mercy, the only difference being he kept insisting he loved her and wanted to settle down with her. God forbid! He hadn't admitted it but she guessed it was him who destroyed Jeremy's picture and tampered with the brakes on his car. He had obviously wanted Jeremy out of the way.

She wondered why he hadn't raped her. After all, there had been plenty of opportunities today and she was in no position to put up a fight. Anyway, whatever the reason, she was thankful he hadn't, although she had a nasty feeling it was what he intended at some point. Please God, was she ever going to get out of this alive? She was more terrified than she had ever been in her life and prayed that someone in her own house would make a connection. Anna knew about the doubts she was having regarding William. Hopefully she would put two and two together.

She tried hard to undo the knots in the rope around her wrists. She could just about reach them with her teeth if she twisted her body at a most uncomfortable angle which wasn't possible to keep up for too long as it killed her back. She worked on her right wrist first as it seemed the looser of the two and if she could get that one undone then it would be easier to do the other as she was right-handed.

With tears of exasperation beginning to fall, she had nearly given up when all of a sudden one of the knots gave way and it became easier to unravel the others.

With a grunt of triumph, she gently pulled her arms down and massaged them. Her wrists were red and sore but she could do nothing about them now. She sat up but still felt woozy and lightheaded and wondered if she could stand up without falling down. But she had to if she wanted to save her life because deep down, she had a horrible feeling that not only was William intending to rape her but at some point, he would eventually kill her too. She had to get out of here and fast. She hadn't heard him moving about the house ever since she woke up so perhaps he was sleeping. She glanced at the gold cross and prayed that he was and she could take him by surprise.

She stood up. Her head spun a bit but within seconds steadied. She knew there was no point in trying the door as she had heard him lock it. She struggled to the window instead. Her heart flipped over when she saw Anna in the garden of No.10 with Charlie, Nellie, Dolly and Rio, trying to get them to have a wee. Jeremy's new Range Rover was on the drive as was her parents' Ford Escort. She wanted to cry, knowing they were all there, probably sick with worry for her. If they only knew she was so damned close.

Anna was on her way back to the kitchen door, the dogs following on behind. In seconds they would be inside and her chance would have gone. She had to get Anna's attention … and now.

The window was locked and the key was missing so there was no alternative but to break the bloody thing. She looked around the room. desperately trying to find a weapon. There was a wooden chair in the corner of the room. She hurried over to grab it and on returning to the window, thanked Charlie under her breath. He was proving reluctant to go indoors and Anna was doing her best to persuade him. Wonderful dog. He would have a couple of extra biscuits when she got home.

With all the strength she could muster with her arms still frightfully weak, she smashed the spindly legs of the stool through the small panes of the sash window, which thankfully weren't double glazed.

"Anna!" she screamed hysterically. "Anna! I'm up here. For God's sake come and get me!"

****

William heard her. He was in the back garden, cutting some red roses to present with the milky coffee he was going to prepare for her at bedtime, with the addition of another couple of sleeping tablets to keep her quiet when he moved her to The Cedars later.

He heard the glass smash. He heard her scream to Anna. He heard Anna scream back. "Oh, my God! Miranda! I'll get Jeremy."

Bugger! The game was up and he had to get away and damned quick. The police would be here in minutes. He dashed indoors, grabbed the BMW's car keys from a kitchen drawer and hurtled back out again and through the cutting in the hedge into the park. He could hear a commotion next door and Miranda was still screaming out of the window.

Shit, shit, shit! He had been so bloody stupid. Why the hell hadn't he taken her to The Cedars last night and kept her there? It had been ludicrous to keep her so close to her own home. If he didn't get caught, he would be bloody lucky and now she knew about his other victims, he would go down for a hell of a long time, probably wouldn't ever be let out again.

He scrambled hastily through the undergrowth and keeping under cover, peered down at the lake. There was very little activity now it was getting dark. The police had given up their search and disappeared and there were just a few people on their way back to the car park.

He kept out of sight in the bushes, running as fast as he dared in case he came across anyone nosing around. His luck held. He reached the woods and hurried along the winding paths, stopping briefly to look back at his house. It was lit up like a belisha beacon, probably swarming with police and all those bloody people next door, including the hated Jeremy.

He seethed with anger as he reached the top part of the woods where a lane led from the main road to the golf course and Linley Close, where stood several beautiful old detached houses. The BMW was under a street lamp on the opposite side of the road. Having changed its number plates, he had left it there when 'Stephen' had supposedly left Leeds and just in case he needed it in a hurry. It didn't look out of place in the area, surrounded by Mercedes sports cars, Volvo XC90's, Audi TT's and a Jaguar E type which would certainly create the most interest.

He jumped in, started the engine and drove it quietly down the lane towards the York road. He had to get to his hideout as fast as possible. That was one good thing. He hadn't told Miranda about it so she couldn't tell anyone else. He should be safe there for a day or so and when the hubbub died down, he could venture further afield maybe. Head for Scotland or Wales with the camper van. Shit! Miranda knew about the camper van and the police would start checking them … and he couldn't go back for the van. Bugger. He only had the bloody BMW and he couldn't live in that! God! What a bloody idiot he had been, not getting her out of Miller Lane last night. He really could kick himself. "Stupid, stupid, stupid," he growled, thumping the steering wheel.

He wouldn't normally have hesitated in driving up the A64 to York but he wasn't going that way now. He had often seen police on that part of the road, stopping people for speeding. He wanted to avoid them at all costs. He headed for Garforth instead, driving slowly and steadily so as not to bring attention to himself. He drove past Lotherton Hall, a beautiful Edwardian mansion run by Leeds City Council, and on to Saxton and then Towton where there had been that dreadful battle in 1461 during the war of the roses when thousands had been killed. He turned left for Ulleskelf. It was a much longer journey this way but with far less chance of being seen and stopped by the police. He eventually came to a crossroads, drove sedately through Acaster Selby and onto Bishopthorpe where he could eventually backtrack towards Appleton Roebuck and his second home.

By the time he reached The Cedars, he was exhausted. He jumped out of the car, opened the gates, drove through and locked them behind him. He drove the car round to the side of the house, opened the garage and left it inside next to the camper van. He locked it and went indoors, drawing all the curtains and making sure the doors and windows were secure. Then he sat on the sofa and tried to stop shaking.

****

They had all charged round to William's house as soon as Anna had burst into the kitchen and yelled that Miranda was next door, not stopping to ring the police although the female constable who was staying with them radioed it through as she ran with them.

They were stalled at William's gates which were bolted from the inside. Jeremy hurled himself against them again and again but all he achieved was a bruised shoulder. Miranda had gone silent which was even more terrifying and Jeremy had never been so scared in his life. He had to get to her.

"We can't wait. He could be doing anything to her in there," he yelled, dashing back for his Range Rover. He had the keys in his pocket. He fired it up, turned it around so fast the gravel spat over the lawns on either side of the drive, and burst out of the gates of No. 10.

"Get out of the way," he yelled. "I'm going to ram the damned things."

He was glad he had bought a Range Rover this time around, the Jaguar might have done the job but not as quickly. He drove straight at the gates. The sound of metal on wood was deafeningly loud but the gates, although badly damaged, creaked and groaned but didn't move. Jeremy did it again, reversing back to the opposite side of the road, revving the engine and letting out the clutch sharply. The Range Rover shot across the road and smashed into the gates. With an almighty bang, they flew open and he drove through at speed, stamping on the brakes in front of the house.

With the police officer, Anna, Sheila, George and Tricia behind him, he tore up the steps to the front door and turned the handle but it was locked.

"Open this bloody door now, William, or I'll break your bloody neck," he yelled.

He gave it two seconds. "Round the back," he panted. They all followed him, assuming that the kitchen door would be the same but were surprised to find it standing wide open. With Jeremy still taking the lead, they dashed up the stairs.

"It's the top floor," Anna panted. "The room at the rear overlooking yours."

Jeremy was there seconds before the rest of them. He threw open the door to find Miranda, sitting on the bed, shaking and crying uncontrollably, rubbing her arms and wrists.

"Oh, Miranda. Oh, my darling," Jeremy exclaimed, rushing over and throwing his arms around her. "What the hell has that maniac done to you?"

****

William was utterly exhausted but deeply worried that he was about to be caught, he couldn't rest properly. He dozed but he was on the alert all the time, listening for sounds of traffic, for police cars arriving at the door but by dawn, nothing had occurred and only the early morning commuters or the odd tractor drove past.

He began to breathe more easily. He turned on the radio to listen to the local news. It was the top item.

"Miranda Denton, the missing professional petsitter from Leeds, has been found safe and well. However, the police are now searching for a William Pemworthy who is also wanted in connection with other crimes and is considered to be dangerous. If anyone knows his present whereabouts, possibly travelling in a motor home, please do not approach but contact your local police station immediately.'

Shit, shit, shit! He would have to stay here now. He could have cried. If only he had brought Miranda with him right from the off. They could have been here for weeks and weeks. Now he was all alone. Hell, he had been bloody stupid this time. All those years, all those crimes and he had never been caught. He hadn't much wriggle room now and he could feel the noose tightening. He frantically tried to think about the best course of action. If he left here in the BMW, he would soon be caught as he would need somewhere to stay. He might get away with it for a while in one of his disguises but it was probably only a matter of time. If only he had brought his passports here, he could have flown abroad at some point, perhaps in a few months when the hue and cry calmed down. If only, if only, if only! Stupid, stupid, stupid! Now he was stuck in the UK with his William disguise, which he would have to ditch because he would be easily recognisable but Miranda and Anna, and Jeremy come to that … and a few other people in Peesdown, knew him as Stephen without it.

Christ, he was done for. His only hope was remaining here, hope the fuss would die down and then make a run for it … how long would that be … a week, a month, two? He had enough food and things to keep him occupied for that length of time but then he would need to go out for more food. He could buy some more disguises online and have them delivered but he still didn't have any paperwork to go with them. No ID, no passports.

However, for the moment it was obvious no-one knew where he was so he was relatively safe for a while but if the worst came to the worst and he was found, he did have a solution, a final way out because whatever happened, he was not going to prison to spend the rest of his life on a sex offenders wing!

****

Miranda told the police everything she could remember. She told them how William had abducted her and then what he had told her about his parents and other victims, and their photos and belongings he had collected. She would never forget seeing the toggle from her duffle coat in his hands as he caressed it. She could never wear that coat again and it would be off to a charity shop the very next day.

Having questioned Miranda, the police searched William's house and grounds. There was no sign of him but a keen-eyed constable noticed the hedge at the bottom of the rear garden had a big gap and there were fresh marks on the ground where someone had crawled through. A search party was sent straight into the park, naturally assuming William was on foot as his van was still in the garage.

Confident he would soon be found, they took their time going through the evidence in the bedroom Miranda had been held in, pulling on rubber gloves and shoe protectors before entering. They took a quick look at the photos of Miranda on the wall before examining the trophy box and scrapbook.

"Looks like we can close the case on poor Tanya, Gov," remarked Sergeant Williams," and it looks like the same can be said for all these other women."

"Yes, Sergeant," replied Inspector Philips. "You can get started on alerting all the necessary authorities in whatever countries they came from. Luckily, he's named them all. That will make it a lot easier. He's certainly been around a bit ... and make a start with Liverpool. His poor parents ... what a little monster they produced."

While they waited for news of his capture in the park, they continued searching his papers. In 'Stephen's' room they found documents for the BMW. In William's study, in the top drawer of his desk, Sergeant Williams discovered the deed poll document with William's change of name from Brownlow to Pemworthy. There was also an advice note from a supplier of white goods, confirming delivery of a fridge freezer to The Cedars, along with the full address.

"Look at this, Guv," he said. "I reckon Pemworthy has a second property. If he's not found around here, don't you think we better pay it a visit? It's not that far away. He might have hitched a lift."

Inspector Philips studied the letter and smiled. "Yes, I think we should."

They gave it until daylight. Search teams had scoured the park and the surrounding area but there was no sign of William. By that time, they had not only pulled the house apart but also the van and the garage and on moving the chest freezer, discovered where William kept his false number plates, his trade signs ... and his passports.

They arrived at The Cedars an hour after dawn, snapping the locks on the gate with bolt cutters and then driving up to the house with lights flashing and sirens blaring. Six officers charged round to the back entrance as Inspector Philips, accompanied by Sergeant Williams and three more constables banged on the front door. There was no answer. He banged twice more before ordering it to be battered in.

William wasn't in the house.

Bugger!" exclaimed Inspector Philips. "This chap's a slippery bleeder ... but he's been here ... the bed's been slept in and by the look of it, he's had a drink or two," he added, sniffing a used glass in the kitchen. "Um. Brandy. Right. Try the garage and search the surrounding fields. He could be hiding out there somewhere."

William was in the garage, slumped on the bed in the rear of the camper van. There was a hole in his head and drying blood on his face. A gun lay by his side. The constable who found the body heaved his guts out on the lawn.

EPILOGUE

No-one ever knew exactly where William had obtained the gun that killed him. The police did tests and discovered it had been stolen from a gun club in Wales but what happened to it between then and when William had it in his possession, there was no knowing.

The police finished searching William's houses and alerted all the authorities where his victims had lived so their families could be informed of what had happened to their loved ones. They also informed his nearest relatives, his paternal and maternal aunts and uncles.

Miranda was utterly appalled to discover that she was executor of his will and he had left all he owned to her. He was an exceedingly wealthy man and he had given her everything he possessed; his houses, his furniture, his vehicles and all the cash in various bank accounts, including those in Switzerland. She was also responsible for his funeral.

Miranda couldn't deal with it. She gave instructions for her solicitor to do what was necessary. He contacted William's relatives in Liverpool but they wanted nothing to do with their nephew, suggesting he should be cremated in Leeds and his ashes scattered in the garden of peace. No-one attended his funeral. Miranda's solicitor dealt with the sale of all William had owned, and the proceeds, plus the cash in his bank accounts, were shared between a homeless charity and the rape crisis centre.

It took Miranda a while to recover from her ordeal. Jeremy had compassionate leave and remained at home with her and if he had to go out for any reason, Anna, Tricia or her parents stepped in so she was never left alone. Jeremy had suggested they sell the house and move as he didn't want Miranda to be constantly reminded of what had occurred. However, she was adamant that they remain, that she would get over it and once new neighbours moved in, it would all be in the past.

So, Peesdown settled down and once it was confirmed William had killed Tanya Philips, and Elsie Makins had definitely committed suicide, the park began to be busy again. However, the police still cautioned vigilance. William's DNA was not the same as that found on the previous rape victim and therefore, a rapist was still at large.

Bob Watkins was now in full charge of the park. He loved his job. He loved watching the women, especially that one in pink lycra. He was going to have her one day!

THE END

LAST WORD

Thank you so much for reading the Peesdown series: Peesdown Park, book 1 and Panic in Peesdown, Book 2. Passion in Peesdown, Book 3 will be available during 2021 and if you would like to be advised as to when, please sign up for my monthly newsletter on the following link:-

www.carolewilliamsbooks.com/sign-up

Also, please could you find a few moments to leave a short **REVIEW**, just a sentence or two and/or a star rating will be fantastic. Reviews can also be placed on Goodreads and my Facebook page - Carole Williams Author, as this will be so helpful, not only to me, but also to future readers.

FURTHER BOOKS BY CAROLE WILLIAMS.

THE CANLEIGH SERIES –

A Yorkshire family drama packed with passionate love, intrigue, suspense, blackmail … and murder!

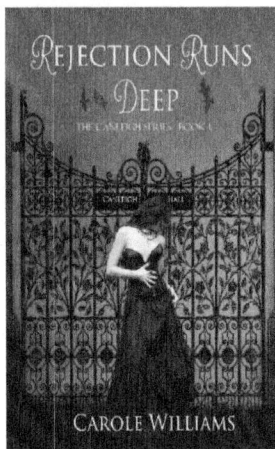

REJECTION RUNS DEEP
The Canleigh Series - Book 1

US: www.amazon.com/dp/B076YZQW57/
UK: www.amazon.co.uk/dp/B076YZQW57/

Lady Delia Canleigh has a difficult childhood, scarred by her mother's scandalous behaviour and the traumatic events it leads to, which results in her suffering a nervous breakdown. She grows into a stunningly beautiful, determined young woman but just as she is about to marry the man of her dreams and gain everything she has ever wanted, her world comes crashing down around her yet again.

Jealousy and rage take over. Her father has denied her the job she has always wanted, her brother will inherit the estate which she considers is rightfully hers, her younger sister is deliriously happy with a most attractive man. Then there is Ruth, her new stepmother, whom Delia despises, and Philip ... the love of her life ... who has let her down so badly. Will he be forgiven or persecuted? Finally, there is the new little heir to Canleigh who causes the biggest problem of all. As Delia's temper simmers, they will all have to be very, very careful!

Delia Canleigh - a woman who will stop at nothing, even destroying her own family, to get what she wants. Is she crazy, is she misunderstood - or is she just bad?

Rejection Runs Deep – the first historical novel in the Canleigh series set at Canleigh Hall in Yorkshire; London, Oxford, Scotland, the Caribbean and America during the mid-1900's until the early 20th century. Delia's Daughter continues the series and Katrina completes it with a truly dramatic finish. The Secret, will soon be available as a free ebook.

A selection of the reviews on Amazon.co.uk for Rejection Runs Deep.

Wow! One of those books that once you get into, you can't put down. The family at Canleigh Hall have one hell of a rollercoaster ride from start to finish. Great glimpses of the Yorkshire stately homes and countryside, mingled with murder, love, sex and yes, rejection! A Yorkshire Dallas!

This is the best book I've read this year! Fast paced and dramatic, with twists and turns and very well written.

Great writing that puts you firmly in Canleigh and the lives of everyone who stayed there.

Wow! Non-stop excitement!

Amazing! I couldn't put the book down, wondering what Lady Delia was going to do next, finding myself wanting to scream at her and hug the rest of the family.

Brilliant: The perfect holiday read: Excellent: Amazing: So many twists and turns: A really good read: An easy exciting read: I was gripped from the first chapter: Un-put-downable: Fantastic: Best book I have read in ages: Excellent author: Look forward to more of her books. Awesome!

NOW FOR THE NEXT TWO EXPLOSIVE BOOKS IN THE CANLEIGH SERIES AND THE BIG QUESTION.

IS LADY DELIA STILL ALIVE?

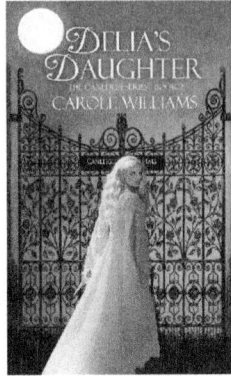

DELIA'S DAUGHTER

The Canleigh Series – Book 2

UK: www.amazon.co.uk/dp/B07G847ZD3/
US: www.amazon.com/dp/B07G847ZD3/

I'll never forget seeing my mother, Lady Delia Canleigh, trying to kill Granny Ruth. I was only four years old at the time and have grown up knowing my mother is evil. Thank goodness I had good people to care for me and help me trust again.

I'm an adult now and in love with Jeremy but he's behaving a little oddly now we are married. I have inherited Canleigh Hall and a fortune to go with it, which was a total shock and a massive responsibility for both of us but I really don't like the way Jeremy is behaving. I can't quite put my finger on it but something isn't right, especially when that friend of his, Matthew, is around … or when he is near Felix, our butler. Both men make me very uncomfortable and even a little scared and I don't know why.

And now I have seen a dangerous glint in Jeremy's eye, just like my mother's, which is highly unnerving. Surely I shouldn't be frightened of my own husband. Or should I?

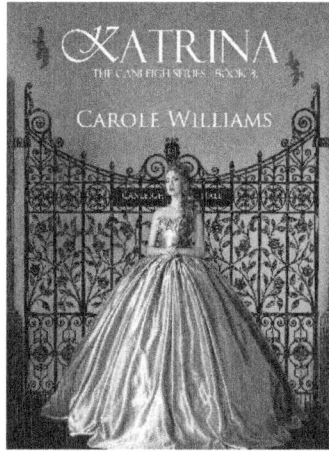

KATRINA
The Canleigh Series – Book 3

US: www.amazon.com/dp/B07QBXWR7F/
UK: www.amazon.co.uk/dp/B07QBXWR7F/

Ever since I was a child I have been fascinated by my evil, stunning beautiful Aunt Delia. My mother, Lady Victoria, is very scared of her sister, is appalled by my fascination with her and is terrified I will turn out the same way. It's true. I do get very angry, very quickly and hate it if anyone thwarts me so does Mother have reason to worry? I'm really not sure. At least she isn't worried about my other obsession with famous actresses, whom I want so very much to emulate.

I did my very best to learn about acting while at school and was extremely lucky to have discovered my drama teacher was a stupid woman and how terrifically easy it was to blackmail her into giving me the best parts in all the plays. Then at eighteen years old, I went to Radley, the best acting school in the country and my life changed dramatically and I had to take a different path to the one I had always wanted.

Now, thanks to my actions, I am in a real predicament and am furious with myself. I have no sparkling career, no money, and no stately home to float around in,or even a decent man to pander to my wishes, although my family have everything. My parents own a sumptuous hotel and are loaded with income from their various businesses but I can't get my hands on any of it until they die, which is far in the future, unless something unforeseen happens ... like an accident ... and then they tell me that I have to share it with my blasted foster sister, Suzanne and her brat, which is totally galling but we will see about that! Then there is cousin Lucy ... who has turned Canleigh into a thriving hotel and is rolling in dough ... and she has a gorgeous man doting on her. I've always been jealous of her. She inherited Canleigh and the huge fortune that went with it at a very young age. It's just not fair!

So, what do I have? My looks. I am beautiful ... everyone tells me so ... and I am going to have to use what I have to get what I want ... fame and fortune. It might take me time and people might get in my way but I will get there. I am determined to. Just watch me!

THE PEESDOWN SERIES

PEESDOWN PARK – BOOK 1
A GRIPPING PETSITTING DRAMA

(A BOOK YOU WON'T WANT TO PUT DOWN – A
BOOK WHICH WILL MAKE YOU WARY WHEN
WALKING ALONE!!

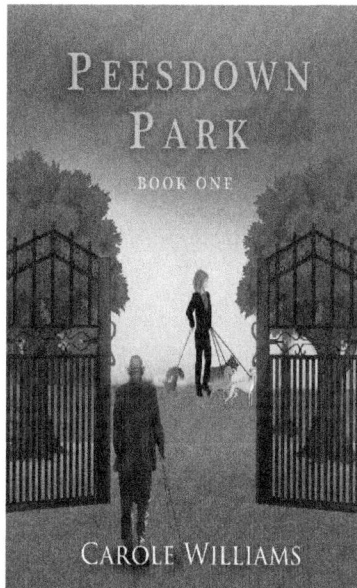

US: www.amazon.co.uk/dp/B08193FHW5

UK: www.amazon.co.uk/dp/B08193FHW5

If you want to make a lot of money, enjoy the outdoors
for most of the day and be your own boss, become a
professional petsitter someone had said. So, Miranda did
... but it wasn't all it was cracked up to be. No-one told

her she would have to take her life into her hands, walking into people's empty houses to feed their cats when they were away with the possibility of bumping into a burglar ... or walking dogs in the woods in Peesdown Park where creepy men lurked about ... and she had no idea she had to be specifically aware of William ... the one man she thought she could trust ...but William was a killer. He had fled the UK after murdering his parents to gain their wealth but now he was back ... and residing near Peesdown Park ... and the locals were blissfully unaware that the nice, friendly old gentleman who integrated himself into the community so well would soon bring terror to their beautiful, normally peaceful recreation area ... and no-one, particularly Miranda, their bubbly petsitter, would be safe for long.

PANIC IN PEESDOWN – BOOK 2

US: www.amazon.com/dp/B08W96FYR5
UK: www.amazon.com/B08W96FYR5

Following a winter cruising the Caribbean, serial killer, William Pemworthy, is back in Peesdown, his sights firmly set on Miranda, the popular, bubbly petsitter but he doesn't want to kill her, he wants to marry her! However, she has just become engaged to the gorgeous Army Major, Jeremy Cross. William is furious and is determined the marriage will not go ahead and if he has to kill Jeremy to prevent it, he will. William enlists the help of his mysterious cousin, Stephen, in persuading Miranda she is marrying the wrong man but his plan doesn't work and unbeknown to them, Miranda and Jeremy are now in terrible danger from both men. Can Miranda overcome the terror that awaits her, will

Jeremy survive to rescue her and will William and Stephen escape justice once more?

Books in the pipeline are Passion in Peesdown, book 3 in the Peesdown series and Darnforth, my next big family drama which begins in Normandy in World War II and then returns to Darnforth, a large Jacobean stately home in England.

To hear when these are available, please sign up to receive my newsletter. You will also receive a free copy of my thrilling short story, YES DEAR along with THE SECRET, the shocking prequel to the Canleigh series.

www.carolewilliamsbooks.com/sign up

You can also follow me on:
Facebook - Carole Williams Author
Instagram - (carolewilliams.author)

Please email me at:

carole@carolewilliamsbooks.com

Many thanks.

Carole Williams.

'Yes Dear'

CAROLE WILLIAMS

Life was hard. She was always playing catch-up, always stressed, always at his beck and call … but he was in for a shock. She hadn't planned it that way. It just happened!!

DON'T FORGET TO SIGN UP FOR YOUR FREE
COPY OF YES DEAR AND THE SECRET.

www.carolewilliamsbooks.com/sign up

AND FINALLY – PLEASE, PLEASE DON'T FORGET TO
AWARD A STAR RATING and/or a REVIEW.
THANK YOU SO VERY MUCH.

Printed in Great Britain
by Amazon